JOURNEY INTO JEOPARDY

Barbara's heart sank as the Earl of Chatworth shut the carriage door firmly, and settled himself beside her.

Now for the first time she realized the full import of being this man's bride. True, he had agreed that this was to be a marriage in name only. But as his eyes slowly traversed her face and figure, she wondered if she had made herself totally clear on this point, and also if this notorious rake could be trusted to tame his well-known desires.

Soon she would find out. Find out what he would do on this their marriage night. And even more troubling, how she would respond . . .

GAYLE BUCK has freelanced for regional publications, worked for a radio station and as a secretary. Until recently, she was involved in public relations for a major Texas university. Besides her regencies, she is currently working on projects in fantasy and romantic suspense.

SIGNET REGENCY ROMANCE
COMING IN MAY 1991

Sandra Heath
Lord Buckingham's Bride

Irene Saunders
The Dowager's Dilemma

Dawn Lindsey
Devil's Lady

Mutual Consent

by

Gayle Buck

A SIGNET BOOK

SIGNET
Published by the Penguin Group
Penguin Books USA Inc., 375 Hudson Street,
New York, New York, 10014, U.S.A.
Penguin Books Ltd, 27 Wrights Lane,
London W8 5TZ, England
Penguin Books Australia Ltd, Ringwood,
Victoria, Australia
Penguin Books Canada Ltd, 2801 John Street,
Markham, Ontario, Canada L3R 1B4
Penguin Books (N.Z.) Ltd, 182-190 Wairau Road,
Auckland 10, New Zealand

Penguin Books Ltd, Registered Offices:
Harmondsworth, Middlesex, England

First published by Signet, an imprint of New American Library,
a division of Penguin Books USA Inc.

First Printing, April, 1991

10 9 8 7 6 5 4 3 2 1

1

Spring, 1808

THE EARL OF CHATWORTH was drunk. He sprawled in his chair, a half-empty wineglass at his elbow and a few cards held loosely in his hand. An untidy mound of chits and gold coins were on the table in front of him. Several of the chits held by the other gentlemen at the table were his. Through the long hours he had both won and lost heavily. At the present, he was down by several thousand pounds.

It was four in the morning. The close air in the gaming room was stale with the smell of spilled wine and greasy smoke from the guttering tallow candles. Through the haze the earl regarded the man seated opposite him. He had disliked the flashy military gentleman upon first meeting, having immediately recognized the rank as dubious and the shady Captain Demont as a professional cardsharp. After observing the gentleman's style of play for some hours, he was equally certain that the man was an adroit cheat. His dislike of Captain Demont had therefore risen to the level of active contempt.

However, there was little that he could say without proof, especially while Captain Demont represented the house. And what a house it was, thought his lordship with a trace of sardonic humor. He had allowed himself to be persuaded by his friends to plunge into the stews abounding about Covent Garden, where it was not unknown for people to simply vanish.

The gentlemen, out for a lark and bent on deep play and dangerous company, had descended into the pit of this most hellish of dives. The Earl of Chatworth knew himself to be well out of his own ken. With the exception of himself and his friends, the clientele was not at all what one would have found in a more respectable gaming house. The majority were cits and rough characters that he thought were likely escapees from Tyburn Tree.

"Well, my lord? Do you play?"

There was a sneer in the military gentleman's brusque tone that rubbed the earl's pride raw. His lordship's cold gray eyes glittered with sudden recklessness. He shoved the mound of chits and coins into the middle of the table. "That, and ten thousand pounds more," he said. Through the brandy fumes clouding his mind, he felt a detached sense of outrage at what he had done. It was madness to bet against the house. But even had he wished to do so, it was too late to recall the bet.

Exclamations rose upon every side. Spectators standing behind the gamesters muttered sharp curses as they jostled one another for the best position to view the game.

Captain Demont's hard face slackened for an instant. Then his jovial expression was fastened firmly into place. "Of course, my lord. I believe that the house can cover that amount." He made to draw the cards, but the earl's hand shot out. Captain Demont looked down in astonishment at the steel fingers that imprisoned his wrist.

"I prefer a new deck, one unopened and uncreased," said the earl softly. He saw the blaze of anger in the other man's eyes, which was as swiftly banked, and he knew that he had made an enemy. There were sniggerings about the table and amid the spectators. The earl released the man's wrist, knowing that his point had been taken, and he sat back slowly in his chair.

"Of course, my lord." The captain snapped his fingers. Without looking around, he took from the waiter a new deck of cards. He tore off the seal and offered the deck with an exaggerated courtesy to his opponent. The earl cut the deck and the captain swiftly shuffled with smooth, unerring skill.

The spectators watched with collective bated breath as the cards were dealt and played. Among them, a heavyset man watched with more than common interest. His mode of dress proclaimed him to be a well-to-do tradesman, and as such, his presence in such an establishment was an anomaly. Members of the rising middle class were conservative and hardworking and as a rule generally eschewed the frivolous pastimes of the higher order.

But Cribbage had chosen to become a regular figure in the haunts that catered to the most hardened gamesters. At first he had been an object of rude curiosity and speculation, but he was now largely ignored. Though for several months he had made a practice of visiting the various gaming hells and dives, he never played. He watched and listened and waited with the patience of the deranged bear that bides its time for the one careless moment that would prove to be its keeper's last.

And now, as Cribbage watched the reckless young lord sprawled in his chair at the gaming table, he sensed that at last he had found what he had been waiting for. He had found his gentleman.

On the last turn of the cards, the Earl of Chatworth lost. There was loud reaction from the spectators, some throwing callous taunts and others words of raucous sympathy. The earl's friends shrugged their elegant shoulders and recommended that his lordship fill up his glass.

The Earl of Chatworth scribbled his initials on some vowels and threw the scraps of paper onto the pile of similar notes and coins that Captain Demont was raking toward himself. "Be damned to you," said the earl shortly with a twist of his lips.

Captain Demont gave an exaggerated sign of acknowledgment. "I thank your lordship most kindly," he said, deadpan.

Cribbage's hard eyes gleamed. Previous to this last bet, Cribbage had taken particular note of who held the earl's earlier vowels of debt. Cribbage glanced contemptuously at the military gentleman. As easily as the earl had done earlier, he formed his opinion of the spurious Captain Demont. He thought there could have been no one he would have preferred to be in possession of that particular handful of paper. Cribbage did not think that the captain would prove to be any great obstacle to his own purposes.

"Perhaps your luck will change for the better with the next game, my lord," Captain Demont said. His mask of joviality had slipped during the quick counting of his winnings and no longer quite concealed his satisfaction at besting the earl.

"I say, not at all the thing to gloat. Lack of breeding, that," said one of the earl's friends in a loud aside to his companion.

The captain heard, and though he gave no indication of it while he shuffled the cards, ruddy color stained his hard cheeks.

The earl had also heard, and he allowed a faint smile to flit over his face at the military gentleman's discomfiture. "Undoubtedly you are right, Captain," he said. He rose from his chair, the triflest unsteady on his feet. "But that is all for me this night, gentlemen." He laughed at his friends' protests that it was still early and they had no desire to quit the table yet. "I am rolled up, gentlemen. But you stay, certainly." He was let go with no further urgings, everyone quite losing interest in a man who had nothing more to wager.

As the earl left the gaming hell and stepped into the cobbled alley, he stumbled. He steadied himself on the lamppost. The cold morning air was a stinging slap in the face, which made him shudder. He glanced around and quickly got his bearings. He walked swiftly in the direction of the Strand, which marked the division of the seamier side of London from that of his own familiar West End.

The fog-laced streets were nearly deserted with but a few malingerers like himself making their separate ways home, while half-seen shadows slid slowly by on nefarious business. Through the fumes of brandy that dulled his mind, the earl was aware that his rich clothing marked him as alien to the area and therefore legitimate prey for any who wished to trouble themselves for the acquirement of a few pounds or a watch fob. Even his elegant coat and breeches had value in this neighborhood, he thought muzzily. He had not realized when he had left the gaming hell alone how vulnerable he would feel.

The earl laughed as he stumbled again on the uneven cobbles. It was all too wonderfully funny. That sense of lurking danger had lent a certain spice to his visit to the gaming hell. But now, with his head fair to splitting with the beginnings of a hangover and lack of sleep, his mouth fuzzy, his eyes grainy from the twice-cursed smoke-filled air of the gaming hell, the earl heartily wished that he had not ventured quite so far off the beaten trail in his search of amusement. He could hardly give a proper account of himself in his present condition if a thug or two took it into their heads to roll him in the gutter.

Such were his bleary thoughts, so that when a shadow materialized beside him, he gave an exaggerated start. However, he saw not the thug he expected, but a woman. She was smiling, and as she drew nearer, the stale scent that she wore filled his nostrils. Her hair wisped about her face and tumbled down over her shoulders, as though she had just risen from someone's bed.

"Fancy meeting you here like this, m'lord. 'Tis fate, to be sure," she said. In the half-light her eyes were hard and calculating. As if by accident the front of her cape fell open, revealing a pale bosom completely displayed by the indecent cut of her muslin gown.

The earl regarded her dispassionately. "My pockets are to let, my dear. Just as well. I'm not one for Covent Garden goods."

With the woman's obscenities ringing in his ears, the earl crossed the once fashionable piazza of Covent Garden toward the Theater Royal, from whence he was able to hail a hackney cab to carry him home.

A few days later Lord Chatworth left his elegant town house on foot and sauntered to a fashionable hotel where one of his friends had lodgings. Viscount Taredell was in and finishing up his morning's toilet. As it so chanced, he was already entertaining a visitor, the Honorable Simon Hadwicke, when the earl arrived.

"Simon, I am glad to see you as well. This will save me from seeking you out later. I have come to claim my vowels off Taredell and I shall do the same with you,'' Lord Chatworth said. To his surprise, both the viscount and Hadwicke said that his vowels had already been redeemed from them.

"A gentleman who introduced himself as your lordship's representative came around yesterday and laid claim to the vowels," said Hadwicke.

Lord Chatworth frowned in puzzlement. "But I never commissioned someone to claim my debts. In fact, I have just this minute come into proper funds."

His friends laughed off the odd circumstance. With a deep shrug, Hadwicke said, "Depend upon it. You were tipsy when you commissioned the man to the errand, and that is why you do not recall the matter."

"Yes, and what is more, that's why you haven't had proper funds until now. You never recalled giving over the blunt to this chap," said Viscount Taredell, frowning at himself in the glass as he carefully placed a diamond pin into the extravagant folds of his cravat.

"What the devil!" Lord Chatworth was more perturbed than before. For the life of him, he could not recall having made any such commission, but there was no other logical explanation for the fact that his vowels had been honorably redeemed. "I am at worse points than I knew when I discover that I can't remember my own orders." He gave a reluctant grin when his two friends laughed at him.

Viscount Taredell turned away from the mirror and mildly requested that Hadwicke toss his coat to him from the back of the chair in which he was seated. Hadwicke did so, and the viscount began the business of shrugging into the tight-fitting garment. Between grunts, he said, "I recommend that you forget the entire matter. That's the ticket when questions that are bound to prove uncomfortable loom on the horizon." He looked in the glass and twitched his sleeve with discontent. "Damn that valet of mine for taking the influenza. Dashed inconvenient, and so I told him."

His complaint was not heeded by the other gentlemen. "Aye, Marcus. What has you in such a pucker? Your honor has been attended to, whether by you or by some poor fool who doesn't know better than to waste his blunt on a frittering nobleman. Come, there is a pugilist expedition down in Friar's Field. If your pockets are too heavy, you may waste your blunt on the betting,'' Hadwicke said slyly.

Lord Chatworth rose instantly to the bait. He gave it as his opinion that he was not any worse than some others he could mention in judging the sport. "We shall see who lays the greater number of losing bets," he said.

"A monkey that Simon takes it," Viscount Taredell said quickly.

"I shall back my lord Chatworth," said Hadwicke with an elaborate bow. "Marcus has a singular talent for playing on the knife's edge of risk, as was witnessed the other night when he bet all against the house."

"That was rather ill-considered, even for you, Marcus," said Viscount Taredell, ushering his friends out of his lodgings and closing the door. "Anyone could see that Demont was cheating. Though how he managed it with a clean deck, I am not certain."

"That was a neat trick, was it not? One can only suspect that the deck was not as clean as its unbroken wrapper testified it to be." Lord Chatworth's hard eyes gleamed. "I should like to meet our Captain Demont again under similar circumstances and take him down a peg or two."

"A laudable ambition, though perhaps one better left to someone with greater luck at cards," Hadwicke said promptly, twirling his cane as he and his companions sauntered out of the hotel.

The earl raised his brows, aware that he had been duly insulted. "I thank you, friend," he said dryly.

"Not at all, my lord," said his closest friend, laughing.

2

LATER THAT SAME WEEK, the Earl of Chatworth agreed to an appointment with his man of business, whose request had been couched in somewhat urgent language. Lord Chatworth had not expected anything of much moment to be conveyed to him in the interview, having long since discovered that what his solicitor found of interest was of profound boredom to himself. But he was not so negligent of his responsibilities that he did not desire to have details brought to his attention, and he was willing enough to put aside his pleasures for the length of the man's visit.

The interview was considerably longer than the earl had anticipated it would be, and not precisely of disinterest. In fact, the Earl of Chatworth's man of business took leave of his master in an exhausted state of mind. He had carried out a particularly unpleasant performance of his duty, and the resulting explosion from the earl had taken long in smoothing over.

As for the Earl of Chatworth, he emerged from the interview in a foul black temper. He had endured more than an hour of subtle reproof while learning the disagreeable truth concerning his negligent handling of his worldly fortunes. It had taken him quite some time to accept the untenable facts, but his man of business had been persuasive and now he stood on the sidewalk outside his town house fully convinced of his own culpable stupidity.

The earl's driver asked his lordship where he wanted to be taken. When Lord Chatworth gave the address, the driver's mouth dropped open. "My lord, be ye certain?"

"Yes," said Lord Chatworth in a savage voice. He jumped

into the carriage and pulled shut the door with unnecessary force.

The driver shrugged and set the horses into the traffic. The carriage's iron wheels rattled over the cobbles, carrying its reluctant occupant deep into the oldest part of the metropolis.

The Earl of Chatworth's destination was the City, that part of London that no proud peer would deign to set foot in.

The City was the financial center of Britain and had existed as such for nearly four hundred years. The streets were narrow and dark, retaining the flavor of the original village of London. Threadneedle, Bishopsgate, Cheapside, Old Jewry, Lombard, Poultry . . .

As the carriage passed through the streets, the earl's lip curled. If he had not been under irresistible duress, there was no power on earth that could have otherwise persuaded him to enter this small area sandwiched between the Bloody Tower and the Temple Bar.

The carriage stopped. The Earl of Chatworth got out and instructed the driver to wait. He swept cold eyes over the faces of the curious who passed by him on the sidewalk and who had instantly recognized him as the stranger that he was, and by will alone he forced them to avert their gazes.

Upon the outside wall of the building in front of him was a plaque with the business stated upon it, as required by law. Without a backward glance, the earl entered the building.

He was shown immediately into the office of the man at whose summons he had come.

The cit was behind his desk. He did not rise upon the earl's entrance, a discourtesy that the Earl of Chatworth perceived as a calculated insult. The cit waved the earl to a chair. "This is indeed an unlooked-for pleasure, my Lord Chatworth," said the cit blandly, leaning back in his chair.

"Indeed, Cribbage? How unlike my man of business to mistake the matter," said the earl grimly.

Cribbage smiled thinly. His heavy face seemed unsuited to such frivolous exercise. His hard eyes did not lighten. "A sense of humor is always an advantage, my lord," he observed.

"I see nothing humorous in this business," Lord Chatworth bit off.

"Ah, but I do, Chatworth," Cribbage said softly. He was aware of the earl's anger at his deliberate lack of respect in addressing his lordship without making use of his title. However, he was obscurely disappointed that his lordship did not call him on it. It would have pleased him to be able to squelch the peer's inbred arrogance. "You realize the irony, of course. Hat in your hand and all of that."

The earl's lips tightened. His eyes were icy. "Quite. I should like to conclude this interview as quickly as possible."

"And I," Cribbage agreed. He tapped a number of parchments under his wide hand. "These are the mortgages to your estates and ancestral home. Also, I have the vowels of honor that you have lost at cards these past two months. The total comes, if I am not mistaken, to several thousand pounds."

Lord Chatworth was white of face as he looked up from the pile of chits. He could scarcely control his rage. "How came you by those?"

Cribbage quirked a heavy brow. "I am a very wealthy man. Hard currency appears much more advantageous to many people than does a handful of worthless chits."

Lord Chatworth could not imagine any of his acquaintances agreeing to such a bargain. It went completely against the gentleman's code of honor. Unless the vowels had been unscrupulously attained, he thought, recalling how two of his friends had said his vowels were redeemed. But the puzzle of the debts of honor was small compared to what else the cit held.

"What is it you want of me?" Lord Chatworth asked harshly. The cit already had the mortgages to his estates, so it was not the land that interested the man. Wild speculations raced through his head. Surely Cribbage must know that he could never raise all at one time the amount represented by his vowels.

"I am a businessman, my lord. I never speculate unless I am certain of a profit. You would have been wise to do the same," said Cribbage, tapping a thick forefinger on the stack of vowels in front of him.

The earl choked back his anger, aware that the cit was deliberately baiting him. But he would be damned before he gave the man the satisfaction of an ill-bred outburst. "What is it you want?" he ground out between his teeth.

Cribbage's hard eyes glittered. "I want your name, Chatworth."

Lord Chatworth stared. The man was mad, he thought. He laughed and replied in clipped contempt, "You damned fool! I could not make you earl if I wished, even if you do hold my life in your hands."

Cribbage smiled coldly. "True, but you can make my daughter a countess."

For an instant of stunned amazement the earl stared into the man's hard eyes. The chair crashed over as Lord Chatworth leapt to his feet. His fists clenched at his sides. "By God, I'll not do it!" All thought of conducting himself with the utmost coolness had evaporated before the outrage. He placed his hands on the desk and leaned over it until his furious gaze was level with Cribbage's eyes. "Hear me, you damned cit. Wreak your worst. I will see you in hell before I will place your common trollop in the *ton.*"

The cit's cold voice cut across Lord Chatworth's anger like rasping steel. "You would see yourself in debtor's prison, your historical birthplace and estates broken up and sold, your tenants turned into homeless beggars, my lord?"

Cribbage's voice had risen with his own smoldering anger at the arrogance and contempt he saw in his lordship's eyes. With an effort he schooled his tone. "All for pride, my lord? I had thought better of a gentleman of honor."

Lord Chatworth was silenced by the picture conjured up for him. It was true that he had not realized the consequences. As the owner of vast estates, it was his inherited responsibility to provide for the health and educational needs of the people who tenanted the land. The holdover from feudal times of the relationship between a lord and his vassals was sometimes neglected in these times, but for the Earl of Chatworth that responsibility had been ingrained in him by both his parents, and in particular by his mother, who had always seen to it that her own example was irreproachable.

At the thought of his beloved mother, now aged and enfeebled by a painful and crippling disorder, Lord Chatworth's heart contracted. The countess resided quietly at the family seat of Wormswood. If Cribbage did as he threatened, her waning days would be concluded in misery and horror. His breathing was hard as he thought of the countess and all those others dependent upon him. "You could not do it, Cribbage."

Cribbage shrugged. He spread his hands. "I am a businessman. What use have I for encumbered estates or debts of honor, my lord?"

Lord Chatworth stared down into the cit's implacable face. Slowly he straightened. He knew now that the man sitting behind the desk would do exactly as he threatened. The earl said softly, "Damn your eyes, Cribbage!"

Cribbage felt a surge of triumph, but he merely nodded as though a point had been won. "Naturally there will be a generous settlement. My daughter commands quite a fortune in her own right. But I am sure you would prefer some arrangement made regarding your mortgaged estates anad your vowels of honor."

Lord Chatworth inclined his head. He felt that he would suffocate if he spent many more minutes in this man's intolerable company. "As you say, Cribbage. I believe our men of business are better equipped to work out the details." He settled his beaver more firmly on his head, his thoughts already racing for solutions. He would pay the devil's price now. But once the bargain was done with, he would be damned if he would remain saddled with an unwanted and vulgar wife. Annulment or event the scandal of divorce was preferable.

"Perhaps you are right, Chatworth," Cribbage agreed. He fingered a pen. "We two are certainly ill-prepared to come to . . . friendly terms."

Lord Chatworth smiled coldly. His eyes were clear as ice. "Believe me when I say that it has been an experience to have done business with you. But remember that I do not easily name any man master."

"That I do believe, my lord." Cribbage's eyes were openly

mocking. "But circumstances seem to have forced you to it."

Lord Chatworth turned abruptly toward the door. He knew that he was but a hairbreadth away from killing the man with his bare hands.

Cribbage's voice came strong behind him. "Chatworth."

The earl turned, one brow cocked. He waited, his expression one of cold distaste. But what the cit had to say was nothing that he could ever have anticipated.

"My daughter may be a trollop. I do not know, nor do I care. That is for you to discover. However, I do not think you shall find her common," Cribbage said.

Lord Chatworth had the capacity to be shocked further than he thought possible. "You speak as though she is but a brood mare," he said.

"So she is," Cribbage responded with a marked sneer. "The most valuable mare in my stable. And I have bought you, my lord, for her stud."

Lord Chatworth spun on his heel. He jerked open the door and it slammed shut behind his swiftly retreating figure.

3

As the hackney cab rolled over the cobbled London streets, Miss Barbara Cribbage had much to reflect upon. Not more than a month before, her father had abruptly summoned her to London. He had kept her kicking her heels for days before he had finally informed her why he had ordered her presence.

He had found her a husband.

Barbara was actually not much surprised by her father's announcement. After all, she had been expecting such news for better than two years.

At age seventeen, at the end of the disastrous Season she had endured, her father had cursed her for not receiving a noble offer. Fortunately for her sensitive hide, her maternal aunt had rather cuttingly reminded her enraged parent that he could not expect a common merchant's daughter to receive a spectacular offer no matter how well the girl was turned out or how well dowered. "For the *ton,* it is bloodline that counts in the end. Barbara has blue blood from only the one side," had said Lady Azaela.

Mr. Cribbage's eyes had bulged with his fury. Though it was impossible for him to publicly acknowledge it, he knew that his despised sister-in-law spoke only the truth. He had run up against the insufferable arrogance of the quality too many times in the past to be mistaken in its scent this time.

"Then take the chit with you and keep her under wraps until I send for her. She may not be thought good enough to be courted as the wife of a peer of the realm, but we shall see what my wealth may purchase for her."

With that awful pronouncement still ringing in her ears,

Barbara had retired with Lady Azaela to her aunt's house in the Derbyshire countryside. She had been very content to resume the quiet life she had led with Lady Azaela Terowne and the succession of excellent governesses and instructors that her aunt had provided for her.

But it had all been only a reprieve. It had come time to once more assume her role as her father's pawn.

For that was what she was, she thought. Her father's one and wholly consuming passion for years had been to become accepted into the *ton*. He had contemptuously brushed aside the consideration of birth in his ignorance of society, believing that the doings of one's ancestors conferred nothing of note upon a man and that it was what a man made of himself that counted.

Mr. Cribbage had been swiftly and brutally disabused of his mistaken notion that wealth alone could provide the entrée into the elite five hundred. He had never forgiven those who had so shredded his pride, and he had become more determined than ever to take his place among those considered England's leaders.

He had sought a noble bride and finally acquired the hand of the daughter of an impecunious lord, in exchange for whom he had paid every outstanding debt owed by the family. He had thought gratitude and the simple business conducted would gain him the social status he desired through his wife's connections. But his wife's family snubbed him and washed their hands of their kinswoman's ignoble fate. She had gone to the altar a sacrificial lamb, and to her family, her new lower station in life made her as good as dead.

Mr. Cribbage had been maddened by this second, and worse, wound to his large pride and ego. His ambition evolved into a consuming obsession. He swore that one day all those who had so grevously insulted him would acknowledge him upon their collective knees.

Before her marriage, Mrs. Cribbage had been a shy, dutiful young woman who had never had a cross word spoken to her. She never got over her terror of, and her secret contempt for, her common husband. Through the years the burden of her sacrifice upon the altar of duty and her family's

abandonment of her weighed ever more heavily upon her
spirit, and when Barbara turned ten years old, she succumbed
quietly to pneumonia.

Mrs. Cribbage's younger sister had defied the general
family wisdom of shunning her and had remained in touch
with her. Lady Azaela Terowne was made of sterner stuff
than Mrs. Cribbage. During the early years of Mrs. Cribbage's marriage, as she gradually learned of Mr. Cribbage's
brutal insensitivities, she had urged her sister to consider the
shocking possibility of divorce. But Mrs. Cribbage had
shrunk from such an appalling course, with its attendant
scandal and the certainty that her husband would never tamely
let her go. Her greatest fear was that if she dared such a thing,
he would out of spite keep their child from her.

"And that I could not bear, dear Azaela. My poor little
Babs. I am the only one to stand between her and Mr. Cribbage, and I am such a poor protectress at that," she had said
with a rare laugh, her hand lovingly caressing her daughter's
glossy auburn curls. She had suddenly looked up, her gaze
fixed with such unusual intentness upon her sister's face that
Lady Azaela was shaken. "Promise me that you will do all
in your power for my Babs," Mrs. Cribbage had demanded.

Lady Azaela had willingly assured her sister that she would
indeed do so, never suspecting that she would be called upon
so soon. Six months later Mrs. Cribbage had breathed her
last and Barbara's nurse had sent an urgent message to Lady
Azaela.

Lady Azaela had suffered herself to endure the first of what
would prove to be through the years her several confronta-
tions with Mr. Cribbage. She had arrived in time for her
sister's funeral, unannounced and unwanted, as her brother-
in-law had made quite plain. But she had ignored his heavy
insults until after the sad business was done and Mrs.
Cribbage at last was allowed her measure of peace.

Then it had come time to turn her considerable personality
to the needs of the living. She had never before had occasion
to observe her niece, who was a little dab of a thing, in Mr.
Cribbage's company. The girl was obviously in terror of her
own father. Lady Azaela's heart had been stung to anger,

but she knew better than to allow her emotions to show. Lady Azaela had not listened to her sister without learning something of Mr. Cribbage. With seeming casualness she had said, "I am willing to take the girl."

"Be damned for your impertinence! The brat belongs to me, to do with as I please," Cribbage had said.

Lady Azaela had shrugged with feigned indifference. "As you wish. She would naturally stand a better chance of achieving a brilliant marriage if she were raised by one intimately acquainted with the social mores of the *ton*. But as you say, she belongs to you. And undoubtedly the expense of providing properly for her would be rather prohibitive, so perhaps this is best, after all."

With that, she had swept out of the drawing room to greet those of the neighborhood who had come to convey their condolences. Mrs. Cribbage had been well liked by those in the lesser society in which she had passed her days, having been one to quietly offer a kindness whenever it chanced that she was able to do so. Lady Azaela hoped that what she had said to her brother-in-law would work to her advantage in the short time remaining before her own departure, or otherwise her promise to her sister would be very difficult to meet.

Mr. Cribbage was a man of decision. He detested his sister-in-law; she represented much of what he despised in the so-called quality. But her words worked upon his obsession to a nicety. He abruptly put forth a business proposition to Lady Azaela. He wanted her to take his daughter and ingrain in the girl all the ways that any well-bred young lady was endowed, and in return he would pay any expenses incurred in the task.

Lady Azaela made a show of hesitation. Mr. Cribbage upped his offer of remuneration and was contemptuous when Lady Azaela accepted the higher consideration. His experience was that any of the quality could be had for a price. One simply had to hit upon the right figure.

When Lady Azaela left her sister's former house, she was accompanied by her niece and the girl's nanny. Babs recalled that she had been a bewildered and frightened ten-year-old girl. She had lost her mother and she was leaving the only

life she had ever known. The future was suddenly filled with
uncertainties, but even so, young Barbara had not been
altogether displeased to be going away. Rather, she had felt
relief that she was leaving her father behind.

The following seven years had been relatively happy ones
for Barbara, marred only by the infrequent appearances of
her father. Mr. Cribbage had remained a terrifying quantity
for her, but she had slowly and unconsciously learned how
to deal with him in the cool manner demonstrated by her aunt.

Lady Azaela thoroughly detested Mr. Cribbage, but she
suffered his intrustions into her well-ordered life because she
was mindful that the man was her niece's legal guardian.
She had tried to have herself named to Babs' guardianship,
but Cribbage would never agree to it, knowing from past
experience never to accede too much to one of the quality.
He believed that one must retain some hold over them to be
able to command their attention. He had early on sensed Lady
Azaela's attachment for his brat, and that, coupled with the
monies he gave to her that he was convinced she could not
do without, were his insurance that she would continue to
acknowledge his importance to the scheme of things.

Babs herself had not dared to completely trust in her aunt
because of the financial arrangement between Lady Azaela
and her father, until the day she realized that Lady
Azaela was neither indigent nor greedy, but was simply
making use of her father's absolute faith in the power of his
money to manipulate him. His continued agreement to leave
his daughter in Lady Azaela's care hinged upon his belief
that he had his sister-in-law in his power.

Mr. Cribbage could never have understood Lady Azaela's
very real compassion for the lonely child and would have
regarded it with such suspicion that he most probably would
not have contemplated letting Babs go to Lady Azaela at all.
But the fact that his sister-in-law did respond to his wealth
assured him of her motives and engendered in him the
mistaken notion that he had a financial hold upon her.

Lady Azaela was a gentlewoman of uncommon shrewdness
and foresight. She knew it was inevitable that one day Mr.

Cribbage would demand the return of his daughter. Lady Azaela had no wish to see her niece completely and forever at Mr. Cribbage's mercy, and she had done what she could to provide for the girl's future.

Lady Azaela carried out to the very letter the promise she had made to her sister upon Babs' behalf. Miss Barbara Cribbage was a most properly educated and socially graceful young lady upon her come-out at age seventeen. Lady Azaela had hoped to milk Mr. Cribbage's obsession with the *ton* to her niece's benefit by tirelessly working to cultivate just those modest connections that would be most advantageous to a young lady whose obvious gently bred manner, lovely face, and considerable dowry could be expected to override the disadvantage of her paternal birth.

But in the end it had all come to naught.

Lady Azaela had planned to lease a residence in a respectable street for the Season, from which she could properly launch her niece into London society. Mr. Cribbage had thought his sister-in-law's notion to be ridiculous. He had not seen the need of hiring a fashionable address. Despite Lady Azaela's protests, Barbara's come-out had taken place in her father's house. The address was well enough, but it smacked unmistakably of the City and *nouveau riche*. The villa itself was appallingly ostentatious, filled with a clutter of ugly bric-a-brac and the most expensive and faddish furnishings that money would buy.

Lady Azaela had been forced to make do. She had banished the worst of the atrocities to the back parlors and bedrooms and softened the impact of the overpowering rooms with satin sheetings and flowers. The musicians and menus were ordered as they should be. Her niece's gowns for the first evening and the succeeding entertainments were in every way quite satisfactory. All in all, she had been rather pleased with the arrangements.

Mr. Cribbage had frowned heavily at Lady Azaela's changes to his house and her studied plans. The functions that Lady Azaela put together were designed to tastefully showcase Miss Barbara Cribbage, but he did not perceive

them that way. Mr. Cribbage thought them palty affairs, and
beginning with his daughter's come-out, he had done all in
his power to arrange things more to his taste.

On the evening of Barbara's come-out, Lady Azaela was
enraged by the unexplained appearance of gold plate,
intrusive musicians, glittering gems nestled in the flower
arrangements, and fountains of champagne. Most of the
changes were not of themselves exceptional, but taken
altogether, a veneer of undoubted vulgarity was visited upon
Lady Azaela's careful efforts.

Through the rest of the Season, Mr. Cribbage flaunted his
wealth. He positively thrust ostentation down the throats of
those of the *ton,* who were eventually put off by the reeking
merchant's taint of the address. Lady Azaela watched,
helpless and virtually impotent to repair the damage, as her
niece was catalogued and dismissed and thereafter forgotten
by polite society.

Babs' first and subsequent only Season ended in complete
and ignoble disaster. She received not one eligible offer,
though there were a few on the unsavory side. Her pride and
self-esteem had received blow after blow. Fully cognizant
of how her father's pretentiousness appeared in the eyes of
those of taste, she had been deeply humiliated and shamed.
It said much of her strength of character and her social
training that she had retained a cool composure in the face
of the amused contempt of those who attended to the progress
of her come-out.

Her exile back to Derbyshire had been a welcome relief.
She had dreaded ever returning to London, which would be
forever for her the scene of her humiliation. Whenever the
thought of her father's determination to make her a branch
of his own twisted ambition had intruded itself into her mind,
she had swiftly and determindedly banished it. Nevertheless,
she had known that the day would come when she would
be forced to return to London.

Lady Azaela had spoken to her niece frankly on the subject.
She had advised Babs not to reject her father's plans for her
out of hand. Instead, Lady Azaela recommended calm assess-
ment of the offer that Mr. Cribbage had gotten for her and

the gentleman behind it. "It is possible that you will be pleasantly surprised. And if not, you always have a home with me," Lady Azaela had said.

Thus Barbara had obeyed her father's summons. She had quietly listened to his command that she was to marry the gentleman he had in mind for her. Then, at the first opportunity she had taken a practical step in heeding Lady Azaela's excellent advice.

Babs smoothed a crease in the skirt of her pelisse. She knew herself to be dressed in the height of fashion. She had dressed carefully for this first meeting with her intended husband, hoping to establish herself as other than a merchant's daughter. However, she could not shake her feeling of nervous dread. It was one thing to accept Lady Azaela's advice as sound; it was quite another to put it to the test and actually pay an uninvited and unexpected call upon a gentleman whom she had never met.

The hackney cab stopped. Barbara got out of the carriage. She quietly requested the driver to wait for her return. For reassurance, she touched a finger to the heavy veil that covered her face. Then she took a deep breath and ascended the steps of the Earl of Chatworth's town house.

She pulled the bell. The door was opened by a porter and she was ushered into the entry hall. She was prepared to give her name as she requested an interview with the Earl of Chatworth, but she was given no chance to do so.

"I shall inform his lordship of your arrival," the porter said. He showed her into a small sitting room and quietly shut the door.

Barbara was disconcerted by the ease of her reception. But she was of a quick intelligence. It was readily apparent to her that the earl had received anonymous female callers such as herself before.

She glanced around the well-furnished sitting room, noting the priceless Ming vase, the sumptuous oriental carpet, the gilded candle branches, the cut-crystal Waterford flower bowl charmingly set off by an arrangement of blushing pink roses, and the striped rose silk upholstery covering the chairs and the settee. The Earl of Chatworth appeared to be a wealthy gentleman, an appearance that she knew was deceptive or otherwise her father could not have gained the leverage that he had claimed to have over the nobleman.

Babs sat down on the pretty settee. Through the mesh of her veil she thoughtfully regarded the portrait hanging over the mantel. The subject of the painting was a gentleman of another age, pomaded and laced in the extravagant style of the century past, whose handsome saturnine features and droop-lidded knowing eyes transcended the canvas and time. The earl's ancestor had definitely been a rakish fellow, decided Babs, and if the porter's high discretion was anything to judge by, so was the present earl.

All the trappings of wealth, probable libertine tendencies of the worst sort, and under her father's thumb, thought Babs. She tugged gently at the strings of her reticule as she reflected. Perhaps she had come on a fool's errand. She had very nearly decided to go find the porter so that she could tell him that she had changed her mind when the door to the sitting room opened.

4

THE EARL OF CHATWORTH ENTERED, shutting the door gently behind him.

Barbara regarded the gentleman with acute interest as he sauntered toward her. Her immmediate impression was favorable, which surprised her.

The earl was younger than she had expected, apparently but a few years older than herself. He was a well-set-up gentleman, broad of shoulder and lean of limb, as was evidenced by the exquisite cut of his morning coat and the close fit of his pantaloons. The earl's attire was finished with an intricately tied white silk cravat and Hessian boots. His dark hair was cut fashionably short and looked to have been impatiently run through with heavy fingers; Babs could not but wonder if it had been the porter's announcement of her own presence that had earned that particular reaction.

However, in the end it was his lordship's face that caught and held her interested gaze. Her eyes flew fleetingly to the portraited gentleman and back again. The present Earl of Chatworth owed much to his ancestor, possessing the same heavy-lidded eyes and aquiline nose, as well as the same half-smile. Babs decided that the knowing arrogance of that smile was particularly unsettling.

"You are safe here, m'dear. There is truly no more need of the veil," said Lord Chatworth, studying his visitor with at least equal interest. The woman was dressed in the high kick of fashion in a well-cut green pelise and matching bonnet. Except for the unmistakable message of the veil, she might have been one of his cousins come to call upon him with another of their constant entreaties to spend more time

dancing attendance on the young debutantes at their boring
soirees.

"I would prefer to keep it for the moment, my lord,"
Barbara said.

The earl's brows drew together in a slight frown. The
woman's husky, well-bred voice was not one that he readily
recalled. He cast about in his memory for a lady with whom
he had had some sort of tryst, but came up with nothing.
He shrugged and moved to lean against the mantel. There
he stood at ease, playing with his fob. Undoubtedly the lady
would herself jog his lamentable memory. "As you wish.
To whom do I owe this mysterious visit?"

"Miss Barbara Cribbage, my lord," she said quietly. She
awaited his lordship's reaction with dread anticipation. It was
all that she could have expected, and worse, and her courage
nearly deserted her.

Lord Chatworth abruptly straightened, dropping his fob
to dangle on its black riband. "You are Miss Cribbage?"
he asked. There was a mingled note of distaste and incredulity
in his voice. His eyes had sharpened and his stare raked over
her with a boldness that would have been insulting at any
other time.

Babs assured herself that she was not shocked or
embarrassed by his inspection. His lordship had as much right
to his interest in her as she had to hers in him. After all,
she had just moments before made much the same assessing
examination of his person.

"Yes, I am Miss Cribbage. You are undoubtedly
surprised, my lord. However, do reflect a moment. I could
hardly consent to marriage without first meeting my
intended," Babs said with a credible assumption of calm.
But her fingers were tight on the strings of her reticule. This
interview was proving every bit as difficult for her as she
had dreaded.

Lord Chatworth smiled thinly at her words. His eyes had
become extremely hard. "Quite. Naturally you wished to
inspect the goods your father has so very kindly purchased
for you." He stared insolently, trying to penetrate the heavy
veil. The woman sounded cultured and she possessed a

youthful figure, yet he could not be certain of her breeding or her age. Those things were apparent only in the eyes and one's countenance, he thought irritatedly.

Babs had flinched at the earl's words, but even as she did, she discovered that his scorn also served to anger her. She said coldly, "Not very elegantly put, Lord Chatworth. However true, you should also know that my father and I disagree vehemently about some of his methods."

"So I see," Lord Chatworth said contemptuously. He picked up his fob again, to swing it from the end of its black satin riband from negligent fingers. "Yet you are willing to be the prize in this farce. You would marry a man you know nothing of for the sake of a title. Pray forgive me for my lack of credulity, m'dear."

It was too much. She had hoped for an alliance of sorts and to reach an understanding, but this haughty ridicule could not be borne. "Lord Chatworth, have you never thought there may be others as equally unwilling as yourself to dance to the piper's tune?"

Babs pressed a gloved hand against her mouth, appalled by her outburst. She was desperately near tears. She fought to regain control of herself, taking deep, measured breaths. Tumbling about in her mind was the clear thought that she should never have come. She had made a horrible mistake. She could never make this arrogant nobleman understand even a particle of what she was feeling, or of her circumstances.

Lord Chatworth watched the woman's rigid figure, at last made sharply aware of her inner distress. He recalled suddenly the cit's aura of overbearing power. "Not even your father can force you into a distasteful marriage, Miss Cribbage," he said gently.

She shook her head. Her hands came together to clench in her lap. "It was so very difficult to come," she said under her breath. She was unaware that she spoke her thoughts aloud.

Lord Chatworth heard the barely audible admission. He moved to sit down beside her on the settee. He took hold of her hands, noting their slender bones even as he gently pried them apart. "My dear girl, your father may be unnaturally hard, but he is no ogre," he rallied in a light tone.

She turned her head, apparently considering him from the concealment of her veil. Dimly through the net he saw a fine-boned face, and was more than ever convinced that Miss Cribbage was indeed a young female. It relieved him of the sneaking horror that she might have been a good deal older than himself. Her fingers moved in his grasp and he released her hands at once.

"Lord Chatworth, what hold does my father have on you?"

The abrupt question and the bald way in which it was phrased took him off-guard. Lord Chatworth drew back, without conscious thought allowing his mouth to fall into its arrogant half-smile. "I cannot see where that concerns you, Miss Cribbage," he said icily.

Barbara had been given hope by his lordship's unexpected display of pity. She was desperate that he not withdraw once more behind his haughty mantle, where he would become once more unapproachable and unreasonable. "But it does, my lord! If I am to marry you, I must know whether you can escape him." Uncaring how he might construe her boldness, she placed an imperative hand on his sleeve. She said urgently, "Neither you nor I must allow ourselves to be trapped into circumstances of eternal dependence upon him."

"I see." Lord Chatworth glanced down at her gloved fingers before his frowning gaze returned to her veiled face. "But your father informed me that you are a wealthy young lady in your own right, Miss Cribbage. I fail to understand your claim of dependence."

She rose hastily from the settee, once more unable to control her agitation. "My fortune has certain restrictions placed against it, my lord. I suppose my father did not inform you that I cannot touch a penny until I am wedded. Even then, I shall be barred from my portion if I marry one who does not meet with my father's approval. If I refuse his choice of husband for me and I remain unmarried at five-and-twenty, my portion will automatically go to a nunnery in France.

I will then have the choice of following it to the cloister or of making my own way in the world.''

She stopped in her restless pacing to turn toward him. "I do not fancy entering service, my lord, so which do you recommend as the more enviable fate—that of governess or as someone's mistress?''

"My word," Lord Chatworth said, stunned.

Babs gave a small ironic laugh. "You see, Lord Chatworth, my father is indeed the ogre. He regards me of very little consequence except as a tool of sorts. Barred from polite society himself, he will go to any lengths to see his seed in the *ton* and thus gain a form of recognition. It was a bitter disappointment that I was not born a male. Then I could have perhaps earned a knighthood in orders or won a title by distinguishing myself in the army.''

There was a strained note in her voice that the earl was not unfamiliar with, given his large experience with women, and he realized that Miss Cribbage was very near tears. He loathed hysterics, and in an attempt to stem any such display, he said harshly, "Do you think you could cease your nervous pacing, Miss Cribbage? I have a great dislike of dramatic females." To his satifaction, there was a sharp intake of breath from his visitor and her head jerked up with the straightening of her carriage.

"I was not aware that I was boring you, my lord. Obviously I should not have come. Pray forgive me for my temerity," Babs said icily. She swept a bare curtsy and turned toward the door. Her elbow was caught abruptly by a firm hand. She glanced up quickly at the earl, surprised that he had detained her.

He looked down at her, his expression grown somber. "Miss Cribbage, pray be seated. I believe you came here to discuss business, and so we shall," Lord Chatworth said.

Barbara hesitated. He gestured toward the settee. Slowly she nodded and returned to the settee, to sink down on the striped cushions. She was somewhat disconcerted when Lord Chatworth chose to seat himself beside her. He placed an arm across the back of the settee so that he faced her.

"In answer to your previous question, Miss Cribbage, your

father holds the mortgages to all but one of my estates, including that of my family's ancestral home. Also, vowels for several thousand pounds lost at cards,'' Lord Chatworth said shortly.

Babs was appalled, as much by the amount as by the disclosure that the earl was apparently a hardened gamester. ''But how ever could he have managed to gain possession?''

''I was told by my man of business that by employing several agents your father bought the mortgages from the unsuspecting holders. He apparently used the same tactics in redeeming my debts for their worth,'' Lord Chatworth said. He paused fractionally. ''Your father has offered clear titles to my lands and possession of my own vowels as bride settlement.''

''I go dearly, then,'' said Babs, not at all gratified by the knowledge. Her clasped fingers twisted painfully. ''I have never been more to my father than an investment, I'm afraid.''

There was a wealth of unhappy undercurrent in her voice, and that more than anything else brought to light for Lord Chatworth with forcible clarity the parameters of her relationship with her father. Lord Chatworth's mouth tightened a moment. He had suddenly a measure of respect for the woman seated beside him that he would not have thought to have been possible only several minutes before.

''We neither of us can afford to indulge in self-pity, Miss Cribbage, if we are to win free of your dishonorable parent,'' he said coolly.

Babs' pulse jumped in her throat at his collective term. His lordship understood, then, and he meant to fight. She stared at his cold expression, noting the firmness of his mouth and the obstinate cast of his jaw. She commented, ''I believe you could be as hard as he.''

Lord Chatworth leaned closer so that his keen eyes could better penetrate through the veil. ''Does that frighten you off, Miss Cribbage?''

''No. It would take a strong man to win over him,'' she said. She searched his lean face and his alert gray eyes, liking and at the same time shivering at the implacable determination she saw.

"Must you continue to hide, Miss Cribbage?" the earl complained. "I hardly think that I can be expected to strike a bargain with a swath of dark net."

She gave the slightest of laughs before she lifted the veil and tossed it back over the brim of her bonnet. She turned to meet his interested gaze.

Lord Chatworth was treated to his first glimpse of her attractive face. A fine sprinkling of pale freckles crossed a straight nose and highlighted flecks of gold in her large green eyes. Her gaze was steady and met his without flinching.

"Does the filly please you, my lord?" she mocked lightly.

Lord Chatworth was unpleasantly reminded of his interview with Cribbage and the man's insulting likening of his daughter to a valuable brood mare. "I do not wed you for your face, Miss Cribbage," he snapped.

"No, it would be for convenience," said Barbara quietly. She smoothed the veil up over the brim of her bonnet. She felt curiously vulnerable without the veil's concealment, but she knew that she must now be able to lay all of her cards on the table if she was to win the full partnership that she so desperately needed. "We both have much to gain. The means is forced upon us, but for success we must use it in tandem and to a common end."

"A marriage of convenience," Lord Chatworth agreed. "And when the purpose is accomplished, the marriage is to be dissolved or not at either of our discretions." He smiled faintly at her nod of agreement. Perhaps this payment of the devil would go far easier than he had first anticipated. The daughter seemed far more reasonable than her parent, and he put his impression to the test. "Further, during the course of the marriage I would not interfere with you nor you with me."

"Excepting in the event of social obligation, of course. Then a mutual agreement of conduct must be negotiated," she said.

His lordship's pleasantness of expression disappeared and he regarded her warily. "Meaning exactly what, Miss Cribbage?"

She smiled and lifted her hands. "Only that I shall be open to your lordship's suggestions if my conduct as your wife does not strike the proper note."

"Agreed, and I shall grant you the privilege of telling me to go to the devil whenever the occasion warrants," said Lord Chatworth. He smiled suddenly. "I like your prosaic attitude, Miss Cribbage. It bodes well for a successful partnership."

Babs laughed, aware that she had both surprised and pleased him. But she swiftly sobered because there was one important point that they had not yet covered. "My lord, there is one other consideration. I do not know how to put it delicately. There is the question of an heir, Lord Chatworth." Faint color rose in her face as she met his expression of open astonishment. She said somewhat unsteadily, "If you agree, my lord, either of our bastards would be eligible to succeed to the title. Or perhaps you would prefer some relation of yours."

Lord Chatworth stared speechlessly at her. His eyes suddenly narrowed as he recalled Cribbage's bland refusal to take insult when he had questioned the daughter's honor. Anger rose in him along with his suspicions. He said softly, "Your bastard, Miss Cribbage? Are you breeding, by chance?"

Babs recoiled, her face flaming. "No, of course not! I only meant that . . . My lord, we do not know how long the arrangement between us must exist. I thought in the instance that one of us should become attached outside . . . if the affair were discreet . . ."

"Ah, I understand." Lord Chatworth considered her unsmilingly for some seconds. "You are a very unusual young woman."

Barbara pulled at the strings of her reticule, a sickening sensation in the pit of her stomach. He obviously found her contemptible. The dark memory of the debacle of her come-out rose to stifle her anew. She could scarcely bear it. "I apologize most profoundly, my lord," she said in a suffocated voice. She avoided his eyes. "It was an ill-considered thought."

"On the contrary, Miss Cribbage."

Her fingers stilled their agitated movement at the approval in his voice. She looked up. Lord Chatworth's smile was almost warm, she thought dazedly.

"Quite practical, actually. I so agree, Miss Cribbage." Lord Chatworth held out his hand. "I believe we shall deal well together. Shall we make it binding?"

Babs responded with a flickering smile and shook his hand in a solemn fashion.

Lord Chatworth rose and walked to the bellpull hanging alongside the mantel. "Would you care to join me in celebration of our prenuptial agreement? A sherry, perhaps?"

Babs rose from the settee, reaching up to replace the veil as she did so. It would cause her acute embarrassment to allow her face to be seen by any of the earl's servants. "Thank you, but, no, my lord. I really must go."

The sitting-room door opened in response to Lord Chatworth's tug on the bell rope and a footman appeared. "My lord?"

"A cab for the lady," commanded Lord Chatworth.

"I have one waiting, my lord," Babs said quickly.

"Indeed? Then I shall not require your services, after all," said Lord Chatworth, dismissing the footman with a gesture. He offered his arm to his visitor. "Allow me to escort you to your carriage, ma'am."

Babs placed her fingers lightly on his sleeve. Lord Chatworth walked her out of the town house down to the street. He handed her up into the waiting hackney cab.

Lord Chatworth detained her for an instant to raise her fingers to his lips in the briefest of salutes. "Until our next meeting," he said quietly. He let go of her hand and shut the carriage door. He stepped back onto the curb as the cab jerked forward into the London traffic.

Babs leaned back against the worn leather of the seat squab. She drew a long breath, feeling oddly shaken now that her visit to the Earl of Chatworth was all over. The die was truly cast, she thought. There would be no turning back.

5

THE ANNOUNCEMENT was duly posted in the London *Gazette* of the banns between Marcus Aurelius Alexander Chatworth, Earl of Chatworth, Viscount Alster, and Miss Barbara Cribbage, heiress. The news caught polite society by surprise.

Lord Chatworth had been a prime catch since reaching his majority, of course, but not even the most wishful of mamas had seriously advised her daughters to dangle after the wild earl. Lord Chatworth was but six-and-twenty and had early on established a reputation for riotous living. It had been assumed that he would not contemplate the advantages of the matrimonial state for some years yet.

Of Miss Cribbage, there were some vague recollections of a brief social debut a few years before, but no one could claim recent knowledge about her.

The unexpected announcement was the *on-dit* of the Season, and the curious speculated on all the possible reasons for the abrupt marriage. There appeared no ready reason for the earl's hasty marriage, other than that Miss Cribbage was said to be extremely well-endowed. The earl obviously was marrying the heiress for her money, since she had few pretentions to society, but no one could say for certain whether the earl was in dire financial straits.

For some years, due to her fragile health, the Countess of Chatworth had preferred to live quietly secluded at the family ancestral estate rather than entertain in town. The cynical had openly wondered whether the countess did not also prefer to be left ignorant of the gossip concerning many of her son's wilder excesses, which she certainly would not

have been if she had been living in London. Speculations
ran rife. Perhaps the Countess of Chatworth was in a poorer
state than had been believed and had requested to see her
only son safely wed before her death, though none could put
forth why a veritable nobody had been chosen to succeed
her ladyship.

The only other possible reason for the earl's abrupt
decision to wed was that there was a child in the offing. That
would certainly explain the odd marriage, if the earl was
concerned about giving legitimacy to an heir. However, the
consensus was that he should have chosen a bride of lineage
as worthy as his own to get a legitimate heir. He need not
go to the finality of marrying the Cribbage girl, even if she
was his mistress and carried his child. He could simply make
proper provision for the child, once born, and pension off
the mother. So society discussed and judged and speculated.

Invitations to the ceremony were eagerly awaited, as
everyone wished to satisfy some of their curiosity concerning
the improbable match. But most were doomed to disappointment. The Earl of Chatworth's marriage was not to be a
grand social function.

The wedding was a private affair held in a small London
chapel with only a few family and friends in attendance. From
his vantage point in his pew, Mr. Cribbage thought it a paltry
affair. He had envisioned an elaborate gala at St. George's
Cathedral, preceded by gilt-edged engraved invitations to
every member of the *ton*, all to trumpet his success to the
world. But his plans had been effectively undermined by the
earl's swift maneuvering.

Mr. Cribbage resentfully eyed the broad back of the
gentleman who was at that moment repeating the sacred vows
that would bind him to his daughter. His lordship had taken
him completely by surprise. Lord Chatworth had cheated him
of his moment of triumph. Mr. Cribbage grunted, recalling
yet again that his lordship had warned him that he "called
no man master." The earl would bear watching, thought
Cribbage dourly.

Lord Chatworth had not deigned to argue the matter of
the wedding arrangements with his future father-in-law, but

instead immediately arranged for the chapel and a minister. He had asked his secretary to send out the necessary notifications to members of his family and those of his friends whom he could trust not to thereafter rush to the gossipmongers. Almost as an afterthought, he had consulted briefly with his intended. Miss Cribbage had readily fallen in with his proposal for a small simple affair. He had half-expected some sort of dust-up, since females were so attached to such things as bridal clothes, but Miss Cribbage had surprised him. He had come away from their second interview with a feeling of satisfaction and the reinforced conviction that this marriage of convenience could suit him well enough.

As for Babs, she sent word posthaste to her aunt to come to London. Ostensibly, Lady Azaela was to aid her in the planning and ordering of her trousseau, but in actuality Babs wished her aunt to be in time to be present at the hurriedly arranged ceremony.

While awaiting Lady Azaela's arrival, Babs and her maid concentrated on putting together a proper wedding ensemble as soon as could be. The seamstresses were adjured to whip up at lightning speed the satin gown and swansdown-trimmed pelisse. The necessity of traveling clothes could safely be set aside, for the earl had made clear that there would not be an extended bridal trip.

Babs shopped for white gloves and satin slippers, camisoles and slips and white silk stockings, a straw bonnet with a white net veil attached to its brim, a reticule knotted of gold string, and myriad other items. She did not count the cost but chose exactly what she wished, with the faintly humorous thought that since it was the only time she was likely to be wedded, she intended to look every inch the fashionable bride in the short time that was allowed to her to arrange it.

Her father approved of her expenditures, seeing glimpses of bandboxes and packages before they were whisked upstairs to Babs' bedroom. Given the bills, he measured the extravagance of his daughter's purchases in direct proportion to how important she was going to appear, which would naturally be a direct reflection on himself. He ordered up a new suit of clothes for himself, and confident in his power, he began to make grandiose plans for the wedding without consultation with either the earl or his daughter. They would accept whatever he chose to give to them.

Mr. Cribbage was not best pleased at the arrival of his sister-in-law, Lady Azaela Terowne, but he recognized the importance of having a member of the quality occupying the bride's pew. He was therefore on his best behavior with Lady Azaela, even going so far as to compliment her on her bonnet and to offer a glass of Madeira to her upon her arrival when she was ushered into the drawing room.

Lady Azaela regarded Mr. Cribbage with a touch of amusement in her sharp blue eyes. She drew off her gloves in a matter-of-fact way. "I am astounded by your affability, sir. We have not dealt so well together in the past."

Mr. Cribbage smiled, hooking his hands into his vest pockets. "Quite true, my lady. However, this morning I have been consulting with caterers in ordering up the wedding feast. Such work has put me into an expansive frame of mind and even your presence cannot mar the satisfaction that fills me at the thought of my daughter becoming a countess." He gave a loud laugh. His black eyes glittered triumph at Lady Azaela. "A countess, my lady! I have bought my daughter—*my* daughter!—a fine title. What say you to that?"

Lady Azaela's eyes became frosty. "Certainly such a title is no less than my sister's daughter deserves." She gathered her gloves and her reticule. "I shall decline the wine, after all, and instead go directly up to see my niece."

Mr. Cribbage made an ironical bow. "Of course, my lady. You will want to inspect my daughter to see that she has not become tainted by her proximity to me."

Lady Azaela did not deign to acknowledge her brother-in-law's rude remark, but swept out of the drawing room and made her way upstairs to her niece's bedroom. She entered on a bare knock, saying, "Well, Babs? What have you to tell me?"

Babs swung around, her green eyes widening in real pleasure. She rushed into her aunt's outheld arms, and unexpected tears rushed to her eyes. "Oh, Aunt Azaela! How very glad I am that you have come."

"There, child, as though I would not," Lady Azaela said

bracingly, touched by her niece's unusual display of emotion. She set her niece away so that she could look at her. "You appear well enough, though perhaps a trifle pale. Are you resting properly, my dear?"

Babs laughed and threw an encompassing glance about the jumble of bandboxes, portmanteaus, and articles of clothing scattered over the bedroom. Her maid had smiled a greeting for Lady Azaela but continued with her task of packing away undergarments and stockings. "Oh, indeed! Lucy and I have been in such a whirl of shopping and planning, you can have no notion. I am so tired that I am hardly able to keep my eyes open through dinner these days."

Lady Azaela snorted, her shrewd glance taking in the telltale circles under her niece's eyes. "So I imagine. Lucy, would you be so good as to bring me a cup of tea?"

"Very good, my lady," said the maid, understanding at once that Lady Azaela wished to be alone with her mistress. She left the bedroom, carefully closing the door behind her.

Lady Azaela laid aside her reticule and gloves and began untying the ribbons of her bonnet. "We shall now have a comfortable cose, dear Babs, and you shall tell me when the wedding is to be. You were rather vague in your letter and downstairs there is your father trumpeting that he is ordering the caterers. I shall require information on everything that has been done to date if I am to eradicate his disastrous influence on the festivities."

"My father is operating under a delusion, Aunt. Nothing that he is planning shall in any way affect my wedding," said Babs, moving aside a couple of opened bandboxes so that her aunt could be seated on the chair beside the bed.

Lady Azaela raised her brows. "You astonish me, my dear. Your father can be most determined, if you will recall," she said dryly.

Babs winced at the reminder of her painful come-out. "True, but the Earl of Chatworth is also a most determined gentleman."

"You interest me most profoundly," said Lady Azaela politely.

Babs laughed, her green eyes twinkling. "Indeed, I had

thought I might. The fact of the matter, dear ma'am, is that his lordship has already finalized arrangements for our wedding. It will be in but a week's time and—''

''A week!'' Lady Azaela all but shrieked in her astonishment. ''My dear, you cannot be serious. Why, there is much to do. Your dress—''

''My dress has just come today. See, here it is.'' Babs lifted the satin and lace gown carefully from the largest box on top of the bed and held it up to herself, one slim arm pinning it against her. A faint smile on her lips, she asked, ''How does it look, Aunt? Shall I appear the usual happy and blushing bride?''

''Oh, my dear,'' said Lady Azaela softly. There was an undercurrent of pity in her voice that her niece could not but detect.

Babs suddenly no longer felt like smiling. She lay back the gown, taking care to fold it within the tissues so that it would not wrinkle. ''Lucy shall put it up later, after she has let down the hem. It was just the slightest bit short, you see, and—''

''Babs, come sit beside me,'' said Lady Azaela. She waited until her niece had settled on the bed beside her and she had taken the girl's hand in hers before she spoke, carefully marshaling her thoughts as she did so. ''I know that this marriage is not precisely what you might have wished for. Oh, every young girl dreams of a dashing gentleman and tender romance. You cannot tell me differently, for I seem to recall something of the sort myself.'' That brought a gurgle of laughter from her niece, which she was glad of. It augered well that Babs retained her sense of humor. ''However, from what you have just told me of the Earl of Chatworth, the match may work very well. He is apparently not one to bow to your father's bullying ways.''

''No, I do not think he is,'' Babs said quietly. ''In fact, I made sure of it before I agreed to accept the marriage. I took your advice, Aunt Azaela. I went to his lordship's town house to meet him and—''

''Babs! I never advised such a course,'' said Lady Azaela, horrified.

Babs laughed in genuine amusement. She shook her head. "Indeed, I know you did not. But it seemed the only course open to me. Pray do not look like that, Aunt. The earl was all that was gentlemanly, once he understood why I had come, and indeed, we were able to come to a very satisfactory agreement."

Lady Azaela regarded her niece with fascinated interest. "What sort of agreement, my dear?"

Babs told her aunt in a few well-chosen sentences the sum of her conversation with the earl. "And that is how it stands. Together we shall fight my father and hope to win free in the end."

"I see." Lady Azaela was silent for a moment, reflecting upon what she had heard. She looked up and squeezed her niece's hand. "You have done well, Babs. It is much better than I could have hoped to come out of your father's intolerable connivings. Perhaps the match will be one that can make you happy, which is, as you know, my dearest wish in life for you."

Babs leaned forward to give her aunt a swift hug. "Yes, I know. And I promise you that I shall be as happy as I possibly can." She straightened and smiled at her aunt. "I am so glad that you have come. You can have no notion how anxious I was that you would not arrive in time to attend the wedding."

"Your father will be very angry," Lady Azaela said quietly. She saw the stiffening of her niece's frame, and her own fingers tightened on the chair arm, relaxing only with an exertion of her will.

"Yes, I know."

That was all that her niece said, but Lady Azaela thought she was familiar enough with the subtle intonations of the girl's voice to know that Babs was badly frightened by the thought of Mr. Cribbage's inevitable fury. He would not take well to all of his plans being usurped by the earl's quick action. Lady Azaela made up her mind. She had not yet completely discharged her duty to her dead sister, she thought. "I shall remain here instead of opening my own house. Your father shall have no choice in the matter, as

I shall say that my house needs to be thoroughly aired before I can possibly move into it.''

Babs gave her aunt a speaking glance. ''Thank you, ma'am.''

As Lady Azaela bethought herself of something further that she wished to say in regards to the bargain Babs had struck with the Earl of Chatworth, the maid returned with the tea tray. ''We shall speak more on the subject of his lordship,'' Lady Azaela said firmly, even as she nodded to the maid.

Babs agreed, though she wondered what Lady Azaela could possibly want to hear. She had told her aunt all that had transpired. However, as the maid went on with the packing and the ladies enjoyed their tea, the conversation shifted pleasantly to other things and Babs forgot her aunt's odd seriousness of tone when she had spoken of the Earl of Chatworth.

6

BABS WAS UNDER tremendous anxiety during the wedding ceremony.

At the eleventh hour she had had second thoughts about the wisdom of marrying the Earl of Chatworth. His lordship was a complete stranger to her. Moreover, he was a gentleman outside her ken, whose morals and manner of life were far removed from her own ideals. She decided that she could not sensibly expect even a marriage of convenience between them to be anything but unhappy for herself and a source of irritation for his lordship.

After a particularly unpleasant interview with her father, who had indeed been enraged to learn that the wedding was to be that same week, she had realized with resignation and despair that her only true recourse was to go through with the sham of marriage. Lady Azaela had interrupted that same confrontation before its ending and had sharply recommended her brother-in-law to take a powder. She would deal with Babs, she said.

Lady Azaela was wise enough to perceive much of the turmoil that stirred her niece's unhappiness. She had taken it upon herself to deliver a short lecture. "I shall not point out the social advantages, Babs, for I know that weighs very little with you. However, you must consider that as the wife of a peer you will not be constrained to endure your father's unwelcome meddling in your life."

"Yes, there is that," Babs had agreed with a somewhat hollow laugh. It was as much Lady Azaela's persuasions as her own good sense that had finally convinced Babs of the

continued wisdom of her original decision to throw in her
lot with the Earl of Chatworth.

And so it was that she found herself elegantly coiffed and
gowned in shimmering satin and fragile lace, standing beside
a man utterly unknown to her with her fingers held captive
in his firm clasp, while her body was shaken by uncontrol-
lable shivers.

As the marriage vows were exchanged, her responses
sounded mechanical and strained in contrast to the earl's firm
voice.

When her new husband lifted her veil, she was white-faced.
As custom demanded, the earl bent to kiss her. Her lips were
cold as ice, but if he noticed anything amiss in her lack of
response, he did not acknowledge it publicly by either word
or expression.

Babs' eyes lifted fleetingly to meet his. He gave her only
a swift, penetrating glance from his remote hard eyes before
he offered his elbow to her. She placed her hand on his
velvet-clad arm. A wink of gold caught her eyes and she
stared at the narrow gold band on her finger. Feeling herself
under observation, she looked up quickly to meet the earl's
inscrutable gaze.

"An odd feeling, is it not?" he said, too quietly for any
but herself to hear. He did not seem to require an answer,
and she was glad of it.

They walked out of the church sanctuary and passed
through the outer doors to the street. Amid the shouted well-
wishers and pelting rice, the earl and Barbara hurried down
the steps and immediately got into the crested carriage that
awaited them at the curb.

The earl had chosen to eschew a reception, again with
Babs' complete concurrence, and so there was nothing to
hold them back from their departure. It was time to embark
on their married venture. Barbara shivered slightly as she
took her seat.

The earl shut the carriage door firmly and without a glance
for her settled himself on the seat. The well-sprung vehicle
started with a jerk, to rattle over the cobbles with a dismaying

sound of finality. The bridal couple, at last free of the eyes of the curious, were able to contemplate their fate.

Babs knew the moment that the earl turned his eyes on her, but she pretended not to notice. She carefully smoothed her gloves over her wrists and even reached up to adjust her veil more smoothly over the brim of her bonnet in order to avoid his gaze. She knew that she was acting in a cowardly fashion, but she could not seem to help herself. It had been terrifying to contemplate marriage, but what she now felt made that emotion pale by comparison. She had finally and irrevocably taken the step that bound her to the gentleman seated beside her.

As though he had read something of her tumbling thoughts, the earl said, "We have done it, Miss Crib—my lady. We have burned our bridges and there is no alternative now but to go forward." There was a trace of grimness in his normally drawling voice.

Babs glanced at him. He sat at ease, his body swaying gently to the carriage movement. There was a frowning expression in his eyes that served to grant her a measure of courage, for she saw that she was not alone in feeling unease over her changed circumstances. "Indeed, my lord. I hope that neither of us has reason to regret the course we have embarked upon." She took a steadying breath as she plunged into what was for her a confidence. "I must admit to a feeling of trepidation. I suppose because it is all so foreign to me. In truth, I never thought to hear myself addressed as 'my lady.' " She attempted to laugh as she shook her head over the vagaries of fate.

"As my wife, you will become used to that, as well as to a great many other things," said Lord Chatworth. His eyes slowly traversed her face and figure, pausing finally on the glint of gold on her finger. Then he turned his head to stare out of the window.

Babs' heart pounded. She wondered exactly what his lord-ship was thinking. His scrutiny had been peculiarly encompassing and the color had risen unbidden to her face during his brief survey of her. It was such a strange,

penetrating stare that she suddenly wondered whether she
had been as perfectly clear as she had thought during their
first meeting. Surely Lord Chatworth had understood that
theirs was to be a marriage in name only. If he had not . . .
the alternative appalled her.

She was not a shrinking miss, nor quite as ignorant as
perhaps she should have been. As a girl in her father's house,
she had seen and heard enough to have gained a fair notion
of what went on between a man and a woman. After her
mother's death—and even before, when her mother had
already become ill—her father had brought various women
into the house. Mr. Cribbage had not cared that he wounded
his wife's sensibilities or that he exposed his impressionable
young daughter to the cruder aspects of life.

Upon Mrs. Cribbage's few and timid remonstrances on
her daughter's behalf, Mr. Cribbage had laughed rudely and
declared that the girl needed educating in her future
marital duties. "She is not like to get it from such a
pale milksop as yourself, madam," he had said bitingly to
his wife.

Mrs. Cribbage had risen from her chair, bright spots of
color in her normally pallid face, and had exited the sitting
room with her husband's hateful mocking guffaws beating
about her ears. Her rare rage had the effect of invigorating
her, despite the weakness of her constitution. The following
morning she had taken Babs and gone for an unprecedented
and lengthy visit to her sister, Lady Azaela. It was during
this time that she had confided so much and exacted the
promise of her sister's aid for her daughter in the event of
her own demise.

In accordance with her sense of duty and out of deep
affection for her niece, Lady Azaela had naturally taken it
upon herself to discover in just what guise this marriage of
her niece and the Earl of Chatworth was taking place. When
Babs had informed her aunt of every detail of the pact agreed
upon between herself and the earl, Lady Azaela had instantly
seen its advantages, but later she had warned her niece that
at times such understandings could be conveniently set aside.
She had proceeded to inform her niece in great detail of what

to expect if his lordship should choose to exercise marital rights, after all.

Babs had listened in shock and amusement, but with immense gratitude as well, for she knew that her aunt spoke of such things only out of great love for her.

Now as she recalled some of Lady Azaela's strictures and explanations, Babs had cause to blush. She glanced again at the earl. She had seen before that he was handsome and that he was possessed with an intriguing hint of recklessness in his eyes and his quick lithe movements. From the first, she had been attracted to him, despite his lordship's unfortunate propensities for gambling and womanizing. Before, her awareness of the earl's attributes had all been academic, but now, this dangerously attractive nobleman was her lawful husband.

She was sitting close enough to him that the clean masculine scent of musk, cloves, and sandalwood was in her nostrils. As she realized this, she was abruptly and newly aghast at what she had done.

She had consigned her future into the hands of a stranger, all on the conditions of a flimsy verbal agreement.

Babs' introspection was so deep that at the earl's touch of her arm, she startled like a timid rabbit. His lordship's brows rose in questioning surprise. Babs flushed. "I—I was thinking, my lord. I am sorry."

Lord Chatworth did not comment upon her nervousness, but instead remarked, "We have arrived, my lady."

Startled, Babs realized for the first time that the carriage was slowing. Despite the knowledge that it revealed a measure of gaucheness, she leaned toward the window for a glimpse of her new home.

The carriage stopped. The door was almost immediately opened by an expressionless manservant in red-and-gold livery. The earl got out and then, as on an afterthought, he turned to offer a hand to his new wife as she descended to the sidewalk. The manservant shut the carriage door and signaled the coachman to drive on, then ran ahead of the earl and the countess up the steps to the open door of the town house.

With her hand lightly on her husband's arm, Babs looked up at the impressive facade of the town house as they ascended the steps. When she had come on her veiled visit, she had not taken particular note of the residence itself because it had not been of importance. But now the town house was to be her home and she found herself quelled by the sheer size of the place.

When she and the earl stepped through the open door and into the front hall, she was astonished to see a long row of servants. The servants stood at quiet attention, their eyes fixed upon the couple who had just entered. The earl was apparently just as surprised as she was by their reception. Babs caught a muttered expletive from him. However, when he spoke it was mildly enough.

"What is the meaning of this gathering, Smithers?"

"The staff has gathered to convey our respects to my lord and her ladyship upon this auspicious occasion," said the butler, bland of face and voice.

"I should have expected something of the sort," Lord Chatworth said softly, an odd smile playing about his mouth. More loudly, he said, "Quite proper, Smithers."

The butler gave a slight bow. He gestured for his lord and lady to precede him and with grave formality proceeded to introduce each member of the staff to the new Countess of Chatworth.

Barbara inclined her head and murmured what was appropriate, all the while acutely aware of her husband's amused expression. As for the members of the household, she met varying glances of scarcely veiled curiosity, of contempt, of critical reserve, even patent hostility. By the end of the formal ceremony, she had fully realized the difficulty she faced in assuming her position as lady of the house. Given the nature of her marriage and her own lack of social stature, the staff would not easily accept her, as they would instantly have done someone of, or near, equal birth to the Earl of Chatworth. Unless Babs completely missed her guess, there was going to be a pitched battle to prove herself worthy of her position, which she had every intention of doing. She had learned well from her aunt that a household must be guided by a firm hand, or chaos resulted.

Babs was not one to give over before the battle was even joined. Her trepidation and awe upon entering the town house evaporated with the stirring of her pride and her anger. She could do nothing about her birth. But she knew very well how to order an efficient household and she was determined that the earl would at least find that she was not lacking in that regard.

She made a mental note to clarify with the earl that anything to do with the ordering of the staff and the house was to be her concern. It would not do to have the squabblings certain to ensue to be constantly appealed to his judgment. She had no wish to have a wedge driven by domestic troubles thrust through the delicate balance of her pact with the earl. From her point of view, there was too much at stake to risk alienation of his lordship.

"Well done," said Lord Chatworth. "Smithers, Lady Chatworth and I shall want sherry in the parlor in half an hour."

"Very good, my lord," said the butler. He shot a steely glance about the still-lingering servants and they all hurried away to resume their various duties.

Lord Chatworth turned to Barbara. "You will naturally wish to change out of your bridal clothes and refresh yourself, my lady. The footman will show you up to your rooms." He raised her gloved hand to his lips in a show of distant courtesy.

Babs murmured her thanks before she turned to follow the footman up the stairs. She knew that the earl did not stand watching her when she heard his quick steps as he crossed the marble tiles of the empty entry hall. A heavy door crashed shut.

Babs suppressed a sigh. It was not at all the sort of marriage she had hoped for, certainly, but she reminded herself that beggars could not be choosers. Her present circumstances had been practically thrust upon her, and she had attempted to make something better of the situation through her understanding with the Earl of Chatworth. It was too early for either of them to have learned to trust the other. Perhaps they never would. If that were to be so, it would come very hard to her to give up all her last dreams of love and warmth and security and respect.

The maid who had served Babs for years in Lady Azaela's house awaited her in the bedroom suite. "There you are at last, my lady," she said, hurrying over to take her mistress's bonnet and veil.

"You speak as though you feared for my very existence, Lucy. But I survive quite well, as you see," Babs said with a touch of humor. She showed her hand with the plain gold band snug about her third finger.

"Not an engagement stone in sight, more's the scandal," Lucy said disapprovingly. She began to undo the scores of tiny buttons that fastened down the back of the white satin gown.

"One could hardly expect the earl to drape me in priceless heirloom jewels, Lucy. After all, this marriage is naught but a business arrangement," Barbara said coolly.

The satin gown slid to the floor and she stepped out of its folds. The maid snorted, snatching up the gown to smooth it carefully before she laid it aside on the bed for later packing away. "That is all very well, my lady, but I should like to see the man who does not have his own notions of what makes a business and what makes a wife." She was busy with the shaking out of her mistress's day gown or she would have seen that Barbara's consternated gaze flew to her face.

After a short pause, while the maid threw the day gown over her head and adjusted it, Babs said, "I am to meet his lordship for sherry in the parlor in half an hour."

Lucy raised her brows. She gave a nod of satisfaction as her fingers flew over the gown's buttons. "At least his lordship has some notion of what is proper. Then maybe some I could mention will see that his lordship means to treat you as his true lady."

Babs met the maid's shrewd glance in the mirror. The expression in her own eyes was unsurprised. "The staff do not acknowledge me."

The maid gave a grim nod.

Babs smiled slightly, recalling all of the careful instructions that had been drilled into her through the years by her aunt. Lady Azaela had never countenanced carelessness, let alone signs of open rebellion, among her staff. Lady Azaela had prepared her niece in every way to be mistress of a large respectable establishment, and those who dismissed her for an ignorant tradesman's daughter would swiftly learn their mistake, Barbara thought.

"I suspected as much when I was introduced to the servants belowstairs. I am despised, Lucy. But I'll wager that before the month is done I shall be mistress of this house. I shan't sit idly by while mismanagement and misplaced snobbery spread like dry rot through the place," she said with quiet evenness.

"Indeed not, my lady," Lucy said, cheered. She set to the pleasant task of rearranging her mistress's fine auburn hair.

7

HALF AN HOUR to the minute, Barbara entered the parlor. The footman who had shown her into the room closed the door behind her. The earl turned from his contemplation of the fire as she walked toward him.

Babs saw that his lordship had also taken the opportunity to trade his bridal clothes for more conservative wear. He had put on instead an afternoon coat, smooth buckskin trousers, and glossy Hessian boots. His cravat was immaculately tied, while his tight-fitting waistcoat was decorated with a collection of fobs and seals at the waist. The Earl of Chatworth was an undeniably attractive gentleman, and when he smiled, as he did now, the countess privately thought she had never met anyone that more fit her romantic fancies.

Lord Chatworth regarded his new wife quizzingly. "A penny for them," he offered, gesturing her courteously to a chair.

Babs laughed, though a faint flush mounted in her cheeks. She gracefully sat down. "I was thinking that I have seldom seen a more attractive gentleman," she said.

The earl paused in the act of pouring their wine. His brows rose and his expression was somewhat sardonic as he said, "Indeed, ma'am! I am flattered that you should say so."

Babs was nettled by his amused tone. As she took the wine-glass from his hand, she looked steadily into his face. "Are you? I cannot conceive why. Afterward one usually does inspect a purchase with a sense of pleasure and perhaps a more critical eye than one did before carrying it home."

Lord Chatworth's brows snapped together and he stared

frowningly at her. Then his expression cleared and he laughed. He leaned his shoulder against the mantel. Lifting his glass, he said, *"Touché,* my lady. I had not thought about it in such terms, but you are right, of course. We have each made what we hope to be a bargain. It is only natural that you should wonder whether I am able to live up to expectations."

Babs took a sip of the sweet wine, letting the pause lengthen to a moment. Lowering the wineglass, she cradled it between her palms. "And you, my lord? Do you also wonder?"

Lord Chatworth regarded her silently. He allowed his eyes to travel over her, from her plaited hair and lovely face with the large green eyes and the delectably curved lips, to her neckline and the hint of shadow there, the small waist and curve of thigh outlined by the day gown.

He saw that his open scrutiny embarrassed her, but she did not drop her eyes when he returned his gaze to her face. He spoke with deliberation. "I, too, have looked over my purchase again, and I experience a sense of undeniable pleasure when I do so."

"That is not quite what I meant," Babs said, her color considerably heightened.

Lord Chatworth smiled in the peculiar fashion that she had taken note of during their first meeting. "I shall be perfectly honest, my lady. I have entered into a marriage that I never wished for and one that I hope will be of the shortest duration. However that may be, I intend to hold by the tenets of our pact. I expect that you will also honor our understanding. You have already proven in more than one respect to be a surprise to me." He paused a moment to regard her more thoughtfully. "Why did you not tell me that Lady Azaela Terowne was your aunt?"

Barbara ran one slender forefinger about the edge of her wineglass. It was a legitimate question and one that caused her a moment of fleeting embarrassment. The truth of the matter was that she had been piqued by the earl's lack of interest in her, but she did not want to admit that to him. She said only, "You did not appear eager to inquire into my antecedents, my lord."

Lord Chatworth barked a short laugh. "No, I suppose that I did not." He tossed off the wine and set the empty glass on the mantel, then seated himself in the chair opposite her. "I owe you an apology, my lady."

Babs looked over at him in some surprise. "In what way, my lord? You have done nothing."

"I have been remiss in my observations in more ways than I thought possible. I should have guessed from the first meeting that you did not spring whole-cloth from the trades. There was an indefinable air in your bearing and your determination that owed itself to good breeding. I have treated you badly, my lady. I have never interested myself in your background. I would like to make amends for that now, if I may," said Lord Chatworth.

Babs was silent for several moments, digesting his remarks. She was not at all sure that she liked his abrupt turnaround. She had no experience to judge by and only her own intuitive sense of preservation to guide her, but she rather thought that the earl's curiosity was more than idle. "I am my father's daughter, my lord. But I owe my sensibilities and my education first to my mother, Amanda Harrowby Cribbage, and after her death, to her sister, Lady Azaela Terowne. Is that what you wished to know, my lord?"

"Then you were not raised in your father's house?" asked Lord Chatworth.

Her fingers tightened about the wineglass. Now she knew exactly what he wanted from her. His lordship was fishing for reassurance that her well-bred appearance was genuine and not merely a thin veneer that would crack under the rigors of her duties as the Countess of Chatworth. In a carefully neutral voice, Babs said, "I was ten when I went to live with my aunt, my lord. I suppose that may be seen as fortuitous, since otherwise I would not have had the benefit of Lady Azaela's mentoring."

Lord Chatworth's keen eyes did not miss the telltale whitening of her fingertips on her wineglass. He suspected that there was something concerning her early childhood that she preferred not to openly discuss with him. He did not begrudge her that, he thought. Any child exposed to

Cribbage's harsh personality must have acquired some sort of resentments, and her mother had died too soon. Perhaps that was the crux of the matter: the poor woman had been driven to her grave by an overbearing vulgar husband, and the sensitive child had naturally blamed her father for it. "I am persuaded that Lady Azaela took you properly in hand," he said.

Babs relaxed at his banal observation, reassured that he did not mean to press her further. "Indeed, my aunt could be quite a taskmaster." A reminiscent smile played about her mouth.

A thought occurred to her and she looked quickly at the earl, who was watching her with a lazy interest in his eyes. "My lord, that brings me to a question that I have wondered about. Ours is a marrage of convenience, and so the traditional roles cannot be taken for granted by me. Exactly what are to be my duties as the Countess of Chatworth? Am I to be complete mistress of this establishment, or shall you wish that I defer to you in every domestic detail, such as the servants' squabblings or the ordering of the kitchen?"

"Good God, no," said Lord Chatworth, taken aback. He was appalled by the very suggestion that he interest himself in the running of the household. "You have free rein, of course. There is Mrs. Sparrow, the housekeeper, to assist you, and Smithers, of course. With their guidance into my habits and particular likes and dislikes, I am certain that you will make a splendid job of it." He spoke with a hearty reassurance that he was not at all positive he actually felt.

Babs smiled, her keen ears picking up the falseness of his tone. She inclined her head in ironic acknowledgment. His lordship was not to know that whatever his reservations might have been, she had every intention of putting his reassurance to her to the uttermost limits. "Thank you for your vote of confidence, my lord. I shall do my utter best, you may rest assured of that."

Lord Chatworth eyed his wife with a hint of suspicion. He did not quite know what had been said, but he sensed that she was hugely satisfied at what had just transpired. "I

shall also require you to act as my hostess from time to time,"
he said slowly.

He was startled by the look almost of panic that darted
into her expressive eyes. Oho, my girl, he thought. So there
is something that you fear, after all. He wondered with
resignation if his wife, with her obvious trepidation at the
mere suggestion of hostessing, would prove to be a disaster
in a social setting. Perhaps her air of breeding would
evaporate and leave only the vulgar underpinnings of her
paternal ancestry.

But then, it hardly mattered. He did not plan on spending
much time in doing the pretty in his own establishment. There
were amusements enough about town so that he did not need
to entertain, and certainly there was a particular lady who
knew just how to entertain him.

At thought of his mistress, the earl's lips curled faintly.
His reception at that lady's hands on the occasion of his next
visit would be interesting at the very least. He had not
informed her of his plans to wed.

Babs wondered at his lordship's strange smile. His eyes
were on her, but she did not think he saw her. She shivered
slightly. There was something in his expression that sent a
frisson up her spine. "My lord? You said something about
hostessing a few gatherings. When may I expect to do so?
I shall naturally wish to address the question of proper
entertainment and the invitations."

Lord Chatworth was brought back from his pleasantly
erotic reverie. He frowned in sudden irritability. "You need
not concern yourself with any of that just yet. I think it more
important that you become better acquainted with society
before setting about a party."

"Of course, my lord," Babs said quietly. She was startled
by the earl's sudden snappishness, but quickly regained her
balance. Her dealings with her father had not led her to
believe that any gentleman was capable of civility for any
great length of time.

Lord Chatworth was unaccountably sorry for his
discourtesy toward his unwanted wife. It was an emotion
as surprising as it was annoying. "I think also that it is

time that we establish a more familiar footing, my dear.''

He was amused that she stiffened, and he smiled, an arrogant mocking-smile expression. ''I do not go back so soon on our agreement, my lady, never fear. Unless you wish it, of course.'' He paused, to give her time to reply, and his amusement was strengthened by her quick shake of her head. ''I meant merely that we cannot go on addressing one another forever with such formality. I think that it is common practice for a wedded couple to make use of each other's Christian names. Especially as we have our unique business arrangement, I think it will facilitate matters if we should practice a little less formality. I am Marcus to my friends.''

Babs smiled a little, wondering with a touch of wistfulness if that was what she was: a friend who chanced to have married him. She thought not, but she could not very well refuse to agree to his suggestion. It would be churlish in the extreme. ''Very well, my lord. I so agree.''

Lord Chatworth smiled. He leaned forward from his chair to offer his hand to her. She laid her hand in his and his strong fingers closed about hers. ''Obviously it will take practice on your part, Barbara,'' he said teasingly.

Her attention was centered on the warm strength of his clasp. How much she wished that she could believe that it was there for her. She said unthinkingly, ''I prefer to be called Babs.''

Even as she sat reduced to speechless amazement by her own unaccountable confidence, the earl nodded. ''Babs it is, then,'' he said, rising from his chair. Still holding her hand, he drew her up to stand with him. ''I hope that this is the beginning of a most profitable relationship for us both.'' He raised her fingers, and his lips brushed lightly across her skin.

The parlor door opened at that fortuitous moment. The earl was still holding her hand as the footman entered. The manservant's quick eyes took in the charming position at a glance, but his expression did not reflect his startled thoughts. ''My lord, you requested to be notified when a reply to your note had been received.''

''Ah, yes.'' Lord Chatworth held out his hand

peremptorily. The footman came over, conveying a silver salver with a single folded note resting upon it. The earl took up the note and broke the seal. He waved the footman out.

After perusing the note swiftly, Lord Chatworth turned to Babs. "I had a bit of business to see to when we got to the house. I hope that you do not mind it, my dear, but I fear that I shall be going out this evening. It is the sort of engagement that I prefer not to put off."

Babs smiled and there was a wealth of understanding in the depths of her green eyes. She had caught the faintest hint of scent wafting off the note. "Of course, my lord. I understand perfectly, and to be truthful, I prefer to make mine an early evening. It has been a very eventful and fatiguing day, as I am certain that you will agree."

Lord Chatworth bowed. His mouth was curled in that peculiarly arrogant smile that so set Bab's teeth on edge. "Quite so. I shall be hard put to do justice to my engagement," he said softly, his thoughts already on his mistress.

Before she could stop herself, Babs made an abrupt gesture of distaste. She realized what she had conveyed to the gentleman standing beside her, and she gave a rueful laugh. "It will be more difficult than I bargained to learn to be the wife that you wish of me," she said.

"I do not think it will be at all difficult to recall once you learn just where the lines are drawn, my dear," drawled Lord Chatworth, annoyed by his wife's temerity in showing her disapproval.

The blood rushed to Babs' face. She bit her lip in vexation. Fortunately for her pride, the footman had already returned to his duty and so was not witness to the heavy set-down she had received. She drew her breath and said, "We have an agreement, my lord, it is true. But I do not think that it includes baiting each other."

"My apologies, my lady." Lord Chatworth bowed once more and he courteously offered his arm to her so that he could escort her to an early dinner. But he once more wore that infuriating smile.

Babs refused to glance at him as they left the parlor.

8

BABS SAW from the serving of the first course that the earl's attention was not really with her. He had a distant expression in his eyes that she thought she knew very well. She had learned long ago as a child that to interrupt her father's reflections was tantamount to requesting an instant rakedown. She had no reason to believe that the earl was any different in his reactions, and so she was extremely wary of giving offense in any way. She replied politely and civilly when his lordship spoke to her, but otherwise she did not elaborate on any topic or introduce conversation of her own.

They talked in a desultory fashion of the wedding, of the various dishes that were set before them, of the probable duration of Lady Azaela's stay in London, but nothing was touched upon concerning the matter that had brought them so abruptly and irrevocably together.

Lord Chatworth was bored out of his mind with his dullwitted wife. He had spent an hour and a half over dinner in his bride's company, making several attempts to launch small conversation, but to all his efforts she replied mostly in monosyllables.

The earl studied her across the table as he drank from his wineglass, and he wondered what he had possibly seen in her at their first meeting to give him the impression of intelligence and suppressed passion. She had been nothing but meek and smiling and unobtrusive the entire evening. She was lovely enough, he supposed, critically surveying an attractive face framed by the stunning auburn hair, her graceful neck and shoulders and rounded bosom. But she was without personality and he discovered that, without some

spark to ignite him, her beauty left him entirely unmoved.
He could scarcely have been more eager to leave her for more
stimulating company.

His thoughts curled idly to the lady to whom he was
engaged that evening. He smiled faintly, and anticipation put
a peculiar edge to his pleasant thoughts.

The covers were removed and his wife was rising from
the table, preparatory to leaving him to his wine, as custom
demanded. "I shall say a good night now, my lord, since
I know that you will be going out later," said Babs.

"Indeed, I shall probably not join you for coffee," he said.

She inclined her head, perfectly understanding that her
company would not be required anymore that evening.

Lord Chatworth rose politely in a show of courtesy as she
walked out of the dining room.

As the door swung shut, he sat down and picked up his
wineglass. At the butler's inquiry, he waved away the suggestion of a fresh bottle of claret. "I shall finish what I have.
That will be all, Smithers," he said.

"Very good, my lord." The butler bowed and exited the
dining room, leaving his lordship to his solitary after-dinner
wine.

Shortly thereafter, the earl also left the dining room, but
he did not rejoin his wife in the drawing room. He went
upstairs to change into evening clothes and emerged to
request that his carriage to be brought around.

Within a very few minutes the Earl of Chatworth settled
into his carriage and rolled away from the town house.

It was not a long ride and quite soon the carriage stopped.
The earl got out and climbed the steps of a fashionable town
house. He rang the bell. The door was opened without delay
and the porter bowed to him, accepting his hat and gloves.
He was expected and was shown immediately upstairs into
a private sitting room decorated in tawny yellow silks. The
bric-a-brac was Oriental, as were the hangings, the carpet,
and the multitude of sofa cushions.

Lord Chatworth had been a frequent visitor to the private
apartment and he was therefore incurious of the mysterious
aura of the furnishings of the room. He poured himself a

glass of wine from the decanter on the occasional table and made himself comfortable on one of the settees. He fully expected to be kept waiting as punishment for his sins, and he was not disappointed.

Some twenty minutes later the hangings that hid one of the doors twitched aside and the lady of the house entered the room. She stood quite still, allowing her gentleman visitor a full span of moments to study her. She was a sloe-eyed, raven-haired beauty, her hair cropped in wispy short curls that enhanced the size of her magnificent eyes. Her sensual mouth was naturally red and was at the moment caught in a delicious pout. She was attired in a revealing gown of thin silk, decorated with a froth of lace at the low décolletage.

Lord Chatworth felt desire rise in him at sight of her exquisite beauty. He made no effort to disguise the expression in his eyes. He smiled, that peculiar smile that hinted at so little and hid so much. "Lady Cartier." His voice was low and caressing.

As she regarded the earl, the lady's own eyes were quite cool. She did not return his smile. She walked toward him and her graceful movement allowed the silk to hint even more vividly that she was wearing little or nothing under the gown.

The earl had risen at her approach and now she gave her hand to him. "Well, my lord?" she asked in a neutral tone.

Lord Chatworth turned over her hand and placed a lingering kiss against her wrist, knowing well how sensitive she was at that particular point. "You are stunning this evening, my lady," he said formally, taking his cue from her own rigid civility. There were twin points of laughter in his eyes as he looked down into her face.

She pulled her hand free and turned half away from him with a petulant shrug. "I think that you owe me at least an explanation, my lord."

Lord Chatworth stepped closer, but he did not actually touch her, allowing his proximity alone to work upon her. His breath ruffled the wisps of hair on the back of her slender neck. "Such formality between us, Beth. You are annoyed with me. I cannot think why, however, unless it is because I am a trifle late for our appointed engagement this evening.

Very well, I shall apologize for my tardiness. Does that satisfy you?''

She rounded on him, her breasts heaving with emotion. Her hands were clenched at her sides. Her dark eyes flashed. "You know very well that it does not, Marcus. I am speaking about your wife." She practically spat the hated word. "Have you any notion what I felt to read in the *Gazette* of your marriage? That you had wedded—and done so without a word to me!"

"I was not aware that I required your permission, my lady," said the earl deliberately.

Lady Elizabeth Cartier heard the chilliness in his tone. She saw how his expression had closed, and at once she changed her tactics. It was not in her plans to permanently alienate him. She laid a hand against his shirt front. "Of course not, Marcus. It was just such a shock, that is all. And I could not but wonder whether I was to be supplanted in your affections," she said softly. Her long nails lightly scraped the fine linen shirt, scoring the warm flesh beneath.

Lord Chatworth bent to place his lips beneath her ear and proceeded to trail a series of light kisses down her neck. She arched her neck like a cat to allow him better access. She gasped when his teeth unexpectedly met in the softness of her bare shoulder. There was controlled passion in his low voice. "My dear Beth, what has my wife to do with this? Or this?" His hands came up to graze her through the gown.

Lady Cartier thought the lady in question had a great deal to do with it. She had long since fancied herself in the role of Countess of Chatworth, and she had been complacently certain that she had the earl firmly caught in her toils. She had thought it merely a matter of time before he came to the point and offered for her hand. The notice of his sudden marriage had destroyed both her hopes and her conviction that he was hers alone.

She held him off a little longer in hopes of learning what she could, but was wise enough to tease him as she did so. She slid her hands up under his coat to push it off his shoulders, which effectively hindered his own distracting explorations. "I was devastated, Marcus," she whispered

against his lips. "I care so desperately for you, you see."
Her hands were busy with his shirt buttons even as she leaned
closer to him.

Lord Chatworth shrugged, as much to relieve himself of
his restrictive garment as to indicate his indifference to her
revelation. "I would not so easily set you aside, Beth. It is
a marriage of convenience, and as such shall not interfere
with our arrangement. Indeed, what is between us is of far
more interest to me." As his coat dropped unheeded to the
carpet, he tore off his cravat. His shirt was pushed open and
her hands slipped inside.

"So I should hope, my lord," she breathed. Her nails
scored his naked back and she pressed close against him.

He laughed low in his throat. His eyes blazed with desire
as he pushed her away so that he could look down into her
half-closed eyes. As she met his gaze, her lips curved in an
inviting smile. "You know well enough how to please a man.
That is more than I ever heard of any wife doing," he said
hoarsely. He pulled her roughly into his arms and his mouth
descended hungrily upon hers.

Much later, Lady Cartier bade a fond farewell to her lover.
After he had left her, she went to the window and lifted one
curtain to await his emergence from her front door. She
watched him go down the steps of her house to enter his
waiting carriage. The streetlamp shone briefly on his face
before he ducked inside. The night was still young and she
should have been disappointed that the earl had not remained
until morning's light. But she had been wise enough not to
tax him about it. It was not in her plans to be seen as
demanding or unfeeling of his wishes.

She would leave that to the earl's wife to provide.

The carriage below rolled away. She dropped the curtain
and turned back into her bedroom, raising her arms above
her head to stretch languorously. The fact of the earl's
marriage had shaken her greatly, but his offhand assurance
and his subsequent actions had left her in little doubt of where
she stood.

This wife of his lordship's was a nuisance, of a certainty,
but she did not think a nuisance that was likely to hinder her

forever. Sometime during their assignation, at a moment
when she had long since discovered a man to be at his most
vulnerable, she had wormed out the information that the earl
had married only to secure a matter of business.

It had surprised her that his lordship should be situated
in such a way that he needed that kind of aid. She had not
known he was in financial straits. But she had also been
pleased. It meant that the wife had brought a fortune with
her, one that now belonged to the earl and much of which
she herself would undoubtedly profit by. So she was content
enough to allow matters to rest as they were for the moment.

As for her former aspirations of becoming the Countess
of Chatworth, she saw no reason to doubt that she still would
not one day capture the prize. Undoubtedly quite unaware
that he had done so, the earl had given her the distinct
impression that his marriage was one that he did not expect
to last. She was too levelheaded to suppose that the wife was
in indifferent health, the sort that might shorten her life span,
but there were such conveniences as annulment and divorce.

Lady Cartier toyed with the idea of annulment. After this
night she had a fair notion that the earl had not bedded his
wife. But that could not be expected to continue forever. If
the wife had any pretension at all to looks, she had no doubts
that his lordship would naturally take advantage of his marital
rights. It was a pity, of course, but one must make the most
of the situation.

Lady Cartier glanced at herself in the long cheval glass
and ran her hands over her curving hips. She rather thought
that his lordship would quickly discover that bedding an
inexperienced wife simply did not compare to making love
to his mistress.

She turned away from the mirror to sit down at her vanity.
A candle burned on either side of its small mirror so that
her face appeared a wan shadow in the light. She chose one
of the lotion pots and opened it. She started to cover her face
with lotion, a ritual that she had made certain her lover had
never been privy to.

Her actions were mechanical as her thoughts pushed on.
Divorce was naturally frowned upon, but she was too

immured to scandal to be quailed by the thought of tying the knot with a nobleman who would dare such social stigma. All in all, the situation could have proven far worse, she thought complacently.

When Lady Cartier eventually rose from her vanity, she bore little resemblance to the siren who had greeted the Earl of Chatworth earlier that evening. Her face and neck were covered with lotion; her hair was tucked tightly under a muslin cap; her hands and arms had been slathered with oil and were completely encased in long cotton gloves.

Lady Cartier got into bed, careful not to disturb her lotions and accoutrements. She always slept late after one of her assignations with the earl, and her maid knew better than to wake her before she was called. She fell into a contented sleep.

9

THE EARL OF CHATWORTH was preparing to go out with one of his friends, the Honorable Simon Oliver Hadwicke, when the package from his man of business arrived. Lord Chatworth took the package from his footman and went into the study, throwing over his shoulder, "Come in, Simon. This won't take but a moment."

Hadwicke followed him into the study and closed the door. He sauntered across the carpet to drop into a chair close to the desk. "Important, is it?" he asked, nodding at the package the earl was opening.

The earl shrugged, a twisted smile touching his lips. He lifted a folded sheet that had been tucked into the package. "If you consider the reason behind my hasty marriage to be important, I suppose it is."

Hadwicke's brows shot up. As much as anyone else, he had idly speculated over why the Earl of Chatworth had chosen to wed so abruptly and in such a hole-in-the-wall fashion, but he had been too well-bred and too much of a friend to press the earl about it. Now he glanced quickly at the earl's face to see if his lordship was joking, but there was no sign of lazy humor in his countenance. Instead, there was a gathering frown on the earl's face as his eyes ran quickly over the sheet of paper. Hadwicke stiffened, aware of a premonitory prickle between his shoulders.

"Damnation!" The earl dropped the sheet to the desktop. He dug through the parchments in the box, glancing at each swiftly. He threw down the parchments in a violent gesture, scattering them over the desk. With one stride he reached the bell rope and tugged it viciously.

"I apprehend that there is a difficulty of some sort," Hadwicke said delicately.

Lord Chatworth barked a short laugh. There was a bitter light in his eyes. "Quite!" The door opened. The footman stepped in, but the earl did not give the man time to inquire his need. He snapped, "I wish Lady Chatworth to join me here on the instant." The footman hurriedly exited, sped on his way by his master's obvious black temper.

Hadwicke rose from his seat, thoroughly convinced that it had come time to make a graceful exit. He knew himself unsuited to be witness of the impending trouble. "Perhaps I should return later, Marcus. I have no wish to become embroiled in your domestic trials."

Lord Chatworth made an abrupt gesture. "No, stay! Your presence must stop me from commiting murder."

Hadwicke stared at him a moment before he gave an uncertain laugh. "Come, Marcus, the jest ill becomes you."

Lord Chatworth smiled, but the expression in his hard eyes was not pleasant. "I scarcely jest, Simon."

Hadwicke was distinctly uncomfortable. He awaited the countess's arrival with increasing unease as he cast several glances at the earl's stony face. He could not recall ever seeing Lord Chatworth in such a patent fury.

The door opened and a lady entered. Hadwicke experienced a distinct shock when he glanced at her. He had glimpsed on the occasion of the wedding the bride's white and strained face when her veil was lifted. She had been stiff and mechanical in her responses, and her demeanor when they had been hurriedly introduced had not led him to believe that she was anything more than a cipher.

The woman who advanced toward them now bore little resemblance to that pale uninteresting creature. The countess was lovely, he thought in astonishment, momentarily forgetting his previous discomfort. She was stylishly dressed and her movements were graceful. There was an inquiring look on her face as she came up.

"My lord? You have requested my presence?" she asked. Her glance touched on Hadwicke in a friendly fashion before returning to her husband's face.

Hadwicke saw the instant that she realized that all was not well. Her green eyes widened and he could have sworn that he glimpsed a fleeting touch of fear in their gold-flecked depths.

"Indeed, madam! You will explain to me the meaning of this." The earl seized her arm and pulled her over to the desk. Unheeding of the strangled gasp that she gave at his rough treatment, he snatched up the note and thrust it under her nose.

Barbara took the paper in her fingers, which unaccountably trembled. She saw that it was a list of some sort and she read it over quickly. Babs realized that she was looking at an inventory of estate titles, undoubtedly those possessed by the Earl of Chatworth.

She lifted her head to meet the earl's cold gray eyes. She gestured in bewilderment. "I do not understand, my lord. What is it you are trying to say to me?" Lord Chatworth's fingers tightened about her arm and she bit off a cry of mingled surprise and pain.

Unnoticed by the couple standing at the desk, Hadwicke took a hasty step toward them. He caught himself before he had actually interfered, however, and he waited in a state of rare indecision. There was a scarcely controlled rage in the earl's eyes that he did not like, but he could hardly believe that his lordship would do the lady a damage while he stood by.

"My dear lady, there is nothing in that list about my vowels. Nor is there any sign of them in the package that my solicitor has sent to me, per my instructions." Lord Chatworth's voice slipped lower, turned menacingly silky. "But I think that does not surprise you."

Babs turned appalled eyes to the open box lying on the desktop. There was a tumbled bunch of papers in and around it. She started to reach out, but restrained the impulse as as her numbed mind realized that the earl must have thoroughly searched through the papers already. His accusations hit her broadside and she protested dazedly, "But that cannot be! You told me that the price included everything—

the titles and the vowels—did you not? There must be some mistake.''

"Yes, and you have made it, my girl. You and that hell-hound father of yours between you!''

Lord Chatworth threw her aside as though he could not stand to touch her any longer. He brushed his hands against his thighs as though they had become soiled.

Babs stumbled awkwardly and she would have fallen except that she was caught by Hadwicke.

She was hardly aware that a stranger's hands steadied her. All of her attention was focused on the Earl of Chatworth and her desperate need to make him believe that she had nothing to do with her father's betrayal. If she could not persuade him, than all that she had hoped to gain through their agreement was utterly destroyed. There could be no basis for trust, nor for a united front against her father and his machinations. In light of what she had just learned, it was more imperative than ever that trust exist between herself and the Earl of Chatworth. "My lord, you must believe me. I knew nothing of this—this—" She gestured at the box and its tumbled contents.

The earl looked down at her, his eyes glacial. His expression was closed and hard. "Save your breath, madam! I do not play the fool twice," he said contemptuously.

As he turned away, Babs caught at his sleeve. She said urgently, "Pray think, my lord! How could I know? My father would never confide what he planned to anyone, let alone to me! You have talked to him—you must know how he regards me—how he detests me!" She broke off on a swift hard intake of breath, almost a dry sob.

His lordship caught her fingers in an ungentle grip. She plunged on before he could fling her aside yet again. "Why did not your solicitor catch the error? Surely he was made aware of what the terms were to be—surely you instructed him!" She saw something shift suddenly in the earl's expression. She broke off, staring up at him.

There was an arrested look in the earl's eyes, and a growing comprehension. "Lord, what a colossal fool I have been,'' he enunciated slowly. He glanced down to see his wife's fearful and anxious expression. Despite the harsh punishment of his fingers, she had still kept hold of his sleeve, apparently determined that he should listen to her. He felt unexpected remorse for treating her so hardily and the nature of his grasp on her hand altered. "I am sorry, my dear. I had not sufficiently thought about it. I am to blame in every regard. As I recall, I left it in your father's hands to contact my man of business and communicate the terms. Obviously he seized the opportunity that I so stupidly granted to him, and arranged matters more to his liking.''

Babs was acutely aware of the difference in the pressure of his fingers; they were almost caressing. The warmth generated within her by his apology astounded and confused her. She instinctively sought to distance herself and she slipped her hand free of his lightened grasp. "I cannot altogether blame you for a natural assumption, my lord." Her attempt at cool graciousness slipped with the appalling realization of their circumstances and she blurted, "How I wish that it had not turned out in such a way!''

"Your consternation cannot begin to compare to the depth of my own regret, my lady," Lord Chatworth said in a clipped fashion, the icy distance in his eyes returning.

Babs was rocked back into her isolated pride. "Of course not, my lord. It was not my intention to imply otherwise," she managed through the constriction in her throat. For a moment she had felt herself truly allied with his lordship, but that had been foolish, she realized.

Lord Chatworth looked at his wife sharply. There was an electric moment of silence as their eyes met and locked. There was something indefinable but arresting in the earl's study of her, and Babs felt difficulty in breathing.

Lord Chatworth broke the contact and with a gesture transferred her attention to the gentleman who had stood as silent witness throughout. "I believe you might recall Hadwicke, my lady. He stood in as my best man at our wedding."

"Oh, Mr. Hadwicke. Of course," stammered Babs, giving the gentleman her hand. She felt the telltale heat rise in her face. She was embarrassed on two counts. She could not honestly recall the gentleman's face, but that was a minor thing to the realization that he had been witness to what had gone on a few minutes before.

Hadwicke was nothing if not a tactful gentleman. He made it easy for her, saying as he took her hand, "I shall not be offended if you do not remember me, Lady Chatworth. It was the fleetest of meetings, and it took place during a most momentous occasion, besides. I could wish, however, that this second opportunity to meet you was not held under still more extraordinary circumstances."

"I could not agree with you more, sir," said Babs. She cast a swift glance up at her husband's face to gauge how her answer had struck him, and she was reassured by the faint smile that touched his mouth.

Lord Chatworth sat down on the edge of the desk. Swinging his booted toe, he regarded the immaculate, mirror-bright polish with a reflective expression. "I trust that I may count upon your complete discretion, Simon." He looked up suddenly, his eyes hard.

Hadwicke smiled lazily at his lordship. There was deep amusement in his voice. "My dear Marcus, need you ask it of me? I would be a fool indeed to jeopardize our long friendship only to add fuel to the gossip wheel." He paused a moment, as though the thought had just struck him, but the laughter in his eyes was unmistakable. "I have a healthy respect for your skill with a sword, besides."

Lord Chatworth threw back his head in laughter. He replied, still grinning, "Indeed! I wish I may see the day that weighs with you. Why, you have only to point that small pistol of yours at me and be done with the business altogether."

"Ah, but that would hardly be sporting. I never miss," said Hadwicke quietly.

The gentlemen smiled at each other in complete understanding while Babs listened with mingled alarm and amusement. "What nonsense is this, my lord?" she demanded, not considering that she was trespassing into the earl's domain. "Why should there be swords and pistols at all?"

"I believe that we frighten the lady, Hadwicke." The Earl of Chatworth slid off the desk. "There is no need to concern yourself, my lady. I hardly think that the occasion shall ever arise where Simon and I must test each other's mettle in such a way."

"True. We respect one another's skills too well," said Hadwicke thoughtfully. He took up the countess's hand and carried her fingers to his lips. Still holding her hand, he smiled down into her eyes. "I shall hope to see you again under more comfortable circumstances, Lady Chatworth. But I think, for now, that I must leave you to his lordship's tender concern. I suspect that there is much that he would like to discuss with you."

As Babs digested that, Lord Chatworth walked with his friend to the door and opened it for him. "I trust you to make my excuses, Simon."

Hadwicke thew a bland glance at the lovely woman who had remained standing next to the desk. "I have only to mention a lady is to blame for your absence, Marcus. None shall put a question past that explanation," he said. He watched curiously as swift color rose in the countess's face. There was something to discover there, he thought. Then he turned and walked out the door.

10

LORD CHATWORTH closed the door. He looked at his wife, and he was surprised that he had labeled her thus. His brows snapped together in sudden irritation. He hardly needed to begin thinking of her as his responsibility. He walked over to her and took her arm. He was surprised and somewhat affronted that she withdrew from his touch. "I shall not eat you. At least, not now," he said.

Babs gave a small laugh. She was impatient with herself. She had reacted to the abrupt and forbidding change in the earl's expression. It was ridiculous to assume that his lordship was even remotely like her father, she thought. She took the hand that he held out to her so peremptorily and allowed him to guide her to the chair that Hadwicke had occupied before her.

Lord Chatworth chose to sit on the edge of the desk, facing her. "Well, my lady? What shall we do now?" he asked politely.

Barbara knew to what he referred. She was unconscious that she twisted her hands in her lap. She shook her head helplessly. "I hardly know, my lord." She raised her eyes to him and he was surprised by the degree of misery in her regard. "I had hoped to be free of him, or nearly so, once we had wed. I never dreamed that he would connive to retain a hold over you. It makes it very difficult, doesn't it?"

Lord Chatworth bit back an overhasty retort. After a short interval, he said instead, "Yes, but that is indisputedly my fault. I think for now we must set aside the fact and concentrate instead on how we may best deal with the possible consequences. Obviously your father wishes to retain some

measure of control over us. I cannot think to what purpose
or what that might entail.''

"But I believe I do," said Babs in a low voice. She looked
away from the earl as she carefully chose her words. "My
father hungers for social recognition above all else, my lord.
That is what he hoped to gain by marrying my mother and
what he hoped to achieve by marrying me to you. He will
demand from you an introduction into the *ton.*"

Lord Chatworth understood from the shaking timbre of
her voice the humiliation she suffered. He reached down to
catch hold of her hands. She looked up at him, her eyes flying
wide and startled. Without thinking about the consequences
of his actions, he pulled her up from the chair and drew her
toward him until she stood against his bent knee. "Babs, you
need not flail yourself so," he said quietly.

Her green eyes suddenly glittered with unshed tears. She
turned her head away from him, a gesture that said as plainly
as if she had spoken that she was ashamed of her own
vulnerability.

Lord Chatworth's mouth tightened. He could not have
given coherence to his feelings, but the fact that she was not
willing to use her tears to gain his sympathy did her no dis-
service in his eyes. His innate protectiveness for those weaker
than himself was stirred. "Babs . . ." He let go of one of
her hands so that he could bring her to him.

At the barest touch of his hand on her back, she flinched.

An instant later she had whisked herself away from him,
coming at last to stand several steps across the study in
apparent contemplation of the titles on a bookshelf. "Were
there any other discrepancies in the prenuptial arrangements,
my lord?" she asked breathlessly, without looking at him.

Lord Chatworth sat quite still. There was a chilly quality
in his expression as he stared at her back. He had been served
a rare set-down and it had not left a pleasant taste in his
mouth. His pride was well and truly stung. But in all fairness
he was forced to concede that she was perfectly within her
rights to refuse his advances, however half-formed they might
have been.

"Everything else was as it should be. The bridal settlement was perfectly within bounds. As for the fortune that your father settled on you upon our marriage, it is quite respectable,'' he said.

He was startled and irritated to hear the edge in his own voice. It surely did not matter one way or the other whether the lady he had married did not wish for him to touch her. He had not tied the knot for that reason, after all. His practiced eyes raked her trim figure as she turned toward him, and he thought that it would not be entirely unpleasant to make of theirs a real marriage. Indeed, after the blow that he had suffered to his ego, he was quite amenable to the notion of initiating his wife into the art of dalliance and seduction.

''My fortune—my lord, that is the answer!'' Babs did not heed the earl's oddly forbidding expression as her enthusiasm carried her back across the room to him. She saw the frowning incomprehension in his eyes and she said impatiently, ''Marcus, do you not understand? You may redeem your vowels and whatever else you owed to my father with the fortune that he has settled on me.''

Incredulity entered his eyes. ''I think not, my dear,'' said Lord Chatworth shortly. ''That is quite out of the question.''

Babs was astonished by the spasm of distaste that had crossed his face. ''But I don't understand! That fortune by law passed into your hands upon our marriage. It is there for the using, my lord.''

Lord Chatworth smiled, but it was the mocking twist of his lips that she so detested. ''Obviously your education regarding a gentleman's honor has been deficient, my dear. I could not take what belongs to you and use it for this purpose.''

''My God, Marcus! You could be free.''

''Could I indeed, my lady! When every day I shall have your face to remind me that I had stooped to stealing in order to be rid of Cribbage. Thank you, but no! I prefer not to place myself in the same category as your less-than-estimable parent,'' he said bitingly.

There was a short silence during which she regarded him with a blank look in her eyes. He had the most startling conviction that he had deeply wounded her. Finally she drew herself up, her chin rising proudly, and he could not any longer divine her feelings behind the cool expression she assumed.

"Forgive my lamentable ignorance, my lord. I did not precisely understand the matter. You have certainly enlightened me. I shall not again forget my place," she said. She turned away to walk swiftly toward the door.

In one stride Marcus reached her. He did not forget how she had stiffened when he had touched her, especially when he saw that she flinched at his sudden proximity. He did not touch her, therefore, but merely addressed her. "Do not come on the high ropes with me, Babs. It doesn't become you," he said measuredly. He saw the spark of anger in her green eyes, and he was glad of it, for the fear that always seemed to spring into the depths of her eyes when he dared approach her vanished with its appearance.

"You are insufferable, my lord," Babs exclaimed. "It is you who has been less than kind and you think nothing of baiting me at every turn. How dare you try to intimidate me when I—"

"Try to intimidate you? My dear girl, if you were any more frightened of me, I dare swear that you would faint dead away from sheer terror," said Lord Chatworth in derision.

"I am not frightened of you."

"Oh, no? Shall we test for the truth of it, Babs?" With one hand Lord Chatworth caught her chin. As he had anticipated, she made an instinctive move to retreat. But now she stood quite still and he was impressed by her self-control. He smiled down into her furious green eyes.

Babs defied him with her returning stare.

The challenge was unmistakable. He could sense the tension in her and he wondered how much of her own mistress she actually was. He had seen so many conflicting sides of her: when she had come to meet with him, he had detected suppressed desperation; when they had dined together, he had dismissed her as dull-witted and inane; when he had accused her of base betrayal, she had determinedly brought him to realize her innocence; when she had been at her most vulnerable, she had nevertheless recognized and drawn back from his advances.

He had never encountered a more complex woman. Nor one that showed herself to be such a challenge to his own pride.

He could hardly recall a time when he had not been pursued by the fairer sex, whether it was for the sake of his face and physical attributes, or for his position and wealth. It scarcely mattered when he had begun to pursue and conquer on his own account; he had long since taken for granted that he need not exert himself unduly to have practically any woman he desired. His reputation was that of a confirmed rake, and he had never experienced any wish to alter it.

The present circumstances hardly gave him cause to regret otherwise. On the contrary, he thought, he had the opportunity to deliver a salutory lesson to a lady whose ignorance of his reputation had led to the insult of his pride.

Lord Chatworth did not take his eyes from his wife's face. He slowly bent his head to brush his lips across hers. The sensation was pleasing, her mouth soft and pliable, her breath sweat and warm.

He caught her mouth more closely. He could feel the tenseness in her body just by the way she held herself, but it scarcely mattered when he found himself able to kiss her without reproof. He broke free of the pleasant exercise to trace her jawline with tiny kisses. His lips touched the sensitive area behind her ear and he lingered. Beneath his mouth, he felt her shiver. He whispered, "Are you not frightened, Babs?"

"No!" There was a breathless catch in her voice.

Lord Chatworth smiled to himself, that peculiar smile that had been bequeathed him. Half-hooded, his eyes glimmered with a rousing desire. He straightened to capture her mouth again, this time allowing himself to show her some measure of his banked passion. Her lips parted under his insistence and he deepened the kiss, savoring the clean taste of her mouth.

His hands came up to cradle her against him. Still he did

nothing more than to draw her closer. She remained stiff in his arms, one of her hands awkwardly pushing against his chest while the other had latched onto the arm that he had placed about her small waist.

At last he let her go, though every part of him had become reluctant to do so. But it was not his intention to seduce her entirely. Not yet, at any rate. His glance dwelled on her parted lips and the breath that came too quickly from between them. It had been a very pleasurable experiment, and one that he intended to pursue in future. He did not believe that she would prove a reluctant participant, he thought complacently.

His gaze lifted to her eyes, where he expected to find uncertainty and dawning passion. Instead, he was startled by the blaze of sheer anger in those green depths. He was not given time to digest the meaning of it, however, for suddenly his head was rocked to one side by a stinging blow.

Lord Chatworth stared at her in stupefaction. One side of his face burned with the imprint of her palm. In the seconds before he had recovered, she had already flown to the door of the study.

She regarded him with complete contempt. "I am not frightened of you. I believe that I have sufficiently proven it, do you not think so, Marcus?" With that she twisted the knob and sailed out of the study.

She sped upstairs to her rooms. When she got to her bedroom, she pulled the bell for her maid and, upon the woman's entrance, asked her help in putting on her walking dress. Within a few short minutes, Babs returned downstairs and walked out the front door in the company of her maid. She had asked that a carriage be brought up to wait on her pleasure, and now she directed the driver to the shops in Mayfair.

She settled back and with a quelling stare at her maid gave the woman notice that she was not in the mood for idle conversation. She badly needed time to think, but she had not felt safe to do so in her bedroom. Foremost in her mind while she had changed had been the uncertainty of whether the earl would follow her. But she had escaped the house without that confrontation and she could breathe easier for a time.

She had lied when she had told the earl that he did not frighten her. But the major portion of her fright was not rooted in his attempt to disconcert and seduce her, which was what had saved her from making a complete fool of herself. She had recognized that he meant to press the issue, and she had gambled that he would not guess the real reason behind her uneasiness whenever she was with him. He had not, which had been proven by his chosen method to overcome her defiance.

Babs thought she had come off from the encounter fairly well, and certainly the earl would think twice before he again trespassed the bounds of their agreement. She bit her lip, worrying at it with her neat white teeth. At least, she hoped that he would do so. She knew so little about gentlemen in general. She had already discovered some differences between her father and the Earl of Chatworth. It would be wonderful indeed if the earl could be relied upon and trusted.

However, she would not hold her breath, she thought with the faintest of smiles. Lord Chatworth was undeniably attractive. If she was completely truthful with herself, she had slapped him as much for his arrogance as her own stupid vulnerability to his experienced charm. And as much as she would prefer to forget it, his lordship was indeed very practiced.

Babs knew very well that the earl kept a mistress. She had seen the missive that first evening, and she had since caught part of the maids' conversation while they were cleaning the upper drawing room. It had been quite clear that Lord Chatworth enjoyed the ministrations of a "high flyer," as one of the maids had put it, and had in the past often entertained ladies in his own home.

Babs' eyes narrowed at the last thought. She might trespass the sweeping terms of their agreement as well. She had no right to interfere with the earl's amorous adventures outside the house, but she was damned if she would welcome his light-skirts into her home. The vigor of her feelings astonished her. She had not realized before how strongly she felt about the validity of her position as the Countess of Chatworth.

11

THE HOUSEHOLD fell quite naturally into a pattern. Each evening the earl dined with his new bride before going out to keep his several engagements. Barbara was left to amuse herself as best she could, and truthfully she had no real desire to accompany his lordship. She was still settling into the oddity of her new position, feeling her way, becoming accustomed to the earl's likes and dislikes, the tempo of the house.

Quietly she observed how the servants did their work. At separate times she talked with the cook, the housekeeper, and the butler. She discovered nothing lacking in the respect or the willingness of the cook and the butler or those under them to accept her orders.

However, the housekeeper was an entirely different matter. Mrs. Sparrow was a large woman whose small hard eyes, hard expression, and girth were all used to intimidate those beneath her. She was efficient in her position and most of the housemaids ran in terror of her.

Besides her obvious unfriendliness of disposition, Mrs. Sparrow had definite ideas of class and quality. The new Countess of Chatworth, to her mind, was not worthy of the exalted position in which she had been placed. The housekeeper held forth to her underlings that her ladyship was an upstart. Mrs. Sparrow allowed that her ladyship had been as clever as she could hold together to have ensnared his lordship, who was known to have an eye for a pretty face and trim waist, but until the earl had committed the folly of wedding this latest of his several flirts, Mrs. Sparrow had

quite believed his lordship quick-witted enough to spot a
honey trap in whatever guise it was offered.

Babs recognized the housekeeper's thinly disguised
contempt. She waited to see if Mrs. Sparrow's disapproval
would extend to disregarding her orders or otherwise
fomenting rebellion among others in the household. Mrs.
Sparrow did not disappoint her. Despite the several talks that
she had had with the woman, the housekeeper did not mend
her manners.

The last straw for Babs was to be told point-blank to her
face that her orders must be laid before the earl before any
action could be taken, and that by a pert upstairs maid.

Barbara had had enough. She had tried to reach across the
natural resentment that the housekeeper must feel in having
another woman take precedence over her own ruling of the
household. She had tried to establish a relationship with Mrs.
Sparrow that would preclude upsetting the household. But
when it came down to having a housemaid refuse her quiet
order because the girl was certain of Mrs. Sparrow'ss
approval in such action, the countess decided that it was time
to cut her losses.

And a loss it would be, she thought as she sent down a
request for Mrs. Sparrow to wait upon her in her sitting
room. Whatever else she might be, termagant and shrew and
snob, Mrs. Sparrow was an excellent housekeeper.

The interview was not pleasant. Mrs. Sparrow was enraged
that the upstart countess was giving her marching orders.
"We shall soon see about this, mistress. I'll warrant that his
lordship will be in a rare taking when I tell him about this
insult," raged the woman.

The countess coolly informed her that the earl had given
herself full sway over the household and that it would not
help her case if she chose to burst upon him with this
particular domestic matter. "In fact, I should have to rescind
the recommendation that his lordship was good enough to
give you, Mrs. Sparrow," she said, holding up a folded
sheet. She had actually penned it herself and had had the
secretary get the earl's seal upon it, but Mrs. Sparrow did
not need to know that. She stared the woman down.

Her cool composure finally convinced Mrs. Sparrow that indeed she had no recourse. The ertswhile housekeeper left on the spot, in possession of her hard expression, her recommendation to another post, her belongings, and her back wages. Quickly following her exit were two housemaids who had been the housekeeper's worst cronies.

The rest of the household was left in a decided stir. In quite a decisive fashion, the new countess had demonstrated her power and firmly established her position. Barbara felt immediately the change in atmosphere when she came into contact with one of the remaining maids. There was more respect and civility than before, and she felt quite triumphant that she had finally won peace in her household.

She thought she should not let it come as a surprise to the earl that Mrs. Sparrow was no longer with them, and she decided to tell him that same morning a somewhat abridged version of what had been taking place with the domestic situation. She did not think that gentlemen greatly cared for the details of such things, but only for the reassurance that their own comforts would continue without interruption. She also wished to ask his lordship for his permission to borrow the services of his secretary, Hobbs, in the necessary inquiries at the various registries in the hiring of a new housekeeper and maids.

Still flushed with her victory, Babs started downstairs to seek out her husband.

The Earl of Chatworth flipped through the morning's post. He abruptly paused and lifted one of the letters free from the rest. He glanced up at his secretary. "That will be all for the moment, Hobbs." The secretary bowed, but already he was forgotten by the earl. Lord Chatworth slit open the envelope with a long silver knife and removed the letter.

The secretary quietly closed the door behind him. As he turned away from the study, he was greeted by Lady Chatworth. "Is his lordship in his study?" she asked, smiling.

"Yes, my lady," Hobbs said, bowing. He was not unfamiliar with his master's moods and he hesitated to send her ladyship into the lion's den. "However . . ."

Babs did not heed the secretary's demur, but turned the knob and went on into the study. Closing the door, she saw that the earl stood at the window in silhouette, one hand on the draperies. "My lord, good morning."

He turned and the sun slanted across his face. Babs saw the temper in his eyes. The words dried on her tongue. She felt her own facial muscles tense. It was her experience that only a communication from her father could bring such an expression to the earl's face. "What is it?" she asked in a low voice.

"It is of nothing to concern you, my lady," said Lord Chatworth in repressive dismissal.

"Of course it must concern me," said Babs. "Anything regarding my father—"

Lord Chatworth laughed shortly, struck by the irony of it. "It is not your father, Babs, but my dear mother."

Barbara grasped the back of a chair. She felt stunned. "Your mother, my lord? But I thought—that is, I assumed—" She stopped, quite incapable of finishing her sentence.

Lord Chatworth had no difficulty in following her. The expression in his eyes became quite bland. "The dowager Countess of Chatworth is very much alive, my lady. She has resided for some years at the family seat, not caring much for London or for society. I naturally wrote to her of our marriage, though I did not expect her to come to London for the wedding."

"I see," said Babs, beginning to feel the stirrings of anger. Her eyes were very bright. "When were you planning to inform me of her ladyship's existence, my lord? Or were you not?"

Lord Chatworth frowned down at the letter that he still held in his hand. "I am in the habit of visiting my mother two or three times a year. I had not thought it necessary to bring you to her attention until we went down to the country for the summer. I had hoped . . . But it seems that her ladyship is taking matters into her own hands." He looked over at his wife to gauge the effect of his announcement. "The dowager countess has written to inform me of her arrival in a fortnight. She has requested that I convey her regards to my new wife.''

Babs numbly sat down in the chair. She stared up at the earl, appalled. Her uppermost thought was that she had just sacked the housekeeper and some of the staff. There was no possible way that she could hire and train new servants and be ready in time for the dowager countess's regal visit. For that was how she envisioned her mother-in-law: a formidable dame of repressive notions and high pride, one who had refused to come to London for her son's wedding to a social nonentity.

''I trust that does not prove an inconvenience to you, my lady?''

There was a note of censure in Lord Chatworth's voice that Babs was quick to hear. She marshaled her expression into one of smiling acquiescence. She could not possibly explain to him now what she had done with the staff. His lordship would only construe her explanation as complaint and incompetence. ''How could it be that, Marcus? I shall be delighted to meet the dowager countess. When did you say that her ladyship will arrive?''

Lord Chatworth regarded her unsmilingly for a moment before he glanced briefly at the pertinent line of the letter. ''On the fifteenth of the month. In less than two weeks.''

Babs rose, saying brightly as she did so, ''Then I must certainly not waste a moment if we are to accord her ladyship the proper hospitality. There are entertainments to plan and—''

''It is not necessary to get up a round of entertainments. My mother dislikes nothing more than a press,'' said Lord Chatworth, going to his desk.

Babs stood facing him, her hands held tight together before her. ''I understand, of course. Then perhaps you will instruct me in how I am to go on to best please her ladyship.''

''Babs.'' Lord Chatworth set aside the letter and looked over at her. ''My mother is not an exacting woman. Quite the contrary, in fact. She prefers a well-ordered household and quiet pursuits. I ask only that her every comfort is seen to, which I am certain the housekeeper is perfectly capable

of supplying. You need not put yourself out to any degree,
I assure you. You may go on with your own pleasures quite
unimpeded.''

"Thank you, my lord, for that most welcome reassurance,"
said Babs, barely able to retain civility toward him.
Apparently her control over her voice was not as complete
as she had wished, for she saw surprise enter his eyes. She
swept out of the study and crashed the door behind her.

Babs ran swiftly upstairs to her private sitting room. She
paced the length of the room, fuming with anger. She had
not been so humiliated since her come-out into society. She
was furious with the Earl of Chatworth. He should have told
her that his mother was still alive. It was her right to have
known. She would have sent off a polite missive to the
dowager countess upon first arriving at the town house as
its new mistress. It was only the fitting thing to have done.

At this point in her angry reflection, Babs stopped short
and stood quite still in the middle of the carpet. The dowager
countess had not come to the wedding ceremony, even though
the earl had written to her and even though her ladyship must
have seen the notice in the *Gazette*. That was what truly
bothered her, Babs thought with cringing hurt. The dowager
countess had apparently so heartily disapproved of her son's
choice that she had refused to condone the marriage by her
presence at the ceremony. And the message of disapproval
had thus been broadcast to the world.

Babs felt the familiar feeling of inevitable disaster wash
over her. It was bad enough that she must skirmish with the
servants to prove herself mistress of the establishment, or
that, whenever the Earl of Chatworth got around to insist-
ing that she entertain, she must hold her head high even
though she knew that there would be whispers behind her
back and smiling malice to her face. Now she had learned
that she possessed a starched-up, prideful mother-in-law who
was not inclined to receive her with anything remotely
resembling approval.

Babs could have screamed aloud with her vexation. But
she would not go down without a fight, she thought grimly.
She would do all in her power to win over the dowager

countess. She thought over the little that the earl had imparted to her about his mother. It became obvious that the first priority was to discover and employ a new housekeeper who could be relied upon to see to the dowager countess's every whim.

Babs was familiar with the tedious business of hiring servants, having observed her aunt do so on more than one occasion. But she could not afford the time that such a process normally took, not with her mother-in-law arriving in less than two weeks.

Babs decided that she could do worse than seek the counsel of her aunt. Lady Azaela might have a few worthwhile suggestions to offer. Babs gave a reluctant laugh. At the very least her aunt could offer her a shoulder to cry on, she thought wryly.

Babs pulled the bell rope, and when a servant answered the summons, she gave orders that a carriage be brought around to the front door and that her maid attend her at once. Barbara went to her bedroom, where the maid helped her out of her morning gown and into a walking pelisse with matching bonnet and lavender kid gloves. Then Babs tripped downstairs and out the door to the carriage. She gave directions for her aunt's establishment before entering the carriage. The footman shut the carriage door and signaled to the driver. The carriage rolled away.

Lady Azaela chanced to be in and she was immediately sympathetic to her niece's dilemma. She said that she had foreseen that something of the sort might happen, since the Earl of Chatworth's house was that of a bachelor and unused to the guidance of a permanent mistress.

"Of course you must have the loyalty of your staff, which will naturally take their cue from the higher echelon of servants. I hope that the housekeeper was the only recalcitrant among the higher staff?" At Babs' nod, Lady Azalea smiled. "As it happens, my own cook's sister, who is visiting her at the moment, is looking for such a position. She appears to be a competent woman, and she has all the earmarks of a loyal and cheerful disposition."

Babs was astonished by her good fortune, but she was not

one to stare a gift horse in the mouth. "Pray produce this paragon," she said with a laugh.

Lady Azaela pulled the bell rope and requested the footman who answered the bell's ring to have Cook's sister sent up immediately to the drawing room.

Upon meeting the worthy Mrs. Fennell, Babs hired her on the spot. She was inordinately pleased and relieved to have her major problem solved so easily for her. The running of the household would again be in firm hands before ever the dowager countess arrived. The shortage of maids was not as pressing an affair. Those left on staff would take up the slack until replacements could be found through the usual way. After Babs made final arrangements with Mrs. Fennell regarding wages and so forth, the remainder of her visit with Lady Azaela assumed a carefree note.

As Babs returned to the Chatworth town house, she reflected that she was extremely fortunate that Lady Azaela had chosen so many years ago to take a small frightened girl under her wing so completely. Life would never have been so simple and gratifying otherwise.

12

BARBARA ENTERED THE TOWN HOUSE and with a smile
acknowledged the porter's greeting. She walked to the stairs
and had already placed her hand on the banister and one foot
on the first step when she heard the Earl of Chatworth call
her name. Babs look around, surprised, and saw that his lordship was standing on the threshold of the open door to the
drawing room. "Yes, my lord?"

"Pray come into the drawing room, my dear. There is
someone that I think you should meet," said Lord Chatworth.

Babs left the stairs and crossed the entry hall to join her
husband. She preceded him into the drawing room and he
closed the door behind them.

A lady was sitting on one of the settees. She met Babs'
startled gaze with an arrogant lift of her brows. "Well,
Marcus? Will you not introduce us properly?"

For an awful instant, the suspicion flew into her mind that
the Earl of Chatworth meant to introduce her to his mistress.
But Babs banished the thought almost as swiftly as it had
come. The earl might be a rake but he was also a gentleman
bred. She therefore smiled at the lady and turned an inquiring
look of her own onto her husband.

Lord Chatworth took his wife's hand and formally escorted
her to a chair. There was banked laughter in his gray eyes,
but he spoke gravely enough. "My dear, allow me to make
known to you Lady Jersey. She is one of the stern patronesses
of Almack's, at whose least displeasure the rest of us poor
mortals quail."

"Pray don't be more of a fool than you can help, Marcus,"
said Lady Jersey sharply, but with an appreciative gleam in

91

her eyes. She turned to the young countess. "What have you
to say for yourself, my dear?"

Babs was taken aback by the lady's forthright, rude
manner. "What can I say, my lady, but that I am most happy
to make your acquaintance," she said warily.

Lady Jersey smiled slowly. She stared at Babs for a
moment and she was not ill-pleased that the young woman's
eyes did not waver from hers. "I like her, Marcus," she
said suddenly, without looking around at the earl. "She has
style and fortitude and she does not toady to one."

Babs was angered to be discussed as though she were not
present. "I thank you, ma'am."

Lady Jersey and Lord Chatworth both laughed. When Babs
glanced up to meet his lordship's gaze, she was startled by
the degree of warmth and approval in his expression. He
reached down to raise her gloved fingers to his lips. "You'll
do, Babs," he said.

"Indeed she will, with my help," said Lady Jersey. "I
intend to sponsor her at Almack's myself, Marcus. That will
put a few noses out of joint, but I shan't care for that." She
smiled again at Babs, whose cool expression was undergoing
swift transition to one of amazement. "You are already a
cause célèbre, my dear, and you have yet to enter society.
Everyone wonders how and why you captured our most
unbridled gentleman, and there are such things said! But I
shan't sully your ears with such malicious gossip. You shall
hear it for yourself before much longer, I'll warrant." She
rose and extended her hand to Babs, and the ladies shook
hands briefly.

Lady Jersey turned to the earl and reached up to buss him
soundly on the cheek. Her eyes were sparkling wickedly as
she glanced slyly at the young countess. "I would watch this
gentleman closely if I were you, my dear. He is too attractive to be allowed to roam loose among the restless hens of
society." She saw that she had managed to ruffle the earl's
composure, and she was still laughing as she sailed out of
the drawing room on her host's arm.

Lord Chatworth returned from seeing out the illustrious

visitor. He still wore the frown that had descended upon his face at Lady Jersey's needling. "Lady Jersey's manners often border on the ill-bred," he said.

"I rather liked her ladyship, actually. She was refreshingly frank," Babs said.

The earl raised his brows. "Indeed! We shall not argue the issue, I think, but rather I shall congratulate you upon making a favorable impression on the lady. Lady Jersey's sponsorship of you into Almack's virtually guarantees your acceptance by society."

"Does it, indeed?" murmured Babs, her thoughts inevitably on a past time when such sponsorship was so sorely needed but unforthcoming to an unknown tradesman's daughter. Certainly her fortunes had changed for the better with her marriage, she thought wryly.

Lord Chatworth found his wife's reception of the signal honor done her somewhat lacking in proper enthusiasm. "Your gratitude is hardly overwhelming, my lady."

Babs was not insensitive to the censorious note in his lordship's voice. "Is it not, my lord? Perhaps that is because I am not so enamored of society as it would like me to be."

Lord Chatworth's brows had drawn hard together and the glance he shot at his wife was impatient. "Come, Babs! Let us have plain speaking between us. The truth of the matter is that you have neither the confidence nor the polish necessary to carry off a high hand against those arbiters of taste and fashion. I recommend that you begin acting the part that better suits you."

"And what is that, my lord?" she asked quietly, though there was a dangerous light in her eyes.

The earl smiled in his mocking way. "Why, that of dutiful wife." His eyes grew cold. "As I told you before, my lady, I expect you to live up to the position I granted to you with that ring upon your finger. I expect grace and dignity and tact from my wife."

"As well as blind eyes and deaf ears," Babs said swiftly.

Lord Chatworth smiled, but the expression did not quite

reach his eyes. "Exactly so, Babs," he said silkily. He stepped close to her and pretended not to notice that she started back from him before she caught herself and stood her ground. There was a scared defiance in her eyes that he found that he detested. "I also expect a proper respect from my wife."

Babs could not quite steady her breathing. "When have I not expressed a 'proper respect,' Marcus?"

"This morning you left the study in a rare tantrum at learning of my mother's arrival," said Lord Chatworth. "I warn you now that I shall not have any rag-mannered harridan presiding at the same table with the dowager countess."

"Is that all?" Babs spluttered on a laugh as she recalled that she had slammed the study door. She saw that her reaction had infuriated him further and she reached up a hand to his arm. "Forgive me, Marcus. But you have no notion what a rarity it is for me to act thus. I suppose that I possess a measure of the same temper that I have occasionally seen exhibited in your own nature."

It was a potent shot and she knew it. She was rewarded for her shrewdness when a reluctant laugh was wrested from him. Lord Chatworth covered her hand with his. He looked down at her, a smile still touching his lips. "You are an intelligent wench, I do grant you that," he said.

He would have said more, but the door to the drawing room was pushed open and a caller was ushered in. Upon seeing who had come in, Babs' face tightened.

Lord Chatworth dropped his wife's hand and turned fully to the gentleman who strode slowly about the drawing room as though on an inspection tour. "Cribbage." The earl's voice was flat of all expression, as was his face. "To what do we owe this visit?"

Cribbage gave the faintest of smiles. His hard eyes left the earl's face to flicker toward his daughter's appalled expression. "Why, is it not usual to call upon the newly wedded couple and offer one's felicitations?"

"Consider that you have done so," said Lord Chatworth.

Cribbage's expression froze; only his eyes remained alive to illustrate his banked fury. Finally he said, "I should like to speak to my daughter in private, my lord."

Barbara made an instinctive gesture of appeal that surprised the earl. She had long since schooled her expression to one of cool inquiry, but she could not disguise the tenseness of her fingers as they slipped about his elbow. Lord Chatworth did not glance down at his wife as he replied to the man whose presence was so obviously unwelcome to her.

"I do not think that I can countenance that, sir." At Cribbage's expression of slack-jawed astonishment, he allowed his twisted smile to come to the fore. "You have forgotten, Cribbage. This lady is no longer just your daughter. She is my wife, and my wishes must take precedence where she is concerned."

Cribbage had himself fully under control again. "I shall not pretend to misunderstand, my lord." His glittering eyes left the earl's insufferable expression of arrogance to settle on his daughter's face.

Babs shuddered inwardly at the promise that she saw in her father's eyes, but she did not glance away from his furious gaze. She held on to the earl's arm like a lifeline, grateful for his presence and his strength. She could never have defied her father in such a way.

Cribbage ground his teeth together but he said not another word. He swung around on his heel and stomped out of the drawing room. For good measure, he pulled the door to with a violent hand that left the air vibrating.

Babs let go of the earl's arm and turned away from him. She still felt shaken and she had no wish for him to see it in her eyes. She had already learned that Lord Chatworth was uncannily prescient where she was concerned.

"I see now where you acquired it."

"What?" Babs turned her head at that, startled.

Lord Chatworth smiled lazily at her. "Why, the art of slamming doors, of course."

She laughed shakily. "I suppose that must be so. But how ungallant of you to point it out, my lord."

"I shall be more ungallant still and inquire why it is that you fear your father so greatly." There was no longer a teasing note in his voice.

Babs turned her eyes aside swiftly, afraid that her expression was too easily read. Though she was not looking at him, she felt when he came up close beside her. His breath ruffled the wisps of hair on her neck that had escaped their plaits. She stepped hastily away. "How ridiculous! Why ever should I fear my father, my lord? I find that I should like some wine. Shall I pour a glass for you as well, Marcus?"

She went quickly to the occasional table and picked up one of the decanters. Her wrist was caught in an iron grip that slowly forced her to lower the decanter back to the table. She did not look around, all too aware of the weight of shoulder and arm that pressed against her and the hand that still imprisoned her wrist. She let go of the neck of the decanter and her fingers closed against her palm.

"All right, Marcus. Since you ask it of me, I shall give you the truth. I have always been frightened of my father. He seemed overpowering and awesome to me as a child, and I suppose that I have never been capable of shaking free of my childish impressions of him." That much at least was part of the truth. She bit her lip, hoping that would be the end of it.

She gasped when he pulled her around and caught her against him.

Lord Chatworth held her by the wrists. He looked down into her wide eyes searchingly. What he saw seemed to satisfy him. He released her and Babs backed a step until she could grasp the edge of the table behind her.

"I shall accept that at face value, my lady. But I must advise you that if I discover you are hiding something from me that will in any way undermine my ability to win free of your father's noisome intrusion into my life, it will go very hard with you," Lord Chatworth said quietly.

"There is nothing—nothing of that sort. I give you my word," said Babs shakily. She had the distinct impression that in him she faced an incalculable danger of a sort that had never before come into her experience.

The earl bowed to her then. His expression did not warm, nor did he utter another word. He exited the drawing room, leaving her still standing against the table and staring at the space he had vacated.

13

THE DAYS PASSED SWIFTLY and the date of the dowager Countess of Chatworth's visit came too soon for Barbara. She awaited her mother-in-law's arrival with scarcely disguised and increasing nervousness. She looked up quickly at any opening of the door during dinner, but each time it was only the next course to be served.

After the covers had been removed, she left the earl to his wine and retired to the drawing room. Several minutes later she was startled when his lordship joined her. The Earl of Chatworth had uncharacteristically elected to remain at home that evening in order to be present when his mother arrived. He was disinclined for conversation and indicated it by opening the newspapers.

The hour continued to advance, the ticking of the clock loud in the silence between herself and Lord Chatworth. Babs had difficulty concentrating on her embroidery and she noticed that the earl could not seem to settle himself comfortably with his newspapers. The butler brought in the after-dinner coffee and later returned to carry it back out. Still the dowager countess had not arrived.

The growing lateness of the hour served to make Lord Chatworth anxious on his mother's behalf, and as a consequence, his countenance was more forbidding than usual.

Babs made an attempt to introduce light conversation, but his lordship was barely civil in his short replies. His impatient eyes strayed often to the clock. Babs saw only that her husband was bored in her company.

She had been surprised when the earl had announced his intention to be present when his mother arrived, but she had supposed that he wished to soften the blow to the dowager countess of meeting her. The thought had not bolstered Babs' sagging self-confidence, and his lordship's subsequent paltry interest in her gambits of conversation, which had long since dwindled to nothingness, confirmed her in the opinion that he regretted his connection to her.

When the long-awaited sounds of arrival came, Babs was in a thorough state of anxiety. She carefully stowed her embroidery hoop and the threads away before she rose slowly from her chair.

"Coming, my lady?"

She looked up to find that the earl had also risen and awaited her impatiently. The ready color rose soft in her face. It had not occurred to her that he meant to escort her to this meeting, and she wondered at the show of courtesy. "Of course, my lord." She hurried to join him at the door.

The earl swept open the sitting-room door and together he and Babs walked into the entry hall.

The porter held open the outer door for the entrance of the arriving party. Candlelight spilled out onto the outside steps. Into the pool of light stepped the butler and a footman, tenderly supporting between them the halting steps of a small frail woman.

The trio came into the entry hall and Babs saw that the lady's face was ashen and that her dark eyes were sunken in twin pools of patient suffering. Barbara's natural compassion was instantly aroused and she instinctively started toward their guest. But she checked herself as the earl bit off an exclamation and strode past her.

Lord Chatworth swept aside the footman and lifted the woman into his arms. "You should not have come, my lady," he said gently but with an undercurrent of anger.

"On the contrary, I should have come much sooner." The dowager countess's voice was firm, belying her obvious frailty. She turned her head and her eyes met Babs' astonished gaze. "My dear, I am so happy to meet you at last. Should you mind it awfully if we put off a more extensive visit until the morrow? I find myself quite unequal to it this evening, more's the pity."

"Of course not, my lady!" Glad of something to do, Babs directed the footmen to take the dowager countess's baggage up to the suite of rooms that she had had prepared for their guest. The earl climbed the stairs with his mother held tenderly in his arms, closely followed by the dowager countess's anxious maid.

Babs thoughtfully returned to the drawing room. She was completely bowled over. All of her preconceived notions of a regal, forbidding dame had been shown to be untrue. She could hardly adjust to the dowager countess's actual appearance. The poor lady obviously suffered greatly from an affliction of the joints. Babs understood now why the earl had said that his mother preferred quiet pursuits to the rigors of society.

The dowager Countess of Chatworth had spoken quite civilly to her, besides, which had relieved Babs of her wary anxiety. She had to smile at the absurdity of her former fears. Perhaps she and her mother-in-law might have a chance of becoming easy acquaintances. Babs did not aspire to hope for more than that.

The butler came into the drawing room to inquire whether she would like a glass of sherry, and Babs said she would. "Perhaps you might bring a glass for his lordship as well," she said on an afterthought. The butler bowed and left on his errand.

Babs took out her embroidery and began plying the needle with the calm that had escaped her earlier that evening. When Smithers returned with the wine and two glasses, Babs thanked him quietly and asked that the tray be set down on the occasional table.

The earl returned to the drawing room some twenty minutes later. Babs saw that he had put on a greatcoat, so that she knew that he meant to go out. Her heart unaccountably dropped, but she smiled up at him. "I trust that her ladyship is made comfortable?" she asked.

"Yes." He saw the bottle of sherry and glanced at her. Without a word he filled the wineglasses and handed one to her, before he went to stand at the mantel, his own glass in hand. "By the by, who is the housekeeper these days?

I had not realized that Mrs. Sparrow had left my employ.''

Babs felt a tide of color rise in her cheeks, but she met his inquiring glance steadily enough. "I accepted the services of Mrs. Fennell ten days ago, after I let go your former housekeeper.''

Lord Chatworth raised his brows. "I had believed that Mrs. Sparrow was perfectly capable, but perhaps I was mistaken.''

"Mrs. Sparrow did not care to be directed by a tradesman's daughter,'' Babs said shortly.

"I see.'' Lord Chatworth contemplated the sherry in his glass, giving it a swirl. He spoke without glancing at her. "I trust that there will be no further such troubles.''

"No, my lord. There will not be.''

He looked up at that and there was the faintest of grins on his lips. "I can well imagine that there will not. You do not strike me as a lady easily able to swallow insult of that sort.''

"No, I suppose that I do not,'' Babs said, uncertain of where he was leading.

Lord Chatworth set aside his wineglass, the sherry untasted. He went to her and took her hand. She looked up at him in surprised inquiry. "I recommend that you recall that sentiment when you begin to go about society. As my wife, you are entitled to respect, but you must also act the part. I do not wish to observe you shrinking away into the nearest corner in trepidation, as you seemed to do while awaiting my mother's arrival.''

Babs gasped, at once angered and appalled by his keen perception. Her green eyes gleamed with temper. "Pray rest assured, Marcus! I shall not shrink into any more corners.''

He laughed then and brushed his lips across her fingers. "Do not wait up for me, my love,'' he said mockingly. Then he was gone in a swirl of greatcoat, the sitting-room door shutting with finality behind him.

Babs threw her embroidery hoop at the uncaring door.

The following morning was nearly spent before Babs received the summons she was expecting from the dowager countess. At once Babs went along to her mother-in-law's room and was admitted by the maid.

The dowager countess gestured for Babs to be seated opposite her, but she waited until her faithful henchwoman exited before she spoke more than a few commonplaces to her daughter-in-law. After seeing that her mistress was made perfectly comfortable where she reclined on a settee, a shawl wrapped warmly about her shoulders against the morning chill, the maid left the sitting room.

The door closed quietly, leaving the ladies to enjoy their privacy. Lady Chatworth smiled at Babs, her gray eyes, so reminiscent of her son's, twinkling. "I am surrounded by solicitous goodwill. I do not begrudge it, for I am fully grateful for the comforts I am thus afforded, but at times it is extremely awkward to appear anything other than a senseless invalid," she said with a touch of self-deprecating humor.

"Oh, no, ma'am, I do not think that anyone could mistake you for less than you are," said Babs. Suddenly aware of how she must have sounded, she flushed. "I apologize if I am impertinent, my lady."

"Not at all, dear child. I am flattered, actually. Not even Marcus grants me such autonomy of being," Lady Chatworth said, laughing. "Now I have embarrassed you. Come, we shall have tea and come to know each other better. Please be so good as to pour. My hands are not as graceful or as capable as they once were."

Babs inclined her head and quietly lifted the pot to do the office. The dowager countess accepted the cup that she handed to her with a word of thanks, before adding, quite coolly, "I was much surprised, as you may have guessed, by my son's hasty missive that he was wedded. I had no notion that he had discovered such a desire in himself. Indeed, I was not aware that he had ever given a thought to it in his life."

Babs was so startled that she slopped a bit of tea out of her own cup as she poured. That annoyed her no end, for she knew very well that how one poured tea counted much in indicating one's degree of breeding. She looked up to meet her mother-in-law's eyes, which were not as warm as she had first believed. In the face of the cool intelligence in those gray eyes, Babs thought it would be the more prudent course to lay everything aboveboard at once.

"I shall be straightforward with you, my lady. I do not believe that his lordship gave any thought to marriage at all before entering into an engagement with me," she said frankly.

"I see. And why should my son change his mind so suddenly upon acquaintance with you, my dear?"

Babs felt twin flags of color unveil in her cheeks. "I think it best that you apply to his lordship for your answer, my lady. For me to comment upon his lordship's motives would be the height of indiscretion."

"What were your motives, Barbara? Pray, do you mind that I call you Barbara? It is not as though we shall always be strangers," said Lady Chatworth.

"I prefer Babs, my lady," said Barbara with determined civility.

"You have not answered my question, Babs," said the older Lady Chatworth.

There was an undercurrent of steel in that gentle voice that Babs readily identified and appreciated. Just so would Lady Azaela have inexorably pursued a tangent of elusive information. She smiled faintly, and her expression, if she had but known it, greatly startled the dowager countess.

"No, ma'am. I know full well that I have not satisfied you. Again, much of what I could say is wrapped up quite firmly with his lordship's business." Babs paused a moment and her finger lightly traced the rim of her teacup. "I shall say, though, that our arrangement arose out of a business necessity. Neither the earl nor myself is personally attached to the other. For more than that, I think it best that you apply to his lordship. I do not wish to say more than he would wish me to."

The dowager regarded her in silent astonishment. She said finally, "My dear child, you are amazingly discreet—indeed, forbiddingly reticent. I assure you, I do not pry where my son does not wish me. I do not interfere with his life, any

more than he interferes unduly with mine. But am I to understand that this is naught but a marriage of convenience,
arising out of some sort of business arrangement between
the two of you?''

Babs could not help smiling at the older woman's palpable
surprise. ''Exactly so, my lady. Is that so unheard of? I had
thought there were many such marriages.''

''Marriages of conveniences, assuredly so, but arranged
by the elders of the receptive families and not by the
principals themselves,'' said the dowager countess, her
emphatic voice stressing her continued astonishment.

Babs only shook her head, laughing a little. Then she
sobered and her frank eyes met the dowager's gaze. ''I hope
that I am not found too entirely below the cut, my lady. I
assure you, though my paternal birth is not what it should
be for one of this exalted position, my mother's family was
quite unexceptionable. My aunt, Lady Azaela Terowne, had
the actual raising of me after my mother's death, and she
attempted most strictly to endow me with the education and
training that a young lady of quality is to possess.''

''Lady Azaela Terowne? I fancy that I know her, or at
least of her,'' said the dowager consideringly. ''She was a
Harrowby, was she not? The eldest Miss Harrowby was once
a bosom bow of mine. It is unfortunate that I quite lost track
of her sometime after her marriage. She was married out
of hand to a quite unacceptable party for familial considera-
ations and thereafter steadfastly refused all my invitations.''

The dowager saw that her daughter-in-law had gone quite
white and in gathering astonishment, she said, ''My dear,
never tell me that your mother was Amanda Harrowby?''

Babs blindly put down her teacup, clattering it in the
saucer. ''My mother—yes, she was the eldest Miss
Harrowby. But I had no notion, no inkling, that she was
acquainted with, or even knew, anyone . . .'' She stopped,
quite suddenly aware that she might burst into tears or betray
her certainty that her mother had deliberately cut herself off
from her high-flying connections as a consequence of her
quite ineligible marriage.

Meeting her mother-in-law's quizzical gaze, Babs made

an effort to regain her equilibrium. "Forgive me, my lady. I was just so surprised by the unexpectedness of the coincidence. I never dreamed that my mother knew anyone in the world, or even that she would be remembered. She was quite secluded from society after her marriage, I understand."

"You mean that she was ostracized by her foolishly proud family, who had made of her a sacrifice to their own gain and then turned their collective backs upon her as though she had become unclean," said the dowager countess brutally.

The older Lady Chatworth saw that she had upset her daughter-in-law, and she stretched out a hand to the younger woman, gently touching her shoulder. "My dear, it is all in the past. I wish now that I had pressed your mother harder to accept my invitations. I might have known you as a child then. But instead, I bowed to her obvious wish to be left to herself; I had come to realize, you see, that she did not desire that I be placed on familiar terms with your father. It was a pity, of course. I missed her very much. But your mother— my dear friend—undoubtedly rests quite easy these days. It is you that we must now consider."

Babs looked up, surprised. She found that the dowager was smiling at her in the most friendly manner imaginable. "What do you mean, my lady?"

"You must tell me all that you have gotten up to since your marriage to my scapegrace of a son," said the dowager countess, raising her teacup to her lips.

Babs could scarcely believe that her mother-in-law was looking at her in such a friendly fashion or that she could truly be interested in such mundane conversation, but obediently she launched into a description of all that she had seen, her visits and shopping trips with Lady Azaela, and even her shaking up of the household.

The dowager countess never appeared to be bored and indeed encouraged her with small comments and questions, so that Babs relaxed and even enjoyed herself. She was surprised when the maid reentered the room to take away the tea tray and to announce that it was time for the dowager countess's nap.

Babs glanced quickly at the clock on the mantel. An hour and a half had passed since she had sat down with the dowager, and she was astonished. "I had no notion of the time, my lady. I have been prosing on for far too long and I do apologize," she said contritely.

"Nonsense," said the dowager countess briskly. "I have enjoyed our little cose immensely. You and I must talk again, quite soon."

Babs knew that she was in a fair way of being dismissed, and so she took leave of her mother-in-law. She left the room without the nervousness that had accompanied her into the interview.

When the maid had shown Babs out, the dowager said, "Macy, I wish to speak to my son. Pray convey my request that his lordship wait upon me at his convenience."

"Yes, my lady." The maid left the room with the tea tray, and when she went downstairs, she relayed her mistress's message.

In due course, the earl was told.

14

LORD CHATWORTH had just come in and was about to go up to change for a dinner engagement when the butler relayed the dowager countess's request. He frowned slightly. His mother's unmistakable command was unusual. "Thank you, Smithers. I shall go up immediately."

Lord Chatworth took the stairs two at a time and made his way to his mother's suite of rooms. At his knock on the door, he was instantly admitted by his mother's maid.

"Ah, there you are, Marcus. Macy, you may go," said the dowager. The maid instantly left the sitting room.

Lord Chatworth's brows shot up in surprise at his mother's abrupt demand for privacy, but he quickly schooled his expression. He was wary now, and wondered again what could possibly have set up the dowager's hackles. He went up to the settee upon which his mother reclined and bent forward to kiss her cheek. She had raised her hand to him and he took it lightly between his own. "Good evening, Mama. You look quite fetching in that cap. Is it new?"

She withdrew her hand to gesture for him to seat himself in the chair opposite. "Thank you, my dear, for the compliment, no matter how insincere it is," she said dryly.

Lord Chatworth grinned. He knew better than to protest against his mother's decisive rejection of his flattery. She was in a rare mood and he was willing to play along with her. "I should not compliment you at all, Mama. It is too fatiguing to attempt to persuade you of my good intentions."

Lady Chatworth smiled and shook her head, her eyes softening a little as she regarded him. "I know full well of your goodness of heart, my boy. I have proof of it every day of my life.''

Marcus snorted, and his lips twisted in a peculiar smile. "Come, Mama! Doing it too brown, are you not? I lead a scandal dog's life, as well you know. You are not so immured at Wormswood that you do not hear of my doings."

"I prefer to turn a deaf ear to the worst stories," murmured the dowager countess. She glanced at her son and her eyes were extremely keen. "One must preserve one's own sense of serenity, I have found. It cannot be left to another to provide."

Lord Chatworth was taken aback by what he could construe only as an unprecedented attack. He and his mother shared an uncommon bond of affection, one that tacitly left unsaid those things that would inevitably have led to argument. He was well aware that his mother did not care for his rakish propensities, and though she sometimes mildly commented upon it to him, she had never attempted to dissuade him out of it, perhaps knowing that she would be wasting her breath. Nor had she ever allowed herself to place blame upon him for giving her pain. At least, not until now. The earl wondered grimly exactly what had so overset her ladyship's usual manner.

"Marcus, I visited with your wife today," said his mother coolly.

He stiffened, now at least certain of where the fault lay. His eyes were hard as he thought of what he would say to his dear wife for her temerity in upsetting his mother. "I take it that it was not a particularly pleasant visit?"

"On the contrary, it was most pleasant. I liked her very much. You could not have done better if you had applied first to me for my opinion. Imagine my astonishment when I discovered that she was the daughter of one of my dearest girlhood friends," said the dowager.

Lord Chatworth sat quite still. That his wife had succeeded in bamboozling his mother he had no doubts at all. The sheer audacity of it angered him. He studied his mother's serene expression. "Surely you did not swallow whole such a fortuitous circumstance as that."

The dowager countess put up her brows and she suddenly bore little resemblance to the frail elderly woman that he had carried upstairs the evening before. "Pray do not be a nodcock, Marcus. I am not yet in my dotage. The connection is there. The girl had no notion that I had been once acquainted with her mother, or for that matter with her aunt, Lady Azaela Terowne." She had spoken sharply, but now she regarded him in a speculative manner. "I begin to understand, I think. Babs told me that yours is a marriage of convenience, built upon a business arrangement. You never thought to look beyond that. My dear cloth-headed son!"

"Thank you, Mama," said Lord Chatworth bitingly. He was furious, but he did not know if it was more with his mother or with his wife. His thoughts pounced on his hapless wife. "It appears that my wife has given away more than she should have. I should have suspected that she would be overawed by you and would bleat out the story, complete with all the ugly details. Damn her eyes! You were not to know of those damnable debts of mine."

There was a long silence, during which Lord Chatworth came to realize two things. Upon his hasty words, the dowager countess's astonished eyes had swiftly risen to his face. As though it was trumpeted, he knew that she had known nothing of what he had spoken about. The other realization was that he had deeply wronged his absent wife, and for some reason that at once shamed and angered him.

"Your debts, Marcus?" The dowager countess's voice was completely void of expression. "Pray, is that the business arrangement Babs spoke of? That your debts were to be paid and in return she would become your wife? I had wondered what was the reason behind your hasty marriage, but I hesitated to pry. But now . . . Yes, now I think that I must have the round tale, if you please."

Lord Chatworth passed an harassed hand through his hair. "I have made a rare mull of it. Yes, since you must know of it now, that was the bargain. Her father approached me with the scheme, which I felt compelled to accept."

"It is a damnable bargain!" Lady Chatworth's voice shook with barely repressed violence. She looked up at her much-

astonished son, her eyes glittering with a frightening degree
of emotion. "That man—her father—he bought himself a
wife in just that way. I often thought of her with true regret.
Dear gentle Amanda, forced into a marriage beneath her and
thereafter shunned by her family and friends. She firmly
denied all my invitations so as not to expose me to that
toadying husband of hers. And now, that man dares to use
that poor girl to promote himself! He dare to use my son!"
She had half-risen in her chair, her hands clutching the arms
to support herself. Her countenance was livid with anger.

Lord Chatworth sprang up and eased her back onto the
settee cushions. "Mama, pray! You are overwrought."

The maid had rushed inside at sound of her mistress's
raised voice, and now he glanced at the woman. "A lemon
water!"

The maid bobbed a swift curtsy and left the room running.

Lord Chatworth turned again to his mother. She had
collapsed against the back of the settee and one hand covered
her eyes. He asked softly, "Mama, are you quite all right?"

She straightened, her hand dropping away. "I am perfectly
all right," she said firmly, but her mouth was still held tight
and her face remained white. "It was but the shock of it all.
Marcus, I insist upon the truth. Does that wicked man retain
a hold upon you?"

Lord Chatworth hesitated, contemplating a lie. But there
was fierce demand in her eyes that he could not deny. "For
the moment only. I shall work free of him before long,"
he said. His jaw tightened in response to his unpleasant
reflections. Cribbage had much to answer for, he thought,
and not the least was the upset given to the dowager countess.
Marcus would not easily forgive himself for inadvertently
giving his mother cause for such shock, but it was Cribbage
whom must bear the brunt of the blame. It was Cribbage
whose influence had poisoned the lives that he touched.

"I trust that you have told me the truth. I shall say no more
about it," said Lady Chatworth. Her voice shook with the
effort required to make such a promise. She caught hold of
her son's sleeve before he could straighten away from her.

Lord Chatworth was surprised by the stern demand in her expression. "I shall say something about Babs, however. She is the daughter of my good friend, and your wife. I shall have her treated as such, Marcus."

He was taken aback by her vehemence. "But of course, Mama. I have naturally allowed her full rein. My quarrel with her father does not extend to her." Even as he uttered the words, however, he suspected that he did not speak entirely true. He spared little thought for it, though, and went on in his reassurances to his mother. "Ours is a marriage of convenience. Babs is free to pursue whatever interests she may get up, just as I am free to continue with my old acquaintances and life. I ask no questions of her, and I am perfectly willing to fork over for whatever bills she may acquire. It is proving a satisfactory arrangement for both of us."

"Is it, indeed! Well, let me tell you that it is not satisfactory in my eyes," said Lady Chatworth sharply. "You have shamefully neglected your duty toward that poor girl. She does not recognize it for herself, but I shall tell you to your head that I was astonished as I listened to her go on about her shopping and her domestic trials, with only visits to Lady Azaela to relieve the tedium. Babs is too young to lead a cloistered life such as mine, Marcus. And that is not the worst of it, my son. You have not made the least push to establish her credibility in society's eyes, nor have you taken the time to learn anything about her. Good God, Marcus, have you any thought for what others think? They shall hardly show proper respect for the Countess of Chatworth when you do not do so yourself."

Lord Chatworth was reluctantly impressed by his mother's reasoning. His sense of duty, at times appearing haphazard to those who witnessed only his excesses, was nevertheless firmly established. His mother was right; he had neglected his duty toward his wife.

He had left her alone every evening, not even inquiring whether she might enjoy accompanying him to a soiree or some other function. His friends had taken to referring to her as the Ghost Countess, which he had previously shrugged aside, but now he saw quite forcibly as good-natured contempt that reflected full upon his own consequence. "Exactly what do you suggest, Mama?" he asked quietly.

Lady Chatworth knew from his mild retort that she had scored her point. "Perhaps an introductory ball and a soiree or two. I shall myself preside in order to lend countenance to my daughter-in-law, who shall desperately need such support if the malicious are to be confounded at this late stage."

Lord Chatworth did not acknowledge the further aspersion to his handling of the situation. "Very well. A ball it shall be. Here is Macy at last with your lemon-water. I shall leave you to rest, my lady." He bowed over his mother's hand and left the sitting room.

As he continued on to his own rooms, a frown darkened his brow. His mother had given him much to think on, and though she had angered him to no small end, he was too fair to lightly cast aside the justice of her sharp observations. It appeared that he would have to bestir himself somewhat in this marriage of convenience, after all.

15

THE EARL CHOSE to join his mother and his wife at luncheon on the following day. He was not uncognizant of his wife's surprise before she managed to school her expression. It only served to point out more strongly the truth of his mother's accusations of the evening before. His mood, which was already one of reluctant compliance to the discharge of his duty, was not improved, and he said abruptly, "It has occurred to me that we have not yet entertained. I have all the tabbies scolding me for being remiss in introducing my wife to society."

Lord Chatworth's glance slid to his mother's face and he saw that she was amused by his oblique and uncomplimentary reference to their discussion the night before. He returned his gaze to his wife's carefully neutral expression. "A ball will do the thing, I believe. Babs, I shall trust you to the details. Pray call upon my secretary for any tasks that you may need him for. He has some knowledge of who are my particular acquaintances, and so forth, so that he can be of aid to you with the guest list."

Babs was dismayed by the earl's pronouncement. She felt totally unequal to the task of putting together a function of the sort that she knew he would take for granted. The very thought of coming face to face with any of those personages who might recall her disastrous come-out two years before made her feel physically ill. But she knew it was expected of her to take up the responsibility, and as she was unable to object, she said tightly, "It shall be just as you wish, my lord."

The earl's brows snapped together. He was impatient of

her obvious reluctance and he was on the point of delivering a curt set-down when the dowager countess spoke up.

Lord Chatworth had not been the only observer of Babs' anxiety, but the dowager came far closer in guessing the reason behind it. "Even though I have been long out of society, I might also be of help to you, my dear. One's first ball can be quite a challenge, as I recall, and I was used to be accounted a fair hostess in my day," she said.

"Thank you, ma'am. I.shall be glad of your advice," said Babs with a fleeting smile. She managed to push down the worst of her fear as she made a civil reply. "I know little about entertaining on a large scale, and even less about those who might expect to receive an invitation. I am not familiar with society, you see."

"You will learn soon enough. It will be a squeeze, I'll wager. If nothing else, curiosity about the new Countess of Chatworth will draw the hordes," Lord Chatworth said indifferently.

Babs was seized by absolute terror when she thought about entering society, and in such a way. Lord Chatworth was undoubtedly right when he said that many would come out of curiosity. She could not forget the horrible experience she had endured during her come-out. Babs shuddered, convinced that once again she would be cast in the role of circus sideshow. Her inner dread must have shown in her face, for the earl's mouth took on that particularly mocking smile. He did not say anything to her, however, for which she was grateful. Instead, he turned to address a question to his mother.

Babs studied his stern profile. It was not the first time that she had traced with her eyes the clean cut of his lean features and the firm set of his mouth and chin. She wondered idly why the earl, who had not seemed particularly interested in entertaining, should suddenly take it into his head to have a ball.

It was then that she finally realized what he was saying. "A week! But that is impossible! I cannot possibly—"

The earl turned his head, his raised brows and cold expression effectively cutting off her ill-conceived protest.

"It shall be held a week from today, my lady," he repeated uncompromisingly.

Babs met his hard eyes. Her own sparked to anger. She made an effort to speak with calm reason. "What you require is quite impossible, my lord. The preparations alone will take nearly that long. There will not be sufficient time to get out the invitations and receive the acceptances. Why, the date would be upon us almost before those who are to be invited are made aware of the ball."

The earl lounged back in his chair. "Nevertheless, that is what I wish. The ball is for your benefit, dear wife, not mine. I am already well acquainted in town."

"Marcus, really!" murmured the dowager countess.

Lord Chatworth ignored his mother's censorious tone. He did not take his eyes from his wife's indignant gaze. For some peculiar reason, her opposition pleased him. He smiled, that flicker of mockery touching his lips. "Surely you will not be terribly disappointed if the function is not as crowded as could be expected."

His shot went home. Babs colored, her high cheekbones taking on an attractive rose that lent emphasis to the anger that brightened her green eyes. She now knew beyond a shadow of doubt that his lordship was aware of her anxiety over entering society. She was humiliated by her self-betrayal and was made all the more furious that he should bait her in such a cruel manner. "You are monstrous," she said in a suffocated voice.

Lord Chatworth straightened, preparatory to rising from the table. "I have never laid claim to a gentle nature, Babs." His voice was brusque and impatient. "You are my lady and I expect you to behave in a fashion worthy of your position. That is my final word on the matter, Babs, and quite within the scope of our previous discussion, do you not agree?"

Babs was silent. With difficulty she arranged her expression to one of cool disdain. "I do not mistake your meaning, my lord."

Lord Chatworth regarded her with detached interest. Her expression had become unreadable and her demeanor would not have given anyone to suspect that she was discomposed.

Only the rigidity of her hands clasped in her lap betrayed her in any significant way. If she reacted with the same cold civility when it chanced to be a *grande dame* who so insulted her, rather than himself, she would be able to hold her own. He had experienced doubts of the wisdom in exposing her to the glaring curiosity that was sure to come their way because of the circumstances of their hasty marriage. Now he thought that she might do, after all.

Lord Chatworth stepped around the table to reach down and raise one of her hands. He spoke his thoughts. "You will do, you know."

Babs' startled eyes flew to his face. His expression of lazy approval took her completely aback. Almost in the same instant she realized that he had for the past several moments deliberately put her out of countenance as a sort of test of her control. Her eyes rekindled and her lips parted on a hasty set-down.

But the earl was too quick for her. He leaned over and lightly bussed her. "There, my lady! Never accuse me of not apologizing for my rude insult," he said with a lurking smile. Not at all put out to meet his mother's quizzical eyes, he bowed to his maternal parent and left the dining room.

Babs sat with flaming cheeks, her thoughts in confusion. How dared he to kiss her like that! It was not at all fair to confound her in such a manner. It was a dastardly liberty on his part, as well as he had known or he would not have smiled in just that way. He was the most infuriating, unpredictable gentleman and he had the most devastating effect upon her equilibrium. Her pulses still hammered with the suspension of her anger and the surprise of his action.

The dowager had for several minutes sat as an interested spectator of the exchange between her son and his wife. Now she regarded her daughter-in-law with a curious expression in her eyes. Whatever else Barbara Cribbage was, the young woman was certainly a match for the earl. A trifle naïve, perhaps, she thought as she looked at the girl's still-flushed face, but she suspected that would quickly become a thing of the past once her daughter-in-law had gained some confidence.

It occurred to her that Babs could become quite a stunning creature, and one who might just give the earl a few perilous moments of unbalance. The thought was an exceptionally pleasing one.

Her son had for too long had matters his own way. Even in her reclusement she had heard stories about him that had given her grave cause for concern. He had always been a dutiful son; that had not changed, nor had his sense of duty toward his dependents. But a wife—and in particular one who bid fair to become a handful from any gentleman's point of view—was something that the earl had yet to come into his realm of experience. It would undoubtedly do him good to have his entrenched notions and habits shaken up a little.

The dowager countess smiled to herself. She signaled the footman, who had returned to remove the covers, and instantly the manservant was at her elbow. With the man's help, she rose from the table.

The older Lady Chatworth smiled at her daughter-in-law, who had risen immediately when she perceived the elderly lady was ready to vacate the dining room. Babs was surprised by the degree of warmth in the dowager's eyes.

"I am going up to rest a while, my dear. Perhaps later this afternoon we shall begin discussing details for the ball, shall we?"

Babs quickly acquiesced in real gratitude. "Thank you, my lady. I shall be glad to wait on you."

"I shall send Macy for you," said the dowager countess. She inclined her head as the footman aided her from the room.

Babs watched the dowager's halting and yet stately exit. Her thoughts turned to the dilemma of the ball and its preparations. A small frown drew her brows together. She was still standing there when the footman returned. He hesitated, then asked, "My lady? Will you be requiring anything else?"

She looked at him quickly. "No, nothing, thank you." Then she, too, left the dining room. She had much to do if she was to get up a ball with suitable decoration, entertainment, and refreshments. And not the least of her concerns was her own appearance. She knew of old that she must make the correct impression, for an unforgiving society could hardly be expected to grant her another chance.

As Miss Cribbage she had not been granted the opportunity to prove herself, but fate had forced upon her the opportunity to redeem herself as best she might in the guise of the Countess of Chatworth. This time around she meant to have things go a little more her way.

Babs had carefully chosen the gown that she would wear for the ball. She knew that she would be the object of all eyes, as would her house and her table. She was determined that there would be nothing that could be pointed to as smelling of the trades.

She smoothed the shimmering violet skirt of her gown, liking the reflection of herself in the cheval glass. The neckline of her dress was low and more revealing than any she had previously worn. Her bosom was emphasized by the thin velvet ribbon that tied under her breasts, its lengths falling to the hem. The sleeves were long and reached over her hands from the wrist bands, establishing a claim to modesty, but the skirt was open in front to reveal the lavishly laced petticoat she wore underneath.

Babs had resisted her maid's urgings to have her hair cropped short in the Titus, the newest fashion from France. Instead, she had requested that her hair be brushed back and caught in a comb highly decorated with precious stones. Her auburn hair was softly plaited at the back of her head while the front had been allowed to remain in soft curls to frame her face. Wisping tendrils escaped about her ears, accenting the amethyst studs she wore.

The maid lifted the necklace that matched the studs. The cool fire of diamonds and amethysts glittered in the candle-light. " 'Tis a beautiful piece, my lady,'' said the maid admiringly as she fastened the necklace about her mistress's slender neck.

"Yes, it is.'' Babs touched the cool stones with her fingers. She stared at herself in the mirror. The earl had sent up the jewel box with the necklace and studs nestled inside and a careless note that it was to mark the occasion of their first ball. He had not presented it to her himself, and for some inexplicable reason that gave her an odd hurt.

Babs lifted her chin. She refined too much upon the manner of the gift. It was enough that the gesture had been made and the house servants had been aware of it. She could sense the difference in attitude in the silent undermaid who had been assisting Lucy with readying her gown, silk stockings, and white gloves. The wariness that had been hers since she had fired the housekeeper and maids was beginning to warm. She had gained some worth along with the earl's largess.

Babs knew from her reflection that she was beautifully turned out. Her hair was dressed *à la Égyptienne,* but she had not had the courage to finish the look. Now she rather thought she would do so. "Lucy, pray bring me the gold beads," she said quietly.

The maid looked at her mistress with an appalled expression. "You'll never be wearing those, my lady. Why, it is positively heathen you'll look."

"Pray do as I say," said Babs. She was acutely aware of the undermaid's scarcely concealed curiosity.

The maid grumbled under her breath but reluctantly brought the beads out of the jewel box. She placed the elaborate tiers of tiny dangling gold beads across her mistress's forehead and brought the ends around to fasten in the plaited hair in back. "There you are, my lady," said Lucy, surveying her handiwork with disapproval but also a grudging appreciation.

The rows of glittering beads swung with the smallest movement of Babs' head as she studied the effect. The scintillating gold brought out the gold flecks in her eyes, charging her large eyes with mystery, and accented her high cheekbones. Her self-critical stare disappeared with the slow smile that warmed her eyes. "I think . . . Yes, I think it will do very nicely." She laughed at her maid's uncertain expression. "I am a countess, Lucy. If I am to be condemned forever for my roots, at least let it be remarked to my credit that I am in the first stare of fashion."

Babs swept out of the bedroom and down the stairs to take

her place at the entrance to the ballroom. She cast a glance inside and was reassured by the beautifully decorated room. Surely nothing could be found wanting in that direction, and as she reviewed the night's menu in her mind, Babs thought she could be confident about that as well. It needed only to be seen what her own reception would be and how many would recall the come-out of an obscure tradesman's daughter two years earlier.

The earl sauntered downstairs and took his place beside her. He gave her an appraising glance. There was agreeable surprise in his eyes. "You appear in great beauty this evening, Babs," he said.

Babs smiled. She had not missed the faint hint of astonishment in his voice. "Thank you, my lord. I had hoped to meet with your approval," she said on a dry note.

She felt rather than saw his swift penetrating look. The first guests were arriving and she was already moving to greet them.

16

AN HOUR AND A HALF LATER, the Earl and Countess of Chatworth left their post at the entrance to the ballroom and began to mingle with their guests. Babs was still tense over what some of her guests might be thinking about her, though few had had the ill-breeding to show other than polite courtesy while the earl stood beside her.

A minor flurry of curiosity was aroused by the entrance of the dowager Countess of Chatworth. Babs turned with the exclamations of the ladies that she was conversing with and watched as a footman and the dowager's maid tenderly settled the old lady onto a settee. Babs was astonished at the extreme formality of her mother-in-law's dress, while the dowager's befeathered turban positively awed her with its magnificence. She had never before seen the dowager countess so turned out.

"Why, there is the dowager Countess of Chatworth! I don't believe she has been in town above a handful of times in the last ten years. I must remember myself to her at once," said one lady.

Her companion quickly said that she also must bring herself to the dowager's attention, and Babs found herself momentarily abandoned.

"I do feel for her ladyship. She will be mobbed for half the night and be burned to the socket as a consequence."

Babs turned her head at the familiar voice. She smiled with genuine gladness as she clasped both of the other woman's hands. "Aunt Azaela! I did not see you arrive or I would have instantly come to you."

"My dear." Lady Azaela placed an affectionate kiss on

her niece's cheek. She then stepped back to inspect her with critical eyes. She gave an approving nod. "You are in looks tonight, Babs. My compliments to your dresser. The style of headdress suits you very well indeed." She glanced around them at the milling company and lowered her voice. "It is going quite differently than the last time, is it not?"

Babs laughed in a bubbling fashion. Her eyes danced a little. "Why, yes, I believe it is. I suspect that a number of those who have graced the ball with their presence do recall something about me, but they are all too polite to say so. Oh, I have been the object of a few cattish innuendos, of course, but I disregard those. You have no notion what protection a title bestows upon one."

"Haven't I, though! And it is no less than you deserve," Lady Azaela retorted tartly. She smiled in a somewhat grim fashion. "It is the beginning of all that I have ever wished for you, my dear girl. I do not intend that it shall end in disaster again. You may rely upon me to aid you in whatever capacity I can."

Babs knew that her aunt referred in part to her father. She smiled gratefully. "I do thank you. I could hardly ask for more. Now, shall I act the proper hostess and hunt up a suitable partner for you for the upcoming set?"

Lady Azaela rapped her niece's arm lightly with her fan. "Puss! As though you are not aware that I have not danced these ten years or more. No, you may instead attend to those who have need of you. I intend to pay my respects to the dowager countess and request her indulgence of a few words on the morrow."

Babs saw her aunt walk off with mixed feelings. She felt suddenly bereft of a comforting presence, which she knew to be illogical. She stood in her own ballroom surrounded by a large company of civil personages who had by their appearance bestowed upon her party just the right touch of success.

From where she stood, Babs could see the Earl of Chatworth's dark head and broad shoulders. His close presence should have reassured her, but she recalled how cavalier he had been toward her in regard to the ball.

Babs straightened her shoulders and turned determinedly to a lady and gentleman that she had not yet spoken to at any length. She would not have the earl remarking later, in that detestable manner that he could don, that she had not lived up to her end of their bargain. She greeted the couple, and after a short interval the trio was joined by a few others.

The Honorable Simon Oliver Hadwicke had casually observed the young Countess of Chatworth during the course of the ball. He had been suitably impressed by the manner in which she handled herself and her duties. There was nothing of the vulgar about her, he thought with satisfaction. He had often wondered whether his friend the earl had made a fatal error in wedding the chit, but now he was rather inclined to give the lady the benefit of the doubt. Whatever her unfortunate connections, they had apparently done her little personal harm.

The set was ending, and after disposing of his erstwhile partner, Viscount Taredell sauntered up to Hadwicke. "How do you, Simon? A fair squeeze, wouldn't you agree?"

"Yes. It is quite a triumph for the Countess of Chatworth's first function," agreed Hadwicke.

The viscount followed his friend's gaze. The new Lady Chatworth was laughing gaily at some sally made by one of her guests and she appeared the very picture of lovely graciousness. "I have never breathed a word to Marcus about his chosen lady. Well, you know how unpredictable he can be. But I don't mind telling you, Simon, that I find Lady Chatworth deuced attractive, despite the rumored connection with trade," he confided.

"I must agree with you, Taredell," Hadwicke said.

A few minutes later, Hadwicke happened to be standing beside the Earl of Chatworth when a mutual acquaintance took himself off, and Simon drew his lordship's attention to the countess. "Your lady appears to advantage this evening," he commented.

Lord Chatworth turned, his curiosity faintly stirred. He saw his bride talking with several people, her eyes sparkling with obvious appreciation, her smile flashing. His attention was more fully caught by the charming picture she made,

her red-gold hair catching fire in the candlelight while his
gift of diamonds and amethysts sparked against her pale
golden skin.

All the evening he had unobtrusively observed her. He had
been pleased by her graciousness in company and he had
quickly relaxed from the spurious anxiety that she would
embarrass him in some way. But at the odd moment it was
her beauty that had caught at his throat, as it did now. He
was startled at how she affected him. However, it was not
in him to give evidence of the direction of his thoughts and
he said only, "Yes, she does." He casually inquired about
the race that Hadwicke had mentioned he would be attending
later in the week.

Lord Chatworth had barely gotten the words out when
there occurred a small commotion at the entrance to the
ballroom. Lord Chatworth turned, his expression mildly
inquiring. On the instant he recognized the bulky gentleman
who was striding into the midst of the startled company. The
gentleman was trailed by two scurrying footmen, upon whose
expressions was registered alarm and dismay.

"What the devil!" the earl bit off. He plunged through
the standing crowd to confront his father-in-law.

As Lord Chatworth reached him, Cribbage showed his
teeth. He was seething with ill-will and thought himself
slighted that he had not received an invitation to his
daughter's first ball. His hard black eyes contemptuously
swept the murmuring company.

"A paltry function, my lord. I had expected better of you
once you had your hands on my daughter's considerable
portion." He had not deigned to lower his voice and he took
pleasure in the angered consternation that entered the Earl
of Chatworth's eyes. Out of the corner of his eye, Cribbage
discerned his daughter's whitening face, but he did not turn
to acknowledge her presence. All of his attention was focused
on the arrogant peer who had yet to learn that he was the
master.

Lord Chatworth could scarcely keep his rage bridled at
the man's deliberate effrontery. He heard the fascinated

horror in the gathering whispers about them and he swiftly signaled the footmen. The footmen leapt forward with alacrity and huge satisfaction to take rough hold of the intruder. The earl said from between his teeth, "We will further our discussion in my study."

"Unhand me, do you hear?" Cribbage made to shake loose of the footmen's hold.

Lord Chatworth bared his teeth. He said very softly, "Come peacefully, or I shall myself wield the horsewhip across your beefy shoulders." There was utter ruthlessness in his silken voice.

Cribbage apparently recognized when he was at a total disadvantage, for he merely shrugged in a contemptuous fashion. Disdaining to notice his escort, he swept around to exit the ballroom.

Babs watched in blind horror as her father and the earl disappeared from sight. Her entire frame shook. She felt as though her whole world crumbled about her. She did not need to look around. She sensed the circle that opened about her as those she had invited that evening drew away from her. She had become the center of stares and supercilious smiles and tittering whispers as all awaited her reaction.

She felt her cold hand drawn through a gentleman's elbow and a low voice spoke in her ear. "Courage, my lady." She glanced up quickly, unfallen tears affecting her sight, but nevertheless she recognized Simon Hadwicke's friendly smile.

"I believe that I have the honor of escorting you in to dinner, my lady," he said in a normal tone.

Her fingers clutched his sleeve and the hand that rested so easily above her own tightened in a warning fashion. Babs gave a jerky nod of acceptance and murmured an incoherent agreement.

"My dear niece, such an appalling heat. Why do we not have the windows opened before going in to dinner?" Lady Azaela stood upon Babs' other side, fanning herself in a leisurely fashion, her expression cool and serene.

"Yes—yes, I think that is a marvelous notion," said Babs

faintly, making the supreme effort to pull herself together. She gestured quickly to a footman and gave the order in a low, even voice.

The horrible spell was broken. Those gathered about began to turn away, looking for their own dinner partners.

Babs nearly sagged with relief. Then high above the lifting conversation came a devastating statement. "Really, my dear, I do not see how she may be countenanced after such a telling spectacle."

The raven-haired lady whose malicious voice had carried such venom gave a sparkling laugh. She looked directly into her hostess's eyes before she deliberately turned her narrow shoulder and with elaborate condescension laid her fingers upon her escort's arm.

Babs felt ready to sink into the floor. Her face had flamed with shame and humiliation, but she refused to allow herself to avoid the gazes of those who turned again to stare at her.

"If I countenance my daughter-in-law with unequivocal approval, then who dares to do less?"

In the astonished silence, the entire company turned. The older Countess of Chatworth stood quite unassisted, her eyes twin points of hauteur. Behind her ladyship hovered her dresser in obvious alarm. The dowager countess's gaze was cold with disdain as she flicked an arctic glance at the offending lady. She cut the lady direct, leaving the woman flushing with fury and humiliation.

Still holding the center of attention, the dowager countess slowly joined Babs. She took her daughter-in-law's hand and reached up to kiss the younger woman on the cheek. With a lurking smile in her eyes, she said quite strongly, "It has been a most delightful party, my dear. I must leave you now, however. The excitement has quite overtaxed me."

"Of course, my lady. I shall visit with you on the morrow," said Babs, recovering.

"That will be delightful, my dear. Good night." The dowager countess left the ballroom in solitary splendor, occasionally giving a regal nod of recognition to acquaintances whom she saw on her way out. Her faithful dresser hurried in her slow wake.

"Well, well. You have a champion, indeed. The dowager is naturally perceived as a formidable ally in the public opinion," said Hadwicke quietly. He smiled down at the lady on his arm. "You'll weather it yet, I suspect. In fact, I would not be at all surprised that this little contretemps does not set the final caveat on a true success."

Babs sighed, shaking her head. She tried to laugh, but it was not a particularly successful attempt. "That I very much doubt, sir. I fear that I am utterly ruined before I am even begun."

But Lady Azaela added her support to Hadwicke's opinion. "I do not think that, Babs. I acknowledge your father's deplorable appearance as a temporary setback at most. But I rather think that the Earl of Chatworth shall take steps to ensure that this sort of unpleasantness does not easily take place again."

In the company of her two allies, Babs continued in to dinner. The menu was pronounced superb by many of those at surrounding tables. She suspected that many of those who went out of their way to compliment her did so to prove that they harbored no ill-will against one who had won such unequivocal favor in the dowager Countess of Chatworth's eyes. Babs knew very well that without the dowager countess's timely intervention she would in all probability have sat down to dinner in a fast-emptying room. As it had turned out, however, she was able to slowly let her guard down and begin to enjoy herself again.

Viscount Taredell had charmingly requested permission to escort Lady Azaela to the table and he now regaled her with several amusing *on-dits*, to which Mr. Hadwicke added his own offerings. Babs was listening with only half an ear while she glanced about the occupied tables. Her roving eyes chanced to fall on the raven-haired beauty who had so nearly caused her complete devastation. She was curious to know who her detractor was, and she turned to Mr. Hadwicke for enlightenment. "Mr. Hadwicke, who is the lady to whom the dowager countess gave such a set-down?"

Viscount Taredell stopped in midsentence, a quick look of consternation entering his eyes. He and Mr. Hadwicke

exchanged a swift and singularly curious glance that made
Lady Azaela's brows rise. The viscount returned to his tale
in a determined manner.

Babs had not been behind in catching the byplay between
the gentlemen. "Come, Mr. Hadwicke. It is a simple-enough
question, surely?" she asked.

Hadwicke shrugged in a casual fashion. He was seemingly
more interested in his lobster than her query. "Yes, I believe
I recall the lady. It is of scarce importance now, my lady."
He turned toward their dinner companions. "Lady Azaela,
her ladyship has told me that you reside in Derbyshire. I
understand it is beautiful country and has excellent hunting."

"Yes, indeed," said Lady Azaela, amused. She was quite
aware that she was being used as a red herring, but she was
not unwilling to play the role. She was too sophisticated not
to have realized the significance of the gentlemen's reluctance
to satisfy her niece's curiosity. She would prefer to allow
her niece to remain in ignorance as long as it was possible.

Babs' idle curiosity had been sharpened by Mr.
Hadwicke's attempt to put her off, and she glanced again
in the direction of the raven-haired lady. Across the heads
of the company she saw the Earl of Chatworth wending his
way among the tables, exchanging pleasantries with the
guests. His lordship's expression was one of bland civility,
and a smile touched Barbara's lips. Lord Chatworth was not
one to give away that he had just come from an unpleasant
interview, she thought.

The raven-haired lady lifted her fan and in obeisance to
the lady's gesture, the earl paused beside her chair. There
was an intimacy in the brief conversation, a certain cast of
expression on the earl's face as he looked down into the lady's
beautiful smiling face, that made Babs' heart suddenly
contract.

She took a shuddering breath, now understanding the odd
glance that had passed between Viscount Taredell and Mr.
Hadwicke. Beyond the shadow of a doubt, she knew who
the lady was without ever having heard her name. She had
just discovered the identity of her husband's mistress.

"Simon, I will know the lady's name."

Her companions all looked at her in surprise. Babs had also heard the hard note in her voice and she summoned up a smile for Hadwicke's quick glance of astonishment. "Should I not know who my detractors are, sir?"

Viscount Taredell scowled uncertainly. "There is something to be said for that, Simon," he said, as much as he would have liked to disagree.

Hadwicke again shrugged as though it was a matter of complete indifference to him. "The lady in question is Lady Elizabeth Cartier. I understand that she is a widow and is greatly sought after for her beauty."

"One can readily understand why, of course," murmured Babs. "She is indeed very beautiful."

"I thought the lady insufferably rude," added Lady Azaela, an appreciative gleam in her eyes for the gentlemen's uneasy shifting in their chairs.

"I suppose much can be forgiven one who is as pursued and courted as Lady Cartier must surely be," said Babs ironically. There was a considering expression in her green eyes as she saw that the earl had left the lady and was swiftly approaching her table.

Viscount Taredell caught sight of his lordship at the same moment, and he greeted him with something bordering on relief. It had made him distinctly uncomfortable to participate in a discussion of the earl's mistress with his lordship's wife and her ladyship's aunt. "Marcus! I am happy to see you, old fellow. You shall not believe it, I expect, but yesterday at the club I saw none other than our friend Captain Demont." He realized abruptly that in his haste to steer clear of dangerous waters he had introduced an equally inappropriate subject. He started to cough in a violent manner and groped for his wineglass.

Simon Hadwicke helpfully gave it into his hand and in a concerned fashion administered a resounding slap to him on the back. The viscount choked on the wine he had hastily gulped and whooped in earnest paroxysm. His eyes watering, he managed to gasp, "Damn your eyes, Simon!"

"Captain Demont? I have not yet had the pleasure of meeting all of your friends, I apprehend," Babs said.

Lord Chatworth rested a thoughtful glance on the hapless viscount before he turned to reply. "He is scarcely a friend, my lady. He is, rather, a Captain Shark whose methods of play are more than suspect."

Babs was silenced by the earl's repressive tone. She thought she understood the matter well enough. Though she was unfamiliar with the term that his lordship had used to describe this Captain Demont, it did not take a great deal of intelligence to gather that the gentleman cheated at cards, nor that the earl had had unpleasant dealings with the fellow in the past.

"At the club, Taredell? I find that most curious," Hadwicke said. He chose to ignore the earl's fulminating glance. "Do you not also, my lord? I suspect our friend has wormed himself into the confidence of someone perhaps overly foolish and quite young."

The viscount had finally recovered and was assuring Lady Azaela of it with some embarrassment. He looked around at Hadwicke's observation and said admiringly, "Why, that is just the thing, Simon." Completely forgetting the tactlessness of the subject, he volunteered, "Demont came in on the sleeve of that young chub of Chesterton's, who should have known better than to vouch for such a swarthy fellow. But I daresay he is beginning to regret it. I understand that he and Demont have been thick as thieves this last fortnight."

Hadwicke looked across the table at the earl, whose expression had grown rather closed. "I discover a desire to pop into the club later this evening. Do you care to join me, Marcus?"

Lord Chatworth's eyes gleamed suddenly. A strange smile began to play about his mouth. "It occurs to me that nothing could give me greater pleasure, Simon."

Hadwicke bowed from the waist and the viscount cracked a laugh of understanding.

The earl politely inquired of Babs and Lady Azaela whether they would like more lobster.

17

AFTER LUNCHEON on the following day, Barbara received an invitation to visit her mother-in-law in her ladyship's rooms. Babs went up to find the lady reclining on her settee. In a low voice, the young countess asked the dresser, "How is her ladyship today?"

The maid shook her head, but she smiled. "Her ladyship is still feeling pulled, but she'll not let onto you, my lady."

"Macy, pray stop gossiping about me and let my daughter-in-law come to me," said Lady Chatworth in a resigned voice.

Exchanging a glance with the maid, Babs went over to the dowager and took the frail hand that the older lady extended to her. "I hope that you are well, my lady," she said.

The dowager chuckled faintly. "I suspect that Macy has already told you that I was made more tired than usual by the exertions of the evening. But I do not regard it. One becomes immured to one's own debilitations, and it did me a world of good to play the *grande dame*."

Babs sat down. "I have not yet thanked you for your role in my rescue from social ruin. The evening would have been a total disaster otherwise."

The dowager countess smiled at her daughter-in-law. "My dear, I do not allow anyone to insult a member of my family in my presence. It was rude and malicious in the extreme." She paused a moment to study the younger woman thoughtfully. "I do have a criticism to take up with you, however. It is my opinion that you refine too much upon your lack of birth."

Babs attempted a light laugh. "I wish that were true, my lady."

Lady Chatworth shook her head. "You are far too sensitive, child, and unnecessarily so. Your mother was a gentlewoman and had as much to do with your birth—indeed, more so—than your father."

"Society is not so forgiving as you, my lady," Babs said quietly. "I do not think that anyone will soon forget my father's disruption of the ball."

The dowager countess laughed. "My dear Babs, you are such an infant. Why, by tomorrow there will be something terribly more salacious and fascinating than the brief appearance of a tradesman at a ball to talk about. You have no notion how this town thrives on gossip. It must always be exclaiming over the latest *on-dit*. Believe me, child, your minor scandal is very much old news. As for society's forgiveness, I have seen two unknown Irish girls of negligible birth marry into the peerage. I do not believe that the ladies suffered for it in the least."

"The Gunning sisters, of course," said Babs, smiling.

Lady Chatworth nodded, also smiling. She made a dismissing gesture. "But that is not the whole point that I wish to make to you, my dear. I most urgently urge you to step out of your father's shadow. If you do not, you will be forever chained to a past that you find reprehensible."

Babs was silent, at once moved by the dowager countess's concern as much as she was disconcerted by the opinions expressed by that redoubtable lady. Finally she said, "You have given me much food for thought, my lady. I cannot assure you that I can do as you say, but I do promise I shall try."

"That is certainly as much as one can ask of you," said Lady Chatworth. She sighed and suddenly looked older than her years. "I should tell you that I shall be leaving toward the end of the week. I long to be home again at Wormswood, and though I have enjoyed meeting you and becoming acquainted with you, I think that I shall be more comfortable away from London."

"I shall be more sorry that I can express to say good-bye to you, my lady," Babs said sincerely.

The dowager countess patted her daughter-in-law's arm. "Pray do not go misty-eyed on me, my dear. Emotional scenes are so fatiguing."

"Yes, of course," said Babs, wobbling on a laugh.

"I shall look forward to Christmas, when you and Marcus will come to visit. It is always a pretty season in the country," said Lady Chatworth.

"I shall anticipate a wonderful visit, ma'am," Babs said. She saw that the dowager was worn out. As she rose, she said a quiet good-bye. She left the dowager countess in the hands of her maid, who was already efficiently tucking a shawl over her mistress's legs as Babs left the sitting room.

When she went downstairs, Babs met the earl, who was just coming in. "Good day, my lord," she said pleasantly. She looked at his face, wondering what he was thinking.

Lord Chatworth nodded to her as he handed his hat and gloves to Smithers. "I see that you have been abovestairs. Have you see her ladyship today?"

"I have just come from your mother's rooms. She is recuperating from yesterday evening," Babs said.

"I thought as much. I shall go up to see her presently," said Lord Chatworth. "Pray join me in the study, my lady. Smithers, coffee."

Babs preceded the earl as he held open the door for her. Lord Chatworth closed the door and gestured her to a chair in front of the hearth. Babs sat down and folded her hands in her lap. She looked up at him with an inquiring expression in her wide green eyes.

Lord Chatworth went to stand at the mantel, his shoulders against it. His glance was speculative. "I have something to relate to you that I am not certain you will appreciate."

"Indeed, my lord? But I shall not be able to say whether it is appreciated or not until I have heard it," Babs said with a smile.

Lord Chatworth gave a laugh. "No, that is true."

The door opened and the butler entered with the coffee.

He served his master and mistress and then quietly left again. Babs did not wait for the earl to speak, but said, "It is about my father, is it not? When you returned to the ballroom last night, I knew from your expression that something had taken place between you."

"I had hoped that I had done better than trumpet my emotions," said Lord Chatworth, frowning.

"I do not think that very many guessed. It was your eyes that gave you away, actually. Your expression was of the blandest," Babs said.

"I am relieved by your reassurance, my lady," Lord Chatworth bowed to her in an ironic fashion. He was silent a moment while she waited, then abruptly he said, "I have given orders that Cribbage is barred from the house. I hope this does not unduly upset you."

"Upset me! Why should you think that it would? Last night my father made an unwelcome intrusion into my life and yours. It is not likely to be the sole instance that he means to do so. Therefore, I am hardly cast down to learn that you have taken the logical course of action to impede him from doing so again. Quite the contrary, in fact. As I told you several weeks ago, I am anxious to be entirely free of him," Babs said.

Lord Chatworth looked at her searchingly. "Are you, indeed? You speak with such emphasis that I am almost compelled to believe you. However, it seems somewhat unnatural to me that a daughter should possess such a violent dislike of her father that she would be eager to cut all concourse with him."

A slight flush rose in her face. "Perhaps my intention does seem unnatural to you, Marcus. But pray believe me when I say that nothing would please me more than to see the back of my father's head and know that I should never need to look into his face again." She broke off, aware that she had spoken with more heat than she had intended. Deliberately she turned the subject. "The dowager countess informed me that she intends to leave us at the end of the week."

Lord Chatworth had been on the point of pursuing the mystery that lay behind his wife's strong dislike of her parent, but this news served to momentarily sidetrack him. "It does not surprise me overmuch to hear it. My mother has not cared for London for several years. She prefers the quiet of the country and her small circle of intimates." He stepped away from the mantel to reach down for his wife's hands. "I wish you would confide in me."

Babs felt unexpected tears start to her eyes. "I do not know what you mean, Marcus."

His lordship's reply dashed the burgeoning of warmth that she had felt at his request. "Anything that I might learn about your father's character is of importance to me in my fight against him. Surely you must see that." Lord Chatworth's voice was as persuasive as he was capable of making it. He had seen the glimmering in her eyes and thought that he had finally penetrated through her guarded exterior.

But Barbara was once more in firm command of herself. She thought that she had more pride than to cast herself upon his chest at the least encouragement, especially when she suspected that he would interpret her vulnerability as an invitation. She gave a laugh and freed her hands. "Yes, I certainly understand that. My father is a formidable opponent in business. You would do better to apply to those who have dealt with him in the City these past several years, for I was still a child when I left his house and I can scarcely be expected to present an informed judgment."

Lord Chatworth regarded her for some minutes. "I suspect that you cheat your own perceptions, my lady." He turned away from her and poured coffee for himself.

Barbara regretted the awkwardness of the moment. She tried to bring fresh life to their discourse. "I trust that your outing to the club with Mr. Hadwicke and Viscount Taredell after the ball proved entertaining."

The earl glanced at her. "It was certainly that," he acknowledged. In order to change the direction of the conversation, he said, "There is a soiree this evening that you might enjoy. I was reminded of it by the hostess, whom I met while out this morning in the park. I shall be happy to accompany you if you should care to attend."

"Yes, I should like to go," Babs said.

He turned, the quick surprise in his eyes. He had not actually had any real expectation that she would accept his off-the-cuff invitation. But quickly his expression schooled itself to one of polite gratification. "I am honored, ma'am. I have a few engagements to see to this afternoon, but I shall return in time to escort you to the soiree."

Babs inclined her head. "I shall look forward to it, my lord," she said, and in truth she was. The dowager countess's observations earlier had struck a responsive chord in her. Her courage had been awakened by that lady's startling view of her antecedents.

In the short time that it had taken her to walk downstairs, she had thought about whom she had become and what she wanted. Certainly neither her new social position nor her own long-held ambitions would possibly allow her to embrace the life of a recluse, even if she had a desire for such. She felt she had at last taken the first step of many that would eventually carry her past the boundaries of her father's long shadow.

"Then I shall wait on your pleasure this evening, my lady," said Lord Chatworth.

18

THE EARL OF CHATWORTH did not see his wife for the remainder of the afternoon, and he dined out. When he returned to change into evening togs, he had quite forgotten he had said that he would act as her escort. He left the town house again without a single thought for her.

When Babs went downstairs and inquired after the earl, she was astonished and hurt to be told that his lordship had left a good hour earlier.

The butler's eyes held a glimmer of compassion after he delivered the information, for her ladyship stood quite still with a blind look in her fine eyes.

Babs began to recover. Her paramount thought was that she had taken such pains over her appearance so that she could do credit to the earl and the effort had been wasted. "I see. Thank you, Smithers," she said in a low, humiliated tone.

The butler cleared his throat deliberately. "My lady, shall I bring coffee to the sitting room?"

Babs looked at the butler. The delicate rose had been driven from her cheeks, but suddenly high color transformed her face. Her green eyes flashing, she said, "I think not, Smithers. Pray call me a carriage instead."

The butler regarded her for a moment in openmouthed astonishment. "But my lady—"

Babs leveled a cold stare on him. "I am attending the soiree this evening, Smithers."

The butler was left with nothing to say. He bowed and did as he was bid. After he had relayed her ladyship's request, he cast a curious glance toward her as she stood waiting, impatiently tapping a foot against the floor. As soon as the carriage came around to the front, he escorted his mistress into it and spoke to the driver. As it drove away, he gave an uncharacteristic shake of his head. He had been astonished by the blaze of sheer temper in the countess's eyes. He would wager that there would be a rare kickup when her ladyship finally tracked down the errant earl.

Babs was still quite angry when she entered the ballroom. She had been a fool to trust in the earl's careless pledge that he would introduce her to a few of his acquaintances so that she might begin carving out her own niche in society. She saw quite clearly that he was an entirely selfish creature, and one thoroughly used to catering only to his own wishes. The fact of their marriage apparently did not lay a particle of responsibility upon the earl's shoulders or appeal to his sense of common courtesy.

Very well, then, thought Babs in a fury. She would make her own way. She had been included in the invitation and she knew that it was not uncommon for a married woman to attend social functions without an escort in evidence.

Her reasonings enabled her to greet her hostess with a reasonable command of herself. But when she turned and saw the sea of mostly unknown faces, several of whom had taken note of her lone entrance with obvious curiosity, Babs felt herself begin to shrink inside. It was one thing to decide to launch oneself into society, but it was quite another to actually do so with grace and fortitude.

As Babs hesitated in the entrance to the ballroom, she made a striking picture. She stood seemingly glancing coolly over the company, all fiery gold from her head to her dress.

One gentleman nudged another. "Gad! Who is the beauty?"

His companion looked around and then stared harder. "Why, I believe that is the new Countess of Chatworth. I haven't had but a glimpse of her previously. She has not been seen much in society. His lordship apparently keeps a close watch upon her, from what I understand."

"That I can perfectly understand. She is a regular dasher," said the first gentleman. Without taking his eyes off the

Countess of Chatworth, he said, "Introduce me, cousin, I beg of you."

"I have not had the pleasure myself, actually," said the second gentleman. "However, I am certain that we must be able to find someone about who might perform the office for us." The gentlemen asked about them of several acquaintances whether the Countess of Chatworth was known to them, and finally they encountered their hostess. She was amused by the urgent request.

"Certainly I shall do so, sirs. I should not wish my guests to remember my little party with anything but the fondest thoughts," she said, and swept them with her toward their object.

Babs was startled to hear her name. She was more startled still when her hostess introduced the gentlemen to her. She smiled tentatively and gave her hand for a brief moment to each. "I am happy to make your acquaintance, gentlemen."

The gentlemen observed at once that the countess appeared somewhat ill-at-ease and instantly set about to make themselves agreeable. Others noticed the trio and drifted up to pay their respects. It was not long before Babs found herself the center of a circle of admiring men. She was unused to such attention, but certainly it was pleasant enough.

She had actually begun to enjoy herself when she at last caught sight of the Earl of Chatworth. He was sitting in an adjoining room at a card table. Standing close to him, with a hand laid possessively upon his shoulder, was a very beautiful woman. The woman was laughing down into the earl's face at something he had said, and as Babs watched, she lightly drew her fan down the earl's jaw in a gesture of obvious intimacy.

The countess drew in her breath, quite unconscious that she did so. Her escort of the moment was not so unobservant, and he looked quickly to see what had drawn her attention. He smiled slightly as he took in the charming tableau. "Lady Cartier is in extraordinarily fine looks this evening," he commented.

Babs looks up swiftly at her escort's face. "What did you say, my lord?"

"Why, I was speaking about Lady Beth Cartier. Are you not acquainted with her, my lady?" asked the gentleman blandly, well aware that he tread where he should not, but curious to hear what the countess might betray.

Babs gave a dismissive shrug of her shoulders. "There are so many with whom I am not yet acquainted, sir," she said unsteadily. She hoped that she gave every appearance of calm, but inside, her feelings were in turmoil. She had no claim on the earl. Their agreement specifically forbade any such claims. But it was hard to reconcile her conception of marriage with the strange and impersonal role that she and the earl had assigned to it.

She requested that her escort show her the fountains. "I have caught but a glimpse of them, but they appeared quite pretty," she said.

Her escort was not unwilling. He rather thought he might enjoy getting the countess off by herself. If he read her reaction to the sight of the Earl of Chatworth and his lordship's mistress correctly, her ladyship was ripe for indiscretion. "Of course, my lady," he said, and walked with her outside onto the balcony overlooking the gardens.

As they paused and slowly moved from one vantage point to another, he maneuvered her ever nearer a secluded corner in the shadows. Before Babs knew what the gentleman was about, he had caught her up into a tight embrace.

She stood for a few seconds, quite shocked, before she tore her mouth from under his. "Sir! Unhand me this instant, I pray you!" But his only answer was a low laugh as he tightened his arms about her.

One of the players at the card table waited until Lady Cartier had drifted off before he directed the earl's attention. "It is not for me to tell you your business, my lord. However, I think it might interest you to observe that your wife is gone off with Ivonhope."

The Earl of Chatworth turned in time to see what was definitely his wife borne off upon the arm of one whom he had no hesitation in labeling a courtcard and a libertine. A singularly dangerous light kindled in his hard eyes. "Has she, by God!" He thereupon extricated himself from the card game and went in search of his wife.

The brandy he had consumed in quantity made his thoughts somewhat groping. He had no idea why his wife was even there. He seemed to recall something now about escorting her that evening to the soiree, but certainly she should not be there, since he had not done so.

The earl paused, at a momentary loss. He scanned the company but did not see his wife with her escort. Then he caught a glimpse of movement on the balcony outside the French doors.

His eyes narrowed in suspicion and he strode through one of the open doors. He swept the balcony with a hard glance and was about to return inside when in the deepest shadows he perceived a couple who were to all appearances making passionate love.

With unprecedented outrage he realized that the lady was his wife. The earl stepped forward. He took hold of the gentleman's shoulder and propelled him backward into the wall. He saw his wife's upturned face; how her expression changed swiftly from relief to bewilderment to fear. Lord Chatworth swung around on the gentleman. "Leave us!"

The gentleman rubbed his shoulder, which had come into bone-jarring contact with the stone. He bowed, quite willing to do as he was ordered, and quietly faded away. He could scarcely believe that the Earl of Chatworth, a renowned rake, should act the jealous husband so convincingly.

Lord Chatworth turned once again to his wife. She had straightened from her frightened posture and faced him with a hint of defiance in her face. "Well, madam?" he asked in freezing accents.

"Thank you for your timely intervention, my lord," Babs said in an unsteady voice. She was acutely aware of his lordship's anger. It was patent in his stance and in his menacing expression. She did not understand why he should be so angry, but that was hardly important. Gentlemen were apparently often subject to unreasonable and ungovernable rages.

The earl stared at her. He gave a short bark of laughter.

"That's rich, by God. I've caught you in another man's arms and you have the temerity to stand there cool as you please and pretend all innocence."

Babs was aghast that he should suspect her of dallying. "But I am innocent! I never encouraged such unwelcome attentions."

The earl reached out to take her elbow in ungentle fingers. "We are going home, my dear wife. I think this evening has seen dissipation enough on your side." He strode into the ballroom, never easing up in his grip on her elbow.

Babs had no choice but to accompany him. She had to hurry to keep up with his long strides and she was humiliatingly aware that their swift passage across the dance floor was causing some comment. But the earl seemed oblivious of the scene that they were causing as he hustled her up to their hostess to take leave of her. After the barest civilities on his part, he escorted Babs outside and called harshly for his carriage to be brought up. He sent an abrupt message of dismissal to the driver of the carriage that Babs had arrived in.

Babs stood beside the stranger who was her husband. He had not let go her arm for even a moment, and his grip remained inexorable. His silence and his tight stance conveyed most graphically that he was furious. She shuddered at the inevitable pictures that such rage made appear in her mind's eye. Her heart hammered in her throat. She felt trapped, but there was no escape from the pitiless gentleman standing beside her.

She ducked into the carriage and moved as far as she could away from him. He settled onto the seat and signaled by a sharp rap on the ceiling for the driver to start up. Once they were well on their way, the earl turned his head to her. "I have yet to hear an explanation of your shameless conduct, my lady."

"It is as I have already told you, my lord. I scarcely knew what the gentleman was about before he—"

The earl gave a sharp crack of laughter. "C'mon! You must do better than that, my lady. I do not easily set aside the evidence of my own eyes. The two of you were twined together like well-rehearsed lovers. I should not be surprised to be handed a bastard in a few months' time.''

Babs drew in her breath sharply at the crudity. ''You are mistaken in me, my lord,'' she said, her voice cold. ''But I see that it is of no use attempting to persuade you of my innocence.'' She resolutely turned her eyes to the window and the passing of the streetlamps.

''What the devil were you doing there in the first place?'' demanded the earl. ''You had no business making an appearance without proper escort.''

Babs was at last truly angered. ''How dare you?'' she breathed, turning back toward him. Her voice gathered in strength, though it trembled. ''Should I have gone tamely up to my sitting room because you chose not to escort me, after all? I am not so puling, my lord. After all, our agreement was to allow each of us the liberty of pursuing our own pleasures. And I chose to attend the soiree, even unescorted as I indisputably was.''

Lord Chatworth was made unreasonably furious by her criticism of him as well as by her defiance. ''We shall talk of how far this agreement may carry you, madam,'' he said, his voice menacing. ''For I will tell you to your head, I shall not have my wife making a spectacle and a scandal of herself.''

''Oh, I do not intend to make of myself a byword, my lord. But neither shall I stay immured in my rooms for the rest of my natural life,'' said Babs.

''Madam, I warn you. I have no intention of being made a cuckold,'' said the earl.

''But that is precisely what you did agree to before we married, my lord,'' she said, carried away equally by her anger and the sting of his unjust position. It was acceptable for him to keep a mistress and consort with all manner of lewd company, but she was not even to be allowed out of the house. ''Do you not recall it, my lord? You agreed to receive my bastard as your own heir.''

There was complete silence from the earl's end of the

carriage. But Babs could hear the harshness of his breathing, and his fury seemed to crackle about the interior of the carriage.

The carriage was slowing. "We have arrived home, my lady. I do not want to further this argument in front of the servants," came the earl's cold voice. "But rest assured that I intend to finish this discussion in the privacy of the drawing room." There was soft menace in his voice.

Barbara felt her anger dry and shrivel away. It was just as though her father sat opposite her, black and dangerous, the ripe rage exuding from him. She started to tremble then and could not stop.

19

THE EARL got out of the carriage first. He handed Barbara down and, without letting go of her arm, silently led her up the steps and into the house. Her panic intensified. She felt herself suffocating and trapped.

In the entry hall, the earl let go of her so that he could give the footman his hat and gloves. Instinctively Babs bolted. Lifting her skirts, she ran like one pursued up the stairs.

Lord Chatworth was left standing, feeling every inch the fool in front of his wooden-faced servants. He watched his wife's precipitate flight with a hard expression in his eyes. When he had heard the distinct crash of a bedroom door, he swung around on his heel and strode to his study. "Brandy," he threw over his shoulder at the expressionless footman.

Once in the study, he threw off his coat and tossed it aside into a chair. He loosened his cravat while he stirred the fire with his booted toe. The footman entered quietly, an open bottle in hand. "Put it on the desk. And bring me another branch of candles. It is bloody dark in here," said Lord Chatworth.

"At once, my lord."

Marcus was alone again with his disagreeable thoughts. He kicked the log, and a shower of red sparks hissed up the chimney and showered out of the hearth. One hot mote landed on his thigh. He swept his hand across the place, but already a tiny hole had been burned. He swore comprehensively.

The footman, who had reentered with the requested candles, was suitably impressed by the extent of his master's vocabulary. When he left the study again, he told his fellow that he had not known the earl was such a stickler when it came to his clothing. "But there it is, Jarvis. His lordship was that perturbed over a tiny spark."

Lord Chatworth's curses might have been triggered by the ruination of his evening breeches, but his thoughts were completely engaged by his wife and the spectacle that she had made of herself that evening. Her subsequent and cowardly avoidance of their *tête-à-tête* had but fed his anger.

The earl swung around and stomped over to his desk. He was determined not to think further about the matter. He had accounts to see to and that was what he would busy his mind with. Lord Chatworth threw himself into the chair behind his desk and opened the drawer to haul out the ledger and its attendant papers. He spread out the accounts in an orderly fashion. Then he poured himself a generous amount of brandy and sat back in his chair to drink it.

His eyes glittered as his thoughts returned to his wife. His pride still smarted from the affront of beholding her wrapped in another man's arms. When he had torn them apart, she had at last seen him and her face had gone quite white with fear. That had maddened him more than anything else. She did not regard anyone else with just that half-defiant, half-fearful expression.

He had scarcely been able to contain his temper while they waited for the carriage to be brought around. He had felt her arm trembling under the grasp of his fingers, and he had been glad of it. She at least had some notion of her position.

On the drive home, she had protested with indignation that she had not been to blame and that she had not encouraged the gentleman's attentions. He had been surprised by the heat with which she had spoken, and it had even given him momentary pause. Once again he heard that suppressed passion in her voice that had led him to draw her out at their original meeting. But then she had reminded him so cuttingly of the terms of their pact and his flash of temperance had vanished.

Lord Chatworth gave a harsh laugh. The lady had done it rather too brown, he thought. He discovered with some surprise that his glass was empty, and he refilled it. He took a drink, his eyes running down the ledger open in front of him. The figures needed working, he thought. He dipped a pen into the inkwell and for a few moments bent to the task. But his mind refused to stay on the numbers. His wife's green eyes and lovely face kept swimming up at him from the paper. With a wrathful oath, he threw down the pen.

He filled his glass again and tossed it down. The brandy burned his throat and spread warmth in his blood. Broodingly he stared across the room at the flickering fire. She was his wife. That was indisputable, regardless of any paltry agreement between them.

His memory played for him again the passionate embrace that he had interrupted. His lips curled in an unpleasant smile. Since he had married her, she had seemed merely to endure his own touch. On occasion she had even winced away from him. Apparently he was not to her taste.

Lord Chatworth threw the wineglass, shattering it against the hearth. His thoughts were furious in tone, fueled alike by stung pride and the brandy he had consumed all evening in the card room. He rose abruptly from the chair and went around the desk. He strode swiftly to the study door. She might encourage the attentions of a lover, but she was still his wife. She appeared to have forgotten that fact. He wrenched open the door, leaving the study to cross the entry hall, and with swift strides mounted the stairs.

Barbara had fled to her bedroom and then waited fearfully for his lordship to follow her. Finally she had realized that he had not pursued her, after all. With an overwhelming sense of relief, she rang for her maid to undress her.

While the maid readied her for bed, Babs reflected unhappily on the morrow. She was not looking forward to her next meeting with the earl. She seated herself at the vanity so that the maid could brush out her hair.

The door crashed open. The maid let out a strangled scream; Babs whirled to her feet, her heart in her mouth. The earl strode in, dominating the room. Babs saw the ugly temper in his eyes and her heart pounded all the harder.

Lord Chatworth saw that she had prepared for bed. She

was dressed in a thin gown and negligee. Firelight outlined her figure through the stuff and he felt the stirrings of desire. Without removing his eyes from his wife, he curtly dismissed the maid.

The maid fearfully glanced at her mistress. "My lady?"

"It is all right, Lucy. You may go." Babs nodded reassurance to the servantwoman, who reluctantly left. The countess turned her gaze back to the earl. Her voice was cool if a bit unsteady. "It is very late, my lord. What is it you want?"

Lord Chatworth laughed shortly. His stare as he looked her up and down was deliberately insolent. "I want you, dear wife," he said with soft menace. He reached out to grasp her wrist, but she instantly twisted free.

"No!" Her green eyes appeared huge in her face. "We have an agreement, my lord. I have your word of honor—"

"My honor, madam! Indeed, and what was my honor to you tonight?" he bit out. He swooped down on her to gather her ungently into his arms. Bending his head, he took rough possession of her mouth.

A stinging blow across the face rocked his head and caused him to loosen his hold. Like a hare, she broke free and ran.

"Damn your impertinence," he shouted, bounding after her. He caught her shoulder and spun her about. Her breath came in dry sobs, her eyes were wild with fear and anger. She fought then like a wildcat, kicking and biting and pummeling him in the face and the body. He could not hold her. She was a blazing inferno of movement, all sharp angles and wicked hits.

An explosion of pain erupted as her knee connected with his groin. Lord Chatworth howled and reacted instinctively. His hand cracked against his cheek.

The blow spun her around, her long hair flying. The negligee and gown ripped down her back under his other hand. She fell heavily against the bedpost and stayed there, dazed, the air knocked out of her.

Lord Chatworth stared down at her bared back. Firelight flickered over healing weals that marred her delicate skin. The silver scars of old beatings shone under the more recent damage. He felt a coldness wash over him, leaving him shockingly sober. He reached down to lift her hair. She flinched away from him, but he held her firmly and yet very gently as he looked closer at her back. His voice shook with mingled fury and disbelief. "Who did this to you?"

"My father."

Lord Chatworth was numbed. "But why?"

She flung up her head to look at him. Angry tears glittered in her eyes. "Does it disgust you, my lord? But the last is almost healed, after all, and he used a flat cane so that he would not break the skin this time. He did not want me bloodied when I went to the altar, for in his queer way he would have considered it dishonorable to have handed over to you damaged goods."

Marcus felt himself shaking. His voice sounded queer even to his own ears. "When we were to be married—he had done this to you then, hadn't he? And when you came to interview me, had he touched you then?"

Her mouth twisted strangely before she averted her face. "My father was not pleased to be cheated out of the spectacle of a wedding he had planned. As for the rest . . ." She gestured, a world of tiredness in her hands and bent head.

She did not look at him again, but only waited for what was sure to come. Her limited experience with men had not led her to believe that they could feel any but the cruelest of emotions, and with her marriage, she had but traded one master for another.

Seconds passed, in which the only sounds were the breaking of the fire log and the earl's harsh breathing. Then she felt her robe eased gently up to cover her bare shoulders.

"I shall not trouble you again."

She heard a quick step and the opening of the door. When she dared to turn, he was gone. She rose, clutching the bedpost for support, and sank down on the bed. Her whole body shook in reaction.

Lord Chatworth hardly knew that he had entered his own bedchamber. He waved aside his valet's attempts to aid him in undressing, his greatest desire at that moment to be left alone. He stood at the mantel, staring into the fire.

He was appalled by what he had learned of his new bride. He had never really given much thought to the reasons behind her own consent to wed him. He had assumed it was simply out of a wish for social gain and the independence of her own establishment, where she might be free of an overbearing father.

Now he fully realized, and from the appalling evidence of his own eyes, that she had been virtually forced into the marriage. When she had come to him beforehand, it had been in a pathetic attempt to guarantee herself some measure of safety from the same sort of tyranny.

Lord Chatworth closed his eyes against his thoughts. He was bitterly ashamed. He had not fully understood then. Not until this evening, when he had tried to force her into his bed, had he begun to understand her panic and desperation. He groaned quietly, recalling that he had struck her. He had proven himself little better than her monster of a father.

After several minutes Lord Chatworth slowly straightened. His hard eyes held a queer light that his scapegrace friends would not have recognized. He vowed that he would not again behave in any fashion that his wife might find objectionable or that would wound her sensibilities. The dowager countess was proven unquestionably right. As his wife, Barbara deserved a great deal more than he had heretofore offered her.

She was blameless in the *contretemps* earlier at the soiree, he thought. It had been he who had overstepped the bounds of their pact and totally disregarded their mutual agreement that granted each the liberty to form their own liaisons.

Though it rotted his pride, he meant in future to step aside for his wife's cisibeo. Hovering on the fringes of that particular resolution was the half-formed thought that he could endeavor to make of himself a much-preferred suitor. He was not lacking in experience and he had the advantage of being married to the lady.

His jaw tightened as he thought of the mastermind behind

their fateful marriage. More than ever before, he was determined to gain freedom from Cribbage's grasp. His hardened determination to do so was now as much for his wife's sake as it had formerly been for himself.

20

THE EARL ACTED SWIFTLY upon his resolutions. When he went down to breakfast, he was determined to proffer his apologies to his wife for his want of conduct, but his good intention was thwarted. Babs was not in the breakfast room. Lord Chatworth assumed that she had risen belatedly and would come down later, so he sat down to his own hearty breakfast of kipper and eggs, steak and biscuits.

Several times during the course of his repast his frowning gaze went to the breakfast-room door, as he was in every expectation of his wife's appearance. He was finishing his coffee when he at last inquired from the butler news of his wife. "Smithers, is her ladyship not coming downstairs this morning?"

"No, my lord. Her ladyship requested that her breakfast be taken up to her room. I understand that her ladyship is not feeling well this morning," said the butler. He had begun to remove the covered dishes on the sideboard; he paused to ask, "Will there be anything else, my lord?"

"No, that will be all," said Lord Chatworth. He lingered over the last of his coffee, reflecting on his best possible course of action. He had the wit to realize the significance of his wife's shunning of the breakfast room. It was obvious to Lord Chatworth that Babs was not in the most amenable of moods. He concluded that his apologies would necessarily have to wait. Whatever his motives, she would very much resent it were he to foist his presence upon her in her rooms. That would smack too much of the scene last night, he thought.

Marcus thought it would be prudent to give Babs time in

which her alarm and anger against him could cool. He was experienced enough to know that if he gave the lady the opportunity to reject his apology out of hand, he would then be forced to endure a sort of armed camp in his own house until she should relent enough to forgive him. He was not enamored of the notion, having a great dislike of such high drama.

Lord Chatworth left the breakfast room and entered his study to pen a short note. He gave the folded sheet into the hand of a footman, directing that the note be carried up to Lady Chatworth. He collected his beaver and left the town house.

The earl sauntered down the walkway in the direction of his club. He knew that two of his cronies could usually be found in the card room at that early hour and he thought that he could contrive to wile away the interim pleasantly enough until such time that he could be reasonably assured of finding Lady Beth Cartier in to visitors. He knew that the lady never rose until noon and that it would be unlikely that even he would be allowed entrance before the appointed hour.

Three hours later and somewhat plumper in the pocket, the Earl of Chatworth left his club. The weather was the clear and sunny sort that encouraged Londoners out-of-doors and there were more than the usual carriages and promenaders on the streets. He was hailed several times by acquaintances in the short distance to Lady Cartier's town house.

Lord Chatworth sent up his card. He was immediately admitted and ushered upstairs to the lady's private sitting room. The door was closed softly behind him.

Elizabeth had posed herself at the parquet mahogany table, one delicate hand on the wine decanter as though she had just reached for it. Her head was turned so that she could direct a glance of inquiry over her slender shoulder, and her lovely face was bathed in the soft light from a branch of candles on the table. "My lord," she purred.

Lord Chatworth was abruptly struck by the absurdity of burning expensive wax candles at the day's zenith. He had not given much thought before to Lady Cartier's penchant for candlelight. The shades in her rooms were already halfway drawn; the lighted candles merely provided the necessary illumination. Candlelight was naturally more flattering to a woman's face than clear honest sunlight. The cynicism of his thought shocked him. "My lady, I hope that I find you well," he said.

Lady Cartier came toward him, both of her hands outstretched in greeting. The warmth in her dark eyes was unmistakable, as was the smiling promise of her full sensual mouth. "I am so glad that you have come, my lord," she said huskily.

Lord Chatworth caught her hands, but he did not turn her hands over to press a lingering kiss into each palm in their usual mating prelude. Instead, he lifted her fingers to his lips in polite salute before releasing her. "I have come on a matter of business only, my lady."

Lady Cartier was disconcerted but she swiftly recovered. She gestured to the settee covered in striped satin for his lordship to be seated. She took her own place against the cushions, tucking her legs under her so that she sat inclined in the direction of her guest. It was a pose that she had found to be enormously inviting to gentlemen.

She was surprised when the earl chose to settle himself at the farthest end of the settee instead of his usual place nearer to her. It was then that she finally took note of the distance of his expression and the considering look in his gray eyes.

Instantly she recalled the disastrous snub that she had delivered to his lordship's wife at Lady Chatworth's own introductory ball and the humiliation of the dowager countess's chilly set-down. She had remained at the ball only to brush through the resulting mortification and to prove to the world that the incident would do nothing to damage her relationship with the earl. She had been satisfied that she had accomplished her purpose when she had been able to draw him over to her chair and hold him in short friendly conversation. As she had hoped it would, that had instantly quelled the tattlers' malicious speculation.

It was now borne in on Lady Cartier that the earl had gotten wind of the whole ill-conceived business and that he was displeased. Lady Cartier damned the tradesman's daughter who had usurped her own coveted place and who had created this misunderstanding between herself and his lordship. However, she was too practiced in the games played between gentlemen and their ladies to allow her spurt of fury to override her cold common sense.

She was determined to retain her hold on the earl and she was confident of her own powers of persuasion. It would take but a show of contrition and the earl would forgive her most magnanimously, for which gesture she would naturally be grateful. Lady Cartier intended to make very certain that her gratitude so satiated his lordship that he would be unable to even look at another woman without thinking of her own exciting bed.

She lowered her head in a graceful fashion. "I know why you have come, Marcus."

Lord Chatworth was taken aback. He had come to the regretful decision of putting an end to the pleasant relationship between himself and Lady Cartier. The lady had had other protectors and so he did not expect there to be much of a scene when he announced his intention, especially when he meant to bestow upon her a lavish parting gift. That his purpose was anticipated, however, pricked his ego. For that reason he spoke in a cooler voicer than he had intended. "Indeed, my lady?"

Lady Cartier raised her head. Her dark eyes glistened with unshed tears. "I have regretted my impetuosity, my lord. I should not have spoken so of Lady Chatworth, I do admit it. It was truly ill-conceived of me."

Lord Chatworth's astonished curiosity was not unnaturally aroused. The swift comprehension that something of moment had occurred between his wife and his mistress, which he had known nothing about, was as quickly followed by a stiffening of his manner. He held his face expressionless. "Ill-conceived, indeed," he said slowly. "I wish you to explain how it came about, my lady."

Elizabeth Cartier felt a surge of triumph at his lordship's quiet tone. The earl was willing to be reasonable, then. He had come to express his displeasure over the incident only out of a sense of the duty owed his wife's position, but he felt no real insult. But she was sensible to the fact that he had not yet granted her forgiveness for her slight to his lady, and so she must continue to play the supplicant for a while.

Lady Cartier's lips parted on a soft sigh. She dared to raise her hand to his jaw and she was not displeased that he caught her wrist. He did not remove her caressing fingers from his face, but merely held her as he waited for her to continue. She shook her head and her lashes swept down as she glanced away. "It is difficult for me, my lord. When I think of you with your lady wife, I think I become a bit mad."

"Do you, my dear? I am flattered," Lord Chatworth said dryly.

As Lady Cartier lifted her gaze to his face, she allowed tears to come to her eyes. "I saw her for the first time the night of the ball and my jealousy sprang into full bloom. Oh, Marcus! Do say you forgive me. I was rattled by the appearance of that vulgar tradesman, or otherwise I would never have said it. I never meant to utter such a cutting aside, truly I did not."

Lord Chatworth silently regarded her. His lids had drooped over his eyes, disguising his thoughts from her. Though nothing showed in his expression, fury coursed his veins. He could guess the sort of thing that Lady Cartier had said.

When he had put down Elizabeth Cartier's name on the guest list that Babs had requested from him, he had not spared a thought for the doubtful wisdom of inviting his mistress to his wife's first function. But of course it had been bound to end in trouble of some sort, especially after Cribbage's histrionic appearance. It said much for his wife's innate pride that she had not complained of such heavy insult to him, but instead had quietly remarked that despite everything she thought the evening had gone off fairly well.

Lord Chatworth had every intention of learning more about the incident that had been alluded to, but not from Lady Cartier. He would not reveal to her that he had known nothing about it. Nor was she ever to know that he had planned to end their relationship on an amicable note with a costly last gift.

As he looked at her, he abruptly felt complete disgust for himself. For the first time he saw the lady for all that she was, and he wondered how he could ever have become so besotted of her wiles. He no longer felt so much as the snap of his fingers for the woman, nor any regret for his decision to sever their relationship. Quite inadvertently Lady Cartier had ripped the scales from his eyes. She had shown him what a true lady should be.

"Marcus? Pray say that you forgive me." Lady Cartier's free hand passed up and down the front of his waistcoat and her fingers teased at the garment's buttons. She looked up at him with invitation in her sultry eyes. "I will gladly accept any punishment that you set for my crime," she said softly.

His lordship's narrowed gaze opened and she was startled by the blaze in his eyes. Before she could comprehend the meaning of his expression, he had grasped her other wrist and pulled her to half-recline against him. His voice was silky. "Will you indeed, my lady? Then certainly I must satisfy your craving for punishment."

She cast a look of startled incomprehension up at him before she found herself flung over his knees. His hand closed on her soft shoulder and his forearm lay heavy across her back. "Marcus! What do you intend?" she blurted, a thread of laughter in her voice.

The first firm blow caught her completely unawares and rendered her speechless. The second swat stung and made her yelp in indignation. "Marcus!"

She struggled and kicked then, but to no avail. Lady Cartier's shrill screams for succor and her lurid curses accompanied each well-placed blow. But the door to the sitting room remainded closed; her ladyship's servants were too well-versed in their mistress's rare entertainments to interrupt.

Lord Chatworth delivered half a dozen swats to his former mistress's shapely bottom. Then he tumbled her off of his lap onto the Oriental carpet and stood up.

Lady Cartier sat on the floor, glaring up at him. Hot tears of rage coursed down her face. "I shall kill you for that, Marcus. Do you hear? I swear to you that I will." He had the effrontery to laugh at her. Lady Cartier paled with fury. She scrambled to her feet, all of her usual poise deserting her.

The earl's voice was quite cold. "You may try, and with my goodwill. However, I suspect that your energies would be better directed toward entrapping another protector as quickly as possible. I know the depth of your extravagances, recall."

His lordship's lips twisted into that peculiarly mocking smile. "Dear Beth, you have just received your parting gift of me." With that, he walked to the door and yanked it open.

A vase smashed against the panels of the door as it was slammed shut.

21

BARBARA FROWNED when she was given the earl's note. She could not conceive why he had written her, unless it was in order to deliver a snappish reprimand for not going down to breakfast and thus putting off their inevitable *tête-à-tête*. However, far from castigating her for her cowardice, the note extended an apology for his lordship's conduct of the night before.

Babs stared at the strong black scrawl. She did not know what to make of it. Surely the earl could not actually have meant what he had penned. Nothing in her experience could have prepared her to believe in the civil words that seemed to leap off the sheet.

"My lady? Will you be wanting the cashmere?"

Babs looked up quickly. She refolded the note and tucked it into her dress pocket. "Yes, Lucy. I seem to feel a chill about me."

The maid placed the fringed paisley shawl about her mistress's shoulders. Babs gave a fleeting glance to the reflection of herself in the cheval glass, assuring herself of the perfection of her auburn curls and the neatness of her long-sleeved dress. The shawl draped elegantly over her shoulders, while the long gold fringes that edged it fell nearly to the hem of her dress. She had chosen the yellow muslin dress for its modest décolletage and simple lines, and she was satisfied that she presented the very picture of the submissive wife.

When she had awakened that morning, she had tingled in every nerve from the memory of the earl's crude entrance into her bedroom and the subsequent fight between them.

She did not understand why he had left again so abruptly, nor why he had done so without chastening her.

She had hidden in her rooms that morning, giving out that she felt a little under the weather. The maid had accepted her excuse without comment, only throwing a single thoughtful glance at the slight bruise on her mistress's cheekbone. After Lucy had served her mistress a tray holding a pot of chocolate and biscuits, she had left Barbara alone with her thoughts.

Babs had dreaded what might be said once she came into his lordship's company, yet she knew that she must face him eventually. She had lingered over her meager breakfast, despising her own cowardice, and then she had rung for her maid to request that a bath be prepared for her.

Babs finished bathing and dressed. She was sitting down at the vanity so that her maid could do her hair when she first saw the bruise marring her cheekbone. Her face tightened. There was little that she could do to disguise the mark. She did not paint her face like some of the ladies she had seen. She could only hope that the bruise would fade quickly. "Lucy, I would like a cloth wet in cold water," she said quietly.

"Yes, my lady." The maid brought the cloth, folded over into a square, and the countess pressed the cool compress to her cheekbone.

It was well after the noon hour when Babs was at last ready to emerge from her bedchamber. The earl was not usually at home during the day, but he would in all probability dine in that evening. She thought she would at least have a few hours before she must see her husband.

Babs touched the pocket of her dress. A small frown gathered her brows. "I am going down, Lucy," she said quietly.

"Very good, my lady."

The countess was just descending the last stairs when the earl emerged from the dining room. She paused, one hand on the banister. Her heart accelerated when she saw the somber look in his eyes. "My lord, I did not expect you to be at home so early in the day."

The earl sauntered across the entry hall to her. Situated on the last step as she was, she was on a level with his gray eyes. Babs felt as though his keen gaze could read her every whirling thought. She held herself warily, for despite the note of apology, she was uncertain of what to expect from him.

He took her hand and raised her fingers to his lips. There was the beginning of laughter in his eyes. "I am set down indeed, my lady! I had no notion that I had so neglected your company."

Babs flushed, at once embarrassed and heartened by his teasing. "It is no such thing, as well you know. I am quite accepting of your pressing round of social commitments."

A peculiar smile touched his face and the expression in his eyes was one that she could not quite read. He drew her down from off the stair. "I am aware of your forbearance, my lady. Upon inquiring, I learned that you had not bespoken luncheon and so I took it upon myself to do so. Shall we go in, my lady?"

"Have you not dined, then, my lord?" asked Babs. She had learned that he usually took luncheon at his club in the company of his peers.

"No, I had a matter of business to sort out instead," he said shortly. His tone held an unusual degree of grimness.

Babs threw up at him a fleeting glance of surprise. But she accompanied him into the dining room without further comment, unaccountably feeling as though she had somehow trespassed. She allowed him to seat her at the table, afterward thanking him quietly for the courtesy.

Lord Chatworth took his place opposite her. After the first course he had been served, he informed the footmen that he and Lady Chatworth could serve themselves thereafter.

Babs cast a glance after the retreating backs of the footmen. She set herself for the discomfort of a *tête-à-tête* before she turned a determined smile on the earl. His lordship sat back at ease in his chair, one arm laid along the table's edge. He held his wineglass in the long fingers of one hand. He was frowning, but he did not seem to be unaware of her presence.

"The soup is quite good, is it not?" she asked in a desultory fashion.

The earl glanced at her. The frowning expression in his eyes deepened as he looked at her. "Is it, madam? I had not noticed." He set down the wineglass and got up from his chair to come around the table.

Babs was rattled by his inexplicable advance, but she was determined not to show it. She looked up at his lordship inquiringly. "My lord? What is it?" Her spoon dropped from nerveless fingers to clatter in the bowl when his hand caught up her chin.

Lord Chatworth turned his wife's face fully to the light that streamed in the tall windows. He had not been mistaken. Across her cheekbone was the slightest darkening of her golden skin. Very gently, he touched it. "I did this."

Babs saw little point in denying it, and her clear green gaze met his eyes. "Yes."

Lord Chatworth released her, turning away. Over his shoulder, he said harshly, "You have cause to despise me, I think. I have over and over treated you with a lack of respect that is appalling." He swung around again and irony shaped his mouth. "You should have sent me to the devil long before this, my dear."

"I haven't wished you at the devil, Marcus, for the simple reason that my life with you has been far more enviable than I could have hoped for under my father's roof," Babs said quietly. She did not know exactly where the conversation was headed, but she sensed that only frank speaking would do now. She found that she was no longer afraid of his lordship or of what he might do. The manner in which he was acting served to give her confidence in the sincerity of the note of apology that was still tucked inside her pocket.

Lord Chatworth barked a laugh, but he was far from feeling amused. "Brutal honesty, Babs! But no less than I deserve." He crossed to her and took her hand. "My lady, I swear to you that I shall behave with all propriety toward you in future. There will be no repeat of last night's offense."

Babs smiled up at him. Intuitively she felt there was no

need to press the matter further. She said gently, "My lord, the soup grows cold. Pray, will you not be seated?"

Lord Chatworth understood and he raised her fingers to his lips in brief salute. "Thank you, Babs."

Thereafter the luncheon progressed to a relaxed, friendly level. The earl set himself to be an amusing companion and he was rewarded by the frequent laughter that he was able to draw out of his wife. At the end, when he had rung for the servants to clear the table, he glanced across at her and said, "I have a capital notion. Why don't you join me in a drive around the park? I have a new leader that I am breaking into his paces. You shall have the opportunity to lend your opinion of the brute's progress."

"Why, I should like that very much," Babs said, surprised and pleased by the unexpected invitation. "I shall go up to change and join you in a few minutes."

Lord Chatworth nodded. "Good. I shall meet you on the front steps in a quarter-hour."

Barbara left the dining room and sped upstairs on winged feet. Her heart sang with happiness. She did not know how it was, but the unpleasantness of the previous evening had all been brushed aside as though it had never been.

With the help of her maid, the countess changed swiftly into a forest-green pelisse and calf boots. She donned a matching bonnet and tied the satin ribbons in a jaunty bow under her left ear. As she left the bedroom, she pulled on kid gloves of palest yellow.

The Earl of Chatworth was already standing on the outside steps when Babs stepped out onto the portico. He smiled at her as he held out his hand. His eyes were appreciative as he glanced over her trimly cut outfit. "You are in fine looks this afternoon, my lady. Allow me to hand you up."

"Thank you, my lord," Babs said. The slightest of blushes had come into her face with his compliment.

Marcus helped her onto the seat of the phaeton and climbed up himself. He picked up the reins and his long whip. After glancing to see that she was comfortable, he ordered the groom at the head of his team to let go of the leaders.

The groom sprang away to the curb and Lord Chatworth turned his team into a stream of carriages, hackney cabs, dray carts, and pedestrians that filled the busy avenue. He flicked his whip, nicking the ears of the leaders, and the pace of the team quickened.

Babs became instantly aware of the earl's driving skill. She watched his gloved fingers as the leathers slipped through them, and she saw how the least movement of his hands was instantly responded to by his horses. Even the off-leader, which Lord Chatworth told her was the new addition to his stables, did not veer from its instruction.

"My compliments, my lord. I had no notion that you were such an expert whip," she said.

Marcus glanced at her, a gleam of laughter in his eyes for the impressed note in her voice. "You are too easily awed, Babs."

"Not at all," she replied instantly. "While living with my aunt, I became a fair whip myself, and so I am an excellent judge of the talent of others."

"Are you indeed! I shall have to put your boast to the test, my lady," said Lord Chatworth as he directed the horses into the park. When the phaeton was on the straightaway, he offered the reins to her.

Babs took the leathers, laughing as she did so. "You may rue it, Marcus," she warned.

"I devoutly trust not," said the earl, grinning. He watched her technique carefully for a few moments before he decided that his sensitive team would take no harm from her direction. He sat back at his ease to enjoy the novelty of being driven by someone else.

Babs cast a gleaming glance of laughter at him around the edge of her bonnet. "What, Marcus? Are you no longer afraid that I might overturn us?"

"Baggage," he said appreciatively. Despite his assumption of nonchalance, she had obviously recognized his initial concern.

Several acquaintances waved at sight of the earl's phaeton. Babs would have slowed to make possible the exchange of pleasantries, but Lord Chatworth directed her to drive on.

She shrugged off the earl's unsociability as merely a whim of his lordship's and one that she was only too happy to indulge. It was rare that she had the opportunity to let down her guard, and she settled herself to truly enjoy the drive. She would have been astonished if she had known the real reason that his lordship chose not to speak to his acquaintances.

The attractive bonnet Babs wore served well to shade her face from the fleeting glances of passersby, but Lord Chatworth had no wish for anyone to come close enough to be able to notice the mark across her cheekbone. The sort of gossip that it would arouse did not fit in with what he planned.

Lord Chatworth intended that their drive in the park was to be well-noted and talked about. He would follow up the unprecedented sight of himself consorting publicly with his wife with several evenings spent at home in her company, at least until the mark on her face had disappeared, and then he would embark on a round of social pleasures with Barbara on his arm. Indeed, he intended to spend an inordinate amount of time with his wife, so much so that it would create a whirl of talk.

Marcus smiled to himself with a touch of mockery. The Earl of Chatworth was not exactly the model for those husbandly qualities that a lady hoped to find in her spouse. On the contrary, he knew that on occasion he had been held up to romantic young misses as just the opposite. He had never paid heed to the accusations of rakehell and libertine that had been leveled at his head, but for the moment at least, such a reputation was a distinct disadvantage to his undertaking.

Lord Chatworth wanted it to become known that he had a most proprietary interest in his wife. That would give Babs a measure of protection from the inopportune wolves of society, such as that gentleman who had taken such liberties with her at the soiree, and it would help to insulate her against the malicious tongues that tended to speak so disparagingly of her birth. It would serve as well to assuage some measure of his own guilt for his offhand treatment of her, for he felt quite keenly that he was partially to blame for Babs' discomfitures because he had not taken steps in the beginning to protect her.

Lord Chatworth reflected that this marriage of convenience had brought difficulties unforeseen by either party when they had entered so easily into their informal agreement. He was very much aware of some of those difficulties, having been brought to realize them through his mother's scolding and Babs' own personality and person.

It was no longer just a question of biding his time before he could manage to extricate himself from Cribbage's power to blackmail him. He had now shouldered responsibility for, and had a duty to, the young woman who sat beside him in the phaeton. She was as much in need of his protection as any other person who had a legitimate claim to it.

Lord Chatworth reached over to take back the reins.

"Why, does your trust fade away so quickly, my lord?" Babs asked, the glint of laughter in her eyes.

"On the contrary, you have proven your mettle to my complete satisfaction," said Lord Chatworth.

"So I should hope, Marcus."

He laughed, and with a smile still lurking about his mouth, he turned the phaeton out of the park and pointed it toward the town house.

22

———

BARBARA RECEIVED A NOTE from Lady Azaela, requesting that she call upon her aunt on Thursday of that week. Babs was made curious by the definite date. Lady Azaela was usually more casual in issuing an invitation to her.

On the appointed day, Babs drove over to her aunt's town house. She was ushered immediately into the drawing room and she saw that Lady Azaela was already entertaining some callers. Babs smiled impartially at the two ladies seated on the settee as she went to her aunt. Lady Azaela had risen at her entrance and they met in the center of the room to exchange an affectionate embrace.

"My dear, you look wonderful, as usual," Lady Azaela said, surveying with approval her niece's fashionable walking dress and chip-straw bonnet.

"And you, my lady," said Babs, sincerely returning the compliment.

"Thank you, my dear. You are most considerate of an elderly lady's vanities," said Lady Azaela, a twinkle in her eyes. Babs laughed, shaking her head. Lady Azaela drew her niece over to the settee from which she herself had just risen, at the same time making certain that her guests knew one another.

"Lady Stonehodge, this is Lady Chatworth. Babs, I do not believe that you have made the acquaintance of Lady Stonehodge and her daughter, Miss Eleanore Stonehodge. They have just traveled up from Derbyshire to partake of the remainder of the Season's entertainments," said Lady Azaela.

Babs smiled in a friendly way, despite the patent hostility

in the older lady's gaze. She could not imagine why Lady Stonehodge should have taken an instant dislike to her on sight, but she supposed that already her reputation of having sprung from trade stock had become known to the woman. "Lady Stonehodge, it is a pleasure," she said evenly.

The lady vouchsafed to her only a stiff bow of acknowledgment.

Babs turned to the daughter, who was regarding her in a manner highly reminiscent of a startled hare. Her civil smile warmed. The girl was obviously just out of the schoolroom, probably no more than seventeen years old, and her expression ill-concealed her timidity. Babs remembered all too well the awkwardness of her own come-out, and she made an effort to set the girl at ease. "Miss Stonehodge, I am most happy to make your acquaintance. Derbyshire is my own beloved county and I have often been homesick for its simpler distractions. However, London has its amusements, too. I hope that we shall see more of each other, perhaps at some of the gatherings?"

The girl blushed fierily and stammered an unintelligible reply. Lady Stonehodge was not so backward as her daughter. "My daughter is not quite out, Lady Chatworth. I do not think that we run in the same society as yourself, moreover." The woman's tone was brusque and rude.

Babs raised her brows at the set-down. She did not fancy being the object of insult and for no good reason that she was aware of. It was but a scant three months since she had come to London to wed the Earl of Chatworth, but in that short time she had become much more confident of her self-worth. She had learned that she did not have to accept the snubs of any who chose to so honor her.

Her voice was cool. "Indeed, Lady Stonehodge? Then there is no more to be said, of course." She turned to her aunt, quite aware of the insufferable woman's reddening face. She had also a fleeting glimpse of the embarrassed distress in the girl's eyes, and for that at least she felt some remorse.

Lady Azaela smiled, not at all displeased by the short exchange. "Actually, there is something more that must be said, Babs," she said with great relish. "By happy coincidence, Lady Stonehodge is the daughter of one of my doltish elder brothers. She and her lovely daughter are your cousins, my dear.''

Babs was stunned. ''I had no notion,'' she said blankly. She looked at Lady Stonehodge, who was obviously having difficulty getting her spleen under control. Babs' own reaction was so mixed that she did not know what she thought. ''My mother never spoke of her family. I had naturally assumed that Lady Azaela was my only relative.''

''I am not at all surprised that your mother never spoke of us, Lady Chatworth. We certainly did not speak of her,'' Lady Stonehodge said with a superior smile.

A dangerous light sparked to life in Babs' eyes. Ice dipped from her tongue. ''Indeed? How mean-spirited of you, to be sure.''

Lady Stonehodge appeared to swell. Beside her, the younger Stonehodge lady made ineffectual imploring sounds. ''Mama, pray!''

''Be quiet, Eleanore! I shall not sit still for this—this—'' Lady Stonehodge appeared momentarily at a loss for words.

''The Countess of Chatworth,'' supplied Lady Azaela. There was warning in her voice. Her expression stern, she captured Lady Stonehodge's startled glance. ''Perhaps it is best to recall who among us possesses the greater social status. Do you not think so, Ernestina? Correct me if I error, but I believe that your stated purpose in visiting me today was to enlist my aid in launching little Eleanore this Season.''

Lady Stonehodge closed her lips in a tight line. She did not look at the elegant young woman whose very existence so offended her sense of propriety. ''Indeed, that is so. I wish Eleanore to have all the advantages to which her birth entitles her. Unfortunately I have few prominent connections myself, but it was within me to hope that I might rely upon you to lend your considerable countenance to her.''

''And so I shall,'' said Lady Azaela. She smiled across at her great-niece, whose youthful face flushed bright with gratitude. ''I enjoy Eleanore's company very much. I am sure that Lady Chatworth will be only too happy to oblige me by taking Eleanore under her wing as well.''

Babs stared at her aunt, nonplussed by the very idea. It was on the point of her tongue to point out that she was not so well-established herself to be able to sponsor a debutante, but Lady Stonehodge's expression gave her pause and she watched her cousin's face in fascination.

That lady was in the throes of strong emotion, but eventually social ambition overwhelmed pride. "I would be most grateful for any such condescension on the countess's part," she said through her teeth, as though the words were wrested forcibly from her.

Babs slowly smiled. She was not untouched by the irony of the situation. "I will be glad to do my small best to make of Eleanore's first Season a triumph," she said.

"That is settled, then," Lady Azaela said in satisfaction.

Lady Stonehodge rose to take her leave, which she did with much graciousness to Lady Azaela. She was a great deal more abrupt in her courtesies toward Lady Chatworth. Miss Stonehodge thanked both ladies in a low sweet voice for their kindness toward her.

"That is quite enough gushing, Eleanore," Lady Stonehodge snapped, and she urged her daughter not to dawdle.

Miss Stonehodge flushed to the roots of her hair. Uttering an unintelligible apology, she scurried after her mother.

As soon as the door had closed behind the two ladies, Babs rounded on her aunt. She was most annoyed to hear Lady Azaela's deep chuckle. "That was the most despicable thing that you have ever done to me, my lady. Just what am I to say to it?"

"Why, nothing at all." Lady Azaela stopped laughing and reached over to squeeze her niece's arm in a gesture of affection. "Dearest Babs, I know it is unfeeling of me to laugh, but your expressions the last several minutes have been priceless. And as for Ernestina's face . . . Why, I have not so enjoyed myself in her presence for quite some time. Do you wish tea, my dear?"

Babs indicated that she did, then said, "Aunt Azaela, why did you never tell me that you and my mother had brothers or that I had cousins? I was never more astounded in my life, I can tell you, and I am not at all sure that I care for the discovery. Lady Stonehodge is not one whom I would willingly choose as a bosom bow.''

''Ernestina is rather hard to swallow,'' agreed Lady Azaela. She handed her niece a cup of tea before she shrugged. ''As for informing you of their existence, would it have made you happy to know that you had relatives who wished nothing to do with you and who were insistent upon pretending that you did not exist? I do not think so, and I still don't. However, sooner or later you were bound to run into Ernestina, or even my brother, though he does not make a habit of coming to London. I thought it best to force the first meeting to occur in private. Our family secrets are not so unknown that the antagonism between you and Lady Stonehodge would have gone unnoticed. And I did not wish you to be any more plagued this Season than you have been with malicious gossip and the ill-will of the curious.''

Babs was thoughtful as she stirred the milk in her tea. ''I suppose that I must be grateful for your protection. But I do wish that it was somehow different. It would have been pleasant to be able to claim relatives that did not think of one as a social pariah.''

Lady Azaela laughed in derision of the idea. ''I hardly think that Ernestina or any of the rest of them will dare to treat the Countess of Chatworth as a social pariah,'' she said cynically.

''No, I suppose not,'' Babs agreed, smiling a little. She looked at her aunt. ''You said that Lady Stonehodge is the daughter of one of your elder brothers. Have I other cousins besides?''

Lady Azaela shrugged her shoulders. ''The eldest brother is long since dead—and quite unlamented by me or anyone else, for that matter. He was a disagreeable skinflint who never married, so you need look no further than that. As for Ernestina, she is one of three daughters, all of whom made merely respectable marriages and presented their respective husbands with several children. Eleanore, whom you have just met, is the eldest of six thriving progeny. At last intelligence, my other nieces have each five children to their credit.''

"My word," said Babs faintly. Her mind was fairly boggled by the stunning information that she had such a population of cousins.

Lady Azaela smiled in understanding. Her faded eyes reflected a lurking amusement. "Pray do not think about it," she advised. "It is not at all important at the moment, you know. Undoubtedly you will gradually meet them all, and I very much doubt that you will have to seek them out. As the Countess of Chatworth, you can expect relations crawling out from under every rock anxious to take advantage of your social precedence, which, by the by, is the single most important reason that Ernestina has taken you in such acute dislike. It affronts her sense of righteousness that a mere tradesman's daughter can claim precedence over the daughter of a baronet, never mind that that same tradesman's daughter is her own first cousin."

"I had guessed as much when I first encountered that stare of hers," said Babs, nodding. A smile played about her mouth and a reflection of her former anger appeared in her green eyes. "It is one thing to show insult to me, but I shall not countenance any slur against my mother. If as you say these relations of mine do come knocking at my door, I shall make it abundantly clear that I have no wish to consort with people who persist in such ill-conceived arrogance."

"I have no objection to that, my dear. However, I do hope that you mean to handle poor Eleanore with gentler hands. She suffers a great deal from her mother's overbearing manner, I suspect. That is why I roped you in as one of her sponsors. I thought you might be good for her self-esteem," said Lady Azaela.

"Stiffen her backbone, do you mean?" Babs asked, amused. She regarded her aunt in great affection. "I shall do my best by my poor cousin. At least she did not seem ready to crush me underfoot, as her mother gave every appearance of wishing to do."

There was a distinctly contemptuous curl to Lady Azaela's lips as she smiled. "I assure you, Ernestina will do nothing to jeopardize her daughter's chances to capture a matrimonial prize. That includes offending you, now that she has been brought forcibly to recognize that you are not any longer a nobody but a 'prominent connection.' "

Babs started to laugh. "Somehow I have never thought of myself as such, but I suppose it is better to be that than lower in the pecking order than Lady Stonehodge. I suspect in that circumstance the lady would make a point of chafing my pride quite unbearably."

Lady Azaela snorted. "Perhaps, and perhaps not. I have made it plain that I am fond of you, and Ernestina does not wish to offend me. She has hopes of inheriting, you see. You stand in the way, of course, and that is another reason to dislike you. Actually, I have been most grateful for the years that you resided with me, as your presence provided me with a most welcome shield from various fawning members of my estimable family. They would not acknowledge your existence, and so they could not bring themselves to come to the house in which you were very much in evidence."

Babs was surprised again into laughter. "I hardly know what to say." Her eyes sparkled with high amusement. "I had no notion that I was so useful, Aunt."

Lady Azaela set aside her teacup. "Oh, you were in another way as well."

There was a strange purring satisfaction in her voice that Babs had never heard before, and when her aunt looked across at her, she was astonished by the positively wicked light in those faded blue eyes.

"My dear, I asked you here not only to be told of your cousins, but because I have a confession," said Lady Azaela.

"Why do I have the distinct impression that you are not in the least contrite about whatever it is?" asked Babs, setting aside her own cup and folding her hands in her lap.

Lady Azaela chuckled. "That is what I have always liked about you, dear Babs. You deal in plain coin, and always did, even as a child. However, I am not so forthright or honest."

"That is the most idiotic thing you have ever said, Aunt Azaela," Babs said, astonished.

Lady Azaela held up her hand. "Wait to hear before you are so generous with your judgment, my dear." She rose to go to a small writing desk and turned the key in its lock. She opened the desk and extracted a folded parchment tied up with satin ribbon. Lady Azaela handed it to her niece. "I wish you to glance over the top page, which is my letter of intent."

Babs glanced at her aunt, her brows knitting. It was such a strange thing for her aunt to give her, for she perceived instantly that the parchment was an official document of some sort. She hoped with a sinking feeling that it was not her aunt's will. She did not want to even think about the dear lady's demise, let alone whether she would profit from it.

Most unwillingly, she slipped off the ribbon and unfolded the document. She went swiftly over the top page as her aunt had requested, and suddenly her face paled.

She looked up with a stunned expression. "Aunt Azaela, is this true?" she whispered.

Lady Azaela nodded, her expression grave but for a telltale tick at the corner of her mouth. "Indeed it is, Babs. Years ago, when you first came to me, I set up a trust for you that would become yours upon the occasion of your marriage or of my demise, whichever came first. It is entailed to you and to your children and therefore would never become a part of a husband's estate. I had hoped to make certain of your independence from your father or from whomever he chose as your next master. I wished to ensure you a bit of happiness, Babs."

"But I can scarcely believe it." Babs looked again at the paper and the figures involved. Her hands shook. Her instant thought was that she held the key to win the earl's freedom from her father.

Lord Chatworth had refused to use her bride portion to redeem his debts of honor, and since by law those monies had passed to his control upon their marriage, she could not do as she wished with the funds without his consent. But the trust that Lady Azaela had granted her was something quite different. She was the sole responsible party and she could do whatever her heart desired.

"Babs, you have not asked me a most telling question.

Are you not the least bit curious where the funds for the trust came from?'' asked Lady Azaela.

''I can see that you must tell me, so I suppose that this is your hideous confession,'' said Babs.

''Quite right it is. I stole those monies.''

Babs stared at her aunt, completely taken aback. She was astounded and confused, first by Lady Azaela's flat and surprising statement, and second by the lady's tone of extreme relish as she had made it. ''I do not think that I quite understand.''

''If you recall, I have a financial arrangement with your father to provide for your upkeep and education. I bargained sharply with him for the highest figure he would accept before I consented to take you.''

Lady Azaela's eyes glittered with the remembered battle. ''Your father flatters himself as an astute businessman, with none his par. But I fancy that it may be said that I got the better of him. You see, I was quite well-placed and I had no need of his persuasions or his largess to take you in. I had already determined to do precisely that. However, I wished to revenge my sister also, and the only way to inflict punishment upon your father was through his obsessive need to make his mark in the *ton*. I gouged a hole in his wallet and through the years I bled him unmercifully. He had no recourse but to allow me to do so, believing as he did that I needed the funds to provide for you and to train you up to be the well-bred prize that he so desperately wanted for his own despicable ambition. Instead of spending the funds on you as it was understood that I would, I placed very nearly every pence in this trust for you. So you see, I literally stole from your father.''

Babs was left bereft of speech by her aunt's story. She could scarcely comprehend the control and the determination that Lady Azaela must have had to call upon to make her plan come to fruition. She could vividly recall several occasions when her father, who made periodical visits to check on his ''investment,'' had broadly insulted and sneered at Lady Azaela for her financial dependence upon him.

Lady Azaela had not ever knuckled down to her brother-in-law, but she had many times swallowed the set-downs that hovered on her tongue until he had climbed back inside his carriage and driven away. Though she had often been reduced to cold rage, never had Lady Azaela said that she would wash her hands of the situation. Babs realized with some humility and a large measure of gratitude that Lady Azaela had not done so even though the option had been there.

Babs' eyes filled with tears. "I cannot begin to tell you how much I love you for what you have done for me," she said.

Lady Azaela reddened and there appeared suspicious moisture in her own eyes. "Come, my dear. Sentimentality has its place, but it is certainly not over tea," she said gruffly.

Babs laughed and threw her arms around the elder lady.

23

WHEN LORD CHATWORTH had rejected the notion of using her bride portion to redeem his vowels from her father, Babs had felt keen disappointment. Though she had learned to accept his lordship's statement that such a usage would violate a point of honor, it had remained incomprehensible to her that, with the means at hand, the earl should remain obligated to her father.

After the debacle at the ball when her father had been hustled from the premises, it had become even more imperative to cut free of his clutches. But she simply had not the least notion of how it was to be accomplished until Lady Azaela had made known to her the existence of the trust.

The earl would not touch her bride portion, but there was nothing dishonorable in her making use of her own trust funds as she wished. Barbara had been able to think of nothing else since the day that Lady Azaela had sprung her surprise.

Babs formed the intention of meeting with her father. She paid a visit to the Bank of England to procure a draft made against the funds that Lady Azaela had given over to her. The amount of withdrawal was left blank on the draft.

Babs rode to the villa in one of the earl's crested carriages, accompanied by her apprehensive and disapproving maid. The porter that opened the door to them recognized Babs. Upon her quiet request to speak to her father, the manservant showed her to her father's study.

Mr. Cribbage was seated at his desk. He looked up, glowering at the interruption.

Babs walked forward, saying, "I know that my visit is

unlooked-for, and I do not expect welcome from you.''

Cribbage had risen from his seat in surprise at her appearance rather than out of any sense of courtesy. As Babs sat down in the chair set in front of the desk, he gestured with a fine irony. ''Pray be seated, Barbara.'' He sat back down and regarded her from under heavy brows, his expression hard. ''You have not come to express any filial feeling, so what is it that you want?''

Babs took a slow breath, feeling as though she was about to plunge into deep cold water. She said baldly, ''I wish to discuss the redemption of the Earl of Chatworth's vowels.''

Cribbage stared at her for a full minute. Then his glance passed to the silent maid who had entered with Babs and had since taken up her station behind her mistress's shoulder. He jerked his head at the servantwoman. ''Get out.''

The maid's set expression did not alter. ''That I shall not, sir. I remain with my mistress.''

Cribbage started to bellow at at the uppish woman, but his bellicosity was arrested by the unexpected sound of his daughter's soft chuckle. His brows snapped together and he stared at her with surprised disapprobation.

''Give over, Father, do. My maid remains. Whatever must be said can be said before her,'' said Babs.

''You have grown impertinent, Barbara. Perhaps you have forgotten that it is I who gives the orders in this house,'' Cribbage said harshly.

''I forget nothing, and most particularly the fact that you deliberately cheated Lord Chatworth,'' Babs said quietly.

Cribbage laughed then, his large white teeth bared. ''The nature of business is to watch one's back. His lordship was content enough to allow me to contact his man of business rather than soil his lily hands with the thrashing out of the details.'' Cribbage shrugged dismissively. ''He was a fool.''

''I concur to a degree.''

Cribbage leaned back in his chair. There was genuine surprise in his eyes, as well as suspicion. ''Do you, indeed!

I would rather have thought that you had succumbed to his lordship's reputed charm, which from all reports is quite well-entrenched among the ladies of the realm.''

Babs ignored the probing stab, knowing from old how her father attempted to discover his opponent's weakest point so that he could better attack. ''Lord Chatworth is certainly a gentleman of charm and of honor. However, practical matters must be dealt with regardless of those estimable qualities. I am here today to do just that.''

''And what do you offer me?'' Cribbage asked in a measured tone.

''I have available to me funds that I feel certain shall cover the full amount of the earl's vowels,'' Babs said.

Cribbage sat quite still for some moments, during which time he stared at his daughter. Her steady gaze did not falter from his, which irritated him. She had always been willful, but she could never withstand his more forceful personality for long. He glanced over her, taking note of the expensive clothes and bonnet, the jewels in her ears and about her neck. She looked every inch a lady of quality.

Fury ignited in him with the hated thought. ''I placed you in your fine position. I made it possible for you to wear fine gowns and jewels and eat from gold plates if it so pleased you. I wedded you into the peerage. Yet you come to me not with words of gratitude, but mealy mouthings about payment of that same peer's debts.'' With each statement his voice became stronger and louder. He had reared over the desk now, his jaw thrust forward, and he shouted directly into her face.

Babs felt herself shaking under the force of his wrath, but she was determined not to allow even a hint of her inner trepidation to escape her. She said in a deliberate and even voice, ''Should I be grateful for not being allowed to say yea or nay to your plans? I think not. But that is past. I have come upon a different matter, and if it is not one you are not willing to discuss, then I shall take my leave.'' She rose to her feet on the words and waited, her brow lifted in an interrogating manner.

Cribbage was astonished. As a child, at the least sign of

his generous rage she had cowered away like the contemptible weak creature that he had always thought her. In later
years, of course, she had tried to carry things off in a braver
fashion. That had been a direct result of her education at the
hands of her aunt. He had regretted at least that much of
his investment in Lady Azaela Terowne's training of his
daughter. But this complete independence of his calculated
fury was something different. She even held herself
differently.

Suddenly he realized of whom she reminded him. In
coloring and build she had always resembled her mother's
family. Now the angle of her head and the way she stood
expressed the same sort of indifference that had always
maddened him when he had dealt with his in-laws.

"This discussion is indeed finished. I shall tell you directly
to your haughty little head that I will never relinquish those
vowels. You and your fine earl are, and will remain, answer-
able to me," he said silkily. "I do not forget insult so readily.
His lordship instructed his servants in my very presence that
I was to be barred from the house. I can therefore hardly
be expected to be in a conciliatory mood."

Babs stared at her father. "I do not believe that has much
to do with your refusal. That is but a convenient excuse. You
never had any intention of keeping your end of the bargain,
did you?"

Cribbage laughed, his anger evaporating with his sudden
amusement. "None at all, Barbara," he said cheerfully. "But
that should not surprise you. I am a successful businessman,
and profit is not garnered through either sentimentality or
weakness. You would be wise to remember that in your
dealings with his lordship, or you will lose much of what
is yours to enjoy at the moment. Those fine trappings and
the stones around your neck will disappear quickly enough
once his lordship recognizes that he is firmly and truly
caught. The earl is not fool enough to squander away his
blunt on an unwanted wife when he has as his mistress a
warm handful the likes of Lady Beth Cartier."

He saw in her eyes proof that he had struck home at last,
and he laughed low in his throat. His eyes gleamed with

renewed malice. ''I find it curious that you come here on
the earl's behalf, for I feel certain that his lordship would
not send you as his emissary. I'll warrant that his lordship
is not even aware of this precious offer of yours. Now,
whatever could be the motive for such an extraordinary
gesture on your part? I wonder—yes, I must wonder whether
you have been fool enough to fall in love with the wayward
gentleman. My poor stupid dear, truly I had thought better
of your intelligence.''

Babs turned sharply to the door. Accompanied by her
maid, she left the study with her father's hateful laughter
ringing in her ears. She was trembling in earnest and her
face had gone white. She walked so swiftly that her
henchwoman was forced to hurry to keep pace.

Babs swept out of the villa and down the steps to climb
into her waiting carriage. The maid scrambled after her and
had scarcely settled herself before Babs rapped on the roof
for the driver to whip up the horses. The carriage jolted
forward, nearly putting the maid onto the floor. Lucy righted
herself with a swift glance at her mistress's closed face.
She expected to see tears, so she was completely nonplussed
by the blazing anger in the countess's narrowed green
eyes.

Babs was not aware of her maid's consternation. She
turned her face to the window and stared blindly outside,
never seeing anything of the teeming London streets.

The interview with her father had ended as badly as
possible. He had not only refused to consider repayment of
the vowels, but he had with diabolical accuracy ripped aside
her own pretenses and brutally and without compassion
forced her to face a truth that she had hidden even from
herself: she had lost her heart to the unfeeling earl.

When Babs arrived at the town house, it was to discover
from the butler that the earl had been asking for her and that
he had been awaiting her return for the past hour.

Babs cast a swift glance toward the closed door of the
study. ''Pray inform his lordship that I shall be with him
directly,'' she said before picking up her skirt and running
quickly upstairs.

Her maid followed, expostulating under her breath at the hurry and scurry to which she had been subjected that day.

Ten minutes later, Babs descended the stairs. She had changed from her bonnet and pelisse into a smart afternoon dress trimmed in yellow ribbons. Her auburn hair had seen a hasty brush. She appeared perfectly cool and collected as she nodded her appreciation to the footman who ushered her into the study.

Lord Chatworth looked up from his contemplation of the records before him. He smiled at his wife before he glanced toward his secretary. "That will be all for now, Hobbs."

The secretary collected the accounts books and bowed himself out of the room.

Lord Chatworth came from around the desk to take his wife's hand. He lightly kissed her fingers. "I missed you this afternoon, Babs. I had not known that you meant to go out."

"I was merely gadding about town today." Babs smiled at the earl. She hoped that he was not nearly so prescient as she had come to think him in the last few weeks. He had several times anticipated her wishes and even her thoughts. She had not enjoyed herself so much in all her life since his lordship had been spending nearly each day with her, spoiling her with drives about the town and private excursions to such points of interest as the Tower and Astley's Circus.

As she looked at him, she thought that it was the fault of his recent attentions that she had so completely lost her head. He was still the Earl of Chatworth, the same gentleman who had agreed to allow her to pursue her own pecadilloes so that he would be free to do the same. He kept a mistress and he gambled and he was a feckless libertine, she told herself. Nevertheless her father had been horridly correct: she had fallen totally and completely in love with her husband.

"Babs, are you quite all right?" His lordship's keen eyes had narrowed as he saw the flicker of unhappiness that crossed his wife's face.

Babs knew herself too inexperienced in falsehoods to be

able to divert him entirely from the truth. "I saw my father today," she admitted.

Lord Chatworth's face hardened. "Did you, indeed! The man had the effrontery to approach you, I suppose."

Babs made a dismissive gesture. She seated herself in a chair. "It is done. Let us talk of something more pleasant."

"I am very willing to do just that," said Lord Chatworth. He sat down on the edge of the desk and began to gently swing his booted toe to and fro. "We are attending the theater this evening, my lady. I hope that meets with your approval?"

Babs' eyes lighted up. "Of course, Marcus! I should like to get out."

He curled his lips in a faintly mocking smile. "I am devastated, madam! I had thought you satisfied with but my estimable company."

Babs rose from the chair, laughing. "Indeed, sir! You have been the meat of my days. But an occasional dessert is not to be spurned."

"Why do I gather that you are thinking of your dinner, madam?" he murmured.

Babs laughed again. She crossed to the door, saying over her shoulder, "I shall count the moments until we meet again, over the soup."

"Minx." Lord Chatworth was smiling as his wife left the study. The last few weeks had passed with astonishing ease.

He had diligently applied himself to the role of husband and faithful escort, fully expecting to be bored out of his head before the fortnight was out. But he had been increasingly surprised by the amount of pleasure he continued to derive from his wife's company. She was a willing and eager companion, one who was not above twitting him for his arrogance or applauding him for some witticism.

Once he had begun to escort Babs about town, he was unsurprised that she gained an instant popularity that she had not known before. It was only to be expected that society's avid curiosity should be roused by the lady who had so absorbed the Earl of Chatworth that he eschewed his old haunts and pleasures. Babs had naturally been wary of the attention, but eventually she had warmed to it. Lord Chatworth had been quite amazed at her quiet transformation into confidence.

That, as well as the message that he had conveyed so very clearly by his actions that he would tolerate no grazing in his pasture, gave him great satisfaction. Barbara had at last attained the respect that her position as his countess had always entitled her.

24

A MONTH LATER Babs herself felt that she had at last achieved some standing of her own in society. She had learned to overcome her shrinking feeling in company, and it had been especially helpful to her to have Miss Stonehodge to consider.

Babs had taken her pledge to sponsor Miss Stonehodge to heart and she had introduced her young cousin to a wider circle of acquaintances than would have normally come in the way of a minor baronet's daughter. Babs knew that Lady Stonehodge could not entirely accept her role as benefactress, but she shrugged it off. Lady Stonehodge's opinion was unimportant to the scheme of her days.

Babs had grown comfortable in her role. Lord Chatworth approved of her, she knew, and it was with real pleasure that she noticed that he appeared content to spend much of his time in her company.

The earl was nearly her constant companion. Their social lives had become a never-ending round of entertainments, which Babs truly enjoyed since Lord Chatworth chose to act as her escort. The earl had become her dearest friend as well, thought Babs, and she could not recall a time when she was happier.

However, there were still matters that lay unsettled between Babs and Lord Chatworth. Her father remained an ever-present black cloud on the horizon, and there was Elizabeth Cartier.

Babs did not forget that Lady Cartier was also a part of the earl's life. Though his lordship seemed to have a preference for her own company, it in no way diminished the indisputable fact that he had not made of her his true wife.

Babs' cheeks warmed whenever she thought about the possibility of Lord Chatworth's taking her into his arms. But it was better to push the thought away, for always accompanying it was the lovely face of his mistress.

The intolerable situation was brought home with force to Babs one evening at a ball. She and Lord Chatworth had finished a waltz and chose to take the air on the balcony. Clouds glided across the velvety night sky and haloed the brilliant moon. Staring up at such sheer magnificence, Babs sighed in utter happiness.

Lord Chatworth set one elbow on the balustrade and regarded her profile. He thought idly that she was particularly beautiful that evening. "A penny for them," he said softly.

Babs glanced at him quickly. "I was thinking that the last few months have been marvelous." She gave a wicked smile. "I do not in the least regret our bargain, my lord."

"Nor do I," said Lord Chatworth, his gaze on her lips. His eyes rose to meet hers.

Babs' heart turned over at the expression in the earl's eyes. She stood quite still, almost mesmerized, as he slowly leaned toward her. His lips descended warmly on hers in a lingering kiss. She became lost in the tumult of her feelings.

He drew away finally, but somehow he had come to stand closer to her than before. His breath was warm against her skin, his voice soft in her ear. "We can deal even better together, Babs."

"My lord . . ." Babs felt the erratic pounding of her heart. She was thrown into a flutter. His simple statement promised so much.

"Babs." His hands slid up her bare arms to her shoulders. The warm light in his eyes rivaled the full moon. Unaccountably shy, Babs averted her eyes from his disturbing regard.

Over the earl's shoulder she saw a lady in silhouette standing at one of the doors to the balcony. The lady moved away from the balcony and the blazing candlelight of the ballroom shone full on the lovely face of Lady Beth Cartier.

Babs felt dashed by a pan of cold water. She withdrew from under the earl's light clasp, saying coolly, "I am perfectly satisfied with our arrangement as it is, Marcus.'' Without waiting for his lordship, she had returned to the ballroom.

Babs now regretted that she had not waited for the earl's reaction. He had never countered her set-down, either then or in the days since. And in light of what else had occurred that same evening, Babs wished the earl had felt strongly enough to push the issue. Then perhaps she could have thrown out to him what she had so regretted overhearing, and thus eased some of the hurt.

However, the friendliness between them was not altered in any way. She and the earl continued with their round of amusements as though she had never given him such short shrift. Indeed, his lordship appeared never to tire of the entertainments and Babs kept private her own wish for an odd evening spent at home.

It came as a shock when Lord Chatworth suggested that they dine in. ''I am rather bored by the frantic pace that we are obliged to keep these days. Would it vex you too much if we were to remain at home for one evening, Babs?'' he asked.

She was startled that he had seemed to read her thoughts so closely, but she recovered quickly enough so that she hoped he did not notice her surprise. ''Of course not, my lord,'' she said. ''I shall speak to the cook about dinner this evening.''

Lord Chatworth nodded. They were rising from the breakfast table and Babs started to precede him from the room. He caught her wrist lightly between his fingers. ''A moment, my lady.''

She looked up at him inquiringly. ''Yes?'' They were momentarily alone in the breakfast room, but soon the footmen would return to clear the table.

Lord Chatworth reached into the pocket of his morning coat. He brought out a small flat leather case and held it out to her.

Babs regarded him questioningly as she took the case. He had let go her wrist and she lifted the lid of the case. Inside, on a background of blue velvet, reposed a diamond pendant

surrounded by pearls on a simple gold chain. Babs stared
at the necklace, stunned. "It is beautiful."

Lord Chatworth lifted the chain. The swinging diamond
caught fire in the morning light. "Allow me, my lady." He
stepped behind her and carried the slender chain over her
head. His fingers brushed her sensitive skin as he fastened
the chain about her neck.

His hands slid to her shoulders and he turned her to him.
He did not remove his hands from her shoulders, but simply
stood there, so close that his boots touched the hem of
her skirt. There was an unreadable expression on his face and
in his eyes a peculiarly penetrating look.

Babs felt the warmth of a blush. She found it difficult to
meet his stare. She lowered her eyes as she touched with
one fingertip the precious stone, which lay cool against her
breast. "It is most beautiful, Marcus. I thank you."

He released her and to her profound relief stepped back.
In a casual tone, he said, "I thought it a pretty trifle that
would please you." He picked up his cup and finished off
the coffee in it.

"It does, very much," said Babs, somewhat breathlessly.
She glanced at his face as he replaced the cup on the table.
She did not know what to make of his behavior. Just a few
moments before he had suggested an intimate dinner and now
he had given her a gift. She dared not attempt to fathom his
reasoning.

Lord Chatworth seemed to read her thoughts again and
his expression lightened with the appearance of his lurking
smile. "Indeed, it is most queer of me to wish the company
of my wife or to bestow a small gift upon her. I normally
reserve such niceties for my mistresses." He saw the quick
aversion of her head and cursed his slip of the tongue.

"Pray excuse me, my lord. I have a great many errands
today," said Babs quietly. All her pleasure in the pendant
and chain was quite destroyed. She had momentarily forgotten that to a gentleman like the Earl of Chatworth such a
gift had little meaning. Doubtless his lordship was quite used
to bestowing such trifles on ladies over the breakfast table.
The thought brought a flash into her eyes, and she did not

glance again at her husband as she started toward the breakfast-room door.

He caught her hand as she made to slip past him, effectively detaining her. "My dear, it was but a joke. And not a particularly well-bred one, at that. Even I have never kept several mistresses, at least not all at once," he said lightly.

She tossed a fleeting glance at him. She threw up her head and met his eyes with a decidedly challenging air. "Indeed, sir! You surprise me. I have heard much concerning your charming manners and stamina in the boudoir. Forgive me, therefore, for my lack of confidence in your present credibility."

Lord Chatworth became for an instant quite still. "Someone has filled your ears with poisonous innuendo. I wonder who, or may I guess?"

Babs flushed slightly. "It is unimportant, after all." She attempted to free her hand, but his clasp tightened about her fingers.

"Ah, but I would know the name of your mysterious source. Come, Babs, confess or it will be the worse for you," he said warningly.

He turned over her hand and lightly stroked the palm with his thumb. He felt her jerk in surprise, and he smiled at her. There was a devilish light in his eyes. "I can be quite persuasive, my dear, which you have yet to discover. Perhaps you should take heed from what you heard from your confidante."

Her eyes flew to his face in shock and consternation.

He said suavely, "I speak of my vaunted stamina, of course. I do not easily give up on an object of interest."

Babs was betrayed into a choked laugh. She had been thinking of something quite other, of which he was apparently all too aware. She smiled faintly. "Very well, sir. I cry craven. I admit to a particularly reprehensible moment of eavesdropping a few evenings past, which I hasten to assure you is not my usual style."

"I am certain it is not," Marcus murmured. He smiled still, but a waiting expression had come into his eyes. "I suppose it is not too much to inquire whom it was who spoke so familiarly of me? My lamentable curiosity, you do understand. One can never rest until one knows the origin of such idle gossip. It is so fatiguing otherwise. My stamina is hard put to carry me through the ordeal.''

Babs laughed in truth then. She found his complaint ridiculous, as she knew that he meant her to. She shrugged in resignation, suspecting that he would not let her go until she had satisfied him. ''It was Lady Cartier and another lady unknown to me. Her ladyship undoubtedly had no notion that I was about.''

Lord Chatworth regarded her unsmilingly for a moment. Then he sighed. ''Babs, I suspect that you know as well as I that Lady Cartier's observations were all for your benefit. She was my mistress, Babs; I do not deny that. But she is no longer, and has not been for some time.''

Babs looked at him while an incredible warmth coursed through her. ''Thank you for telling me that, Marcus.'' She smiled suddenly, trying to dispel her own vulnerability. ''I have preparations to see to for this evening if we are to sit down to a decent dinner. I must hurry off or I shall not accomplish all that I should.''

''Of course,'' agreed Lord Chatworth. He smiled at his wife and raised her fingers to his lips. ''I also have several matters to attend to today, but nevertheless I shall count the hours until we dine together this evening, my lady.'' He drew her to him and kissed her lightly.

The footmen entered at that moment and Babs flushed to be caught in such an intimate posture. ''Really, my lord! One would think you an accomplished flirt,'' she said flippantly. She whisked herself free and left the breakfast room with a lightened step.

Babs spent the morning in a happy haze. She consulted at great length with the cook to decide just the perfect meal to place before the Earl of Chatworth. That exercise took up most of the morning. She also received a few morning callers. She greeted her visitors with a graciousness not at all tainted with her usual reserve, which led one of the ladies to remark later that the countess was in bloom.

After luncheon, Babs occupied herself agonizing over just

the right gown and the necessary accessories. The earl's gift must be worn, of course, and the careful choosing of her dress evolved about the diamond-and-pearl pendant. Her maid was nearly driven to distraction in the trying on and the rejection of more than a dozen gowns before Babs settled upon one of organza silk.

The gown was deceptively simple in cut, being high-waisted and narrow of skirt. The half-round sleeves fell off the shoulders and the décolletage plunged, so that Babs' shapely breasts appeared to be the only deterrent to the gown slipping completely away.

Lucy dubiously eyed the shocking bodice. "My lady, perhaps another gown? Might I suggest the blue satin or the yellow—"

"No, it shall be this one. It is perfect," Babs breathed as she stared at her reflection. Her shoulders rose like smooth alabaster out of the puffed silk sleeves, and her bosom nicely rounded the silk. The sophistication of the gown was an incredible foil for the simplicity of the gold chain and pendant that lay against her bare skin.

She had bought the revealing gown months ago, but she had never worn it. She had realized the gown was too daring by half. Disgusted by her own cowardice, she had made certain that the gown had been thrust to the back of her wardrobe so that she would not be reminded at sight of it of her faintheartedness.

Now she was immeasurably grateful that she had put it aside. This was a gown made for a special evening. As she looked in the cheval glass at the reflected fire of the diamond pendant, she began to hope that it would be a very special evening, indeed.

"Lucy, I wish something new done with my hair. Something very elegant and very simple," she said.

"Of course, my lady. Nothing could be easier," said Lucy with awful sarcasm. Nevertheless, she made shift to discover a style that met the completely opposite requirements demanded by her mistress.

In the end, Babs regarded her reflection with awe. "Lucy, you have outdone yourself," she murmured. Her hair was pulled into a loose knot at the back of her head and the locks were left to wisp free about her face and shoulders. The glorious mane glinted red-gold and rivaled the pendant for fire.

"It is a true creation, if I may say so, my lady," Lucy said, extremely pleased with herself.

Babs impulsively hugged her servantwoman, shocking the maid to such an extent that she was made speechless. The countess laughed as she left the bedroom and went downstairs.

25

BABS PRETENDED not to notice the footman's dropped jaw as she passed, but she was pleased, nevertheless. It was just the sort of effect she had hoped for, though it remained to be seen whether the Earl of Chatworth was to be as susceptible.

The footman leapt to open the drawing room door for her. Babs murmured her thanks and stepped into the room. The earl was standing with his back to the door as he stirred the fire with his boot. At sound of her entrance he turned. He stared at her. A light kindled deep in his eyes.

Babs had anxiously awaited his lordship's reaction. She was uncertain whether his stillness was altogether flattering. Attempting not to reveal her nervousness, she walked toward him. "Good evening, my lord," she said quietly. She was glad when her voice came out more calmly than she felt.

"My lady." Lord Chatworth took her hand. His salute was a brief brush of his lips across her fingers. He kept hold of her hand while his glance traveled over her from head to toe.

Babs met his somber gray eyes steadily enough, but she felt the pulse beating erratically in her throat.

"You are in exquisite looks this evening, Babs," he said, the timbre of his voice deepened.

She inclined her head in civil acknowledgment as relief flooded over her. "Thank you, my lord."

She had meant to address him by his Christian name, but somehow to do so would bring them into an unbearably intimate juxtaposition that she was not ready to assume.

When she had put on the revealing organza silk gown, it

had of itself put her on a much more intimate footing with the earl than she had realized. Babs was inexperienced, but there was a crackling electricity in the air that any woman would have sensed. Her heart pounded with the headiness of it.

Lord Chatworth drew her near. He smiled into her wide green eyes. "I am flattered, my lady," he said quietly.

"What?" Babs asked in confusion. She seemed unable to catch her breath when he looked at her like that.

He lifted his hand and his fingers brushed her soft skin as he picked up the pendant. "I am flattered that you think so much of my small token," he said.

"It is quite beautiful," said Babs. She could not think coherently, not when his hand was sliding upward along the gold chain. His fingers warmly encompassed her slender neck. His thumb caressed her jaw.

"Shall we go in to dinner?" asked Lord Chatworth softly.

His eyes were half-hooded, partially curtaining the light in their depths. He stood close, so close that she felt the warmth of his breath on her lips.

"Please," she whispered. Neither of them thought she spoke of dinner.

The moment hovered and then was dashed altogether as the door to the sitting room opened. "My lord, pray forgive the intrusion . . ."

The earl let go of Babs and she moved hurriedly away from him, her cheeks hotly coloring. "What is it?" Lord Chatworth bit out, his brows snapping together in extreme annoyance.

The hapless footman was thrust aside by a stiffened arm. The burly figure who entered paused inside the doorway to study the scene. Babs stood at one end of the mantel, her eyes turned to the fire. The heat of the flames could account for the warmth in her face, but the visitor was not persuaded that it was so.

Cribbage turned his shrewd gaze on his son-in-law and bared his teeth in a tight smile. "So, Chatworth. I had hoped to catch you before you had gone out, but instead I find you dining at home. This unexpected domesticity is illuminating, to say the least.'' There was a wealth of malice in his voice as his eyes traveled again to his daughter's face.

Lord Chatworth stepped forward, as much to shield his wife as to draw the man's attention. He was furious that the man had even been allowed entrance, but that circumstance would have to be dealt with later. ''What brings you here, Cribbage?'' he asked coldly.

''Why, what should bring me but the small matter of your vowels? Social invitations are few and far between, are they not?'' Cribbage asked.

''You have found me, then. State your business in short order, Cribbage. I have more pleasant ways to occupy my evening than to barter words with the likes of you,'' said Lord Chatworth.

Cribbage's narrowed eyes glittered. ''That is undoubtedly true, my lord. Brevity suits my purpose as well. In a few days' time there will be a vote coming up in the House pertaining to trade matters. You will cast against it, my lord.''

Babs had turned to listen to her father. She made an inarticulate sound and her eyes flew to her husband's face.

The Earl of Chatworth stiffened. His face was expressionless except for his eyes. His eyes were cold, hard, and quite brilliant with anger. ''Forgive me if I seem more than a little startled. You have caught me unawares. You will, no doubt, understand when I refuse your request,'' he said, quite softly.

Cribbage gave a sharp bark of laughter. ''You do not disappoint me in the least, my lord. Your pretty arrogance is exactly as I anticipated.''

His veneer of joviality dropped away. There was heavy menace in his voice. ''The vote shall be cast as I wish, Chatworth, or I shall publish to the world the appalling nonpayment of your vowels, which you will recall I still hold. I believe that gentlemen of the quality refer to them as debts of honor, do they not? How distressing it would be to watch the blackening of your reputation, my lord.''

Lord Chatworth was tight-lipped. ''Get out, Cribbage. Before I have you tossed out.''

''I am all accommodation, my lord,'' said Cribbage with

weighted irony. His glance touched once more upon his daughter. "As for you, my dearest Barbaraa, I am glad to see you in such fine looks. That gown . . . 'tis fit for a gentleman's mistress." With his last barb, he swung on his heel and strode swiftly out.

There was a long uncomfortable silence. Babs felt almost physically ill. She was bitterly aware of an ashlike taste in her mouth. She felt as though she had been trounced and mauled and dirtied by her father's presence. She could not take her eyes from her husband's face, which had gone quite still and remote.

The butler entered the sitting room. His expression was one of worried contrition. "My lord? I am most sorry, my lord, for failing to divert the gentleman. The footman is new and I was not at my post."

The earl seemed to shake himself. As though from a long distance, the barest of smiles briefly visited his face. "I do not blame you, Smithers. Mr. Cribbage is a determined personage, as I well know."

"Yes, my lord," Smithers said, relieved. He straightened, regaining his normal equanimity. "Dinner is served, my lady."

Babs was released from her awful suspension. She moved toward her husband, who still had not moved. "Thank you, Smithers. We shall not be a moment."

The butler bowed and went out. Babs turned to her husband. She bravely pinned a smile to her lips despite the remoteness of his expression. "Shall we go in, my lord? I do not think that Cook will be happy to hold back serving." Her voice was a little shrill and she swallowed nervously.

Lord Chatworth turned his head. He regarded her with a frowning gaze, very much as though she represented a problem just brought to his attention. His voice was very cool. "You go ahead to dinner, my lady. I shall be along directly. I have a matter to attend to first."

Babs felt her eyes sting, but pride would not allow her to let him see her distress. "Of course, if that is what you wish, my lord."

"For the moment, it is what I wish," said Lord Chatworth.

Babs swept a light curtsy and with erect carriage walked away from him. In the dining room she continued to preserve her countenance as she informed the footmen standing ready to serve that his lordship would not be joining her until later. She sat down and quietly indicated her preferences as the first course was served.

Her gaze slowly went about the well-laid table. Branches of burning candles cast a soft yellow glow over the silver serving dishes and gave vibrant life to the fresh-cut flowers arranged in a crystal bowl in the center of the table. Across from her own place was an unused table service and an empty chair.

Almost blindly, Babs looked down at her soup bowl. She had no appetite left, but she picked up her spoon. It would not do to have the servants gossiping because she refused to eat.

Babs forced himself to swallow a portion of each dish that was served her. She hardly knew what she consumed. It did not matter. She could not taste anything over the ashes of her hopes for the evening.

The earl did not join her during the soup, or for the first course of meat pies and the side dishes of vegetables, or for the entrée of braised beef and chestnut gravy. Babs plowed through despite her misery, keeping up a smiling front for the benefit of the footmen, who efficiently went about their duties.

It had been going on for some time before the significance penetrated her conscious thoughts, but the countess heard again the closing of the front door and the murmur of voices. Swift footsteps in the hallway trod past the closed door of the dining room, then the sound of another door opening.

Unmistakably, she heard the Earl of Chatworth's voice. "Ah, here is Hasford at last. You are always among the last, sir."

There were several male voices raised in easy laughter before the sound was muffled by the closing of the door.

Babs stared at the apricot tart that the footman offered to her. Suddenly she pushed herself away from the table. Her napkin fluttered to the carpet. "I do not wish for anything more, not tonight," she said. Without waiting to gauge the result of her abrupt behavior, she swiftly left the dining room.

As she crossed the entry hall, there came another burst of laughter from the earl's private study. Babs lifted her skirts, and with the delicate silk crushed in her hands, she ran quickly up the stairs.

She fled to her bedroom and slammed shut the door. Babs leaned against the hardwood panels, choking back the threatening tears. She heard the door that led to the maid's closet open and she straightened, wiping quickly at her eyes.

"My lady?"

Babs turned, putting on a credible smile. "There you are at last, Lucy. Come help me. I have learned to detest this gown. It has been an extravagant waste, as you told me at the time that I bought it." She turned to the vanity as she stripped the jewels from her ears and the pendant from her neck. She looked at the pendant for a moment, then allowed the slender gold chin to slither from her fingers to the dresser.

"Of course, my lady." The maid looked questioningly at her mistress's averted face, but she knew better than to pry into what did not concern her. In silence, Lucy undressed her mistress and readied her for bed. She picked up the hairbrush, but at a swift gesture from her mistress she paused. "Yes, my lady?"

"Leave it. I shall not require you again tonight, Lucy," Babs said coolly. She stared at herself in the mirror, then her eyes rose to meet the maid's concerned gaze. She forced herself to smile. "I wonder whether my father would appreciate a visit on the morrow. He has not had me to shout at for some time."

The maid chuckled. "Aye, that is true, my lady." She turned away to pick up the discarded silk gown. It was sadly crushed, she saw, and she shook her head. She went to the door, pausing only to wish her mistress a good night.

Babs returned the sentiment, but with a somewhat twisted smile. She rose from the vanity to pace the carpet. The semitransparent lace negligee she wore floated about her as she moved restlessly from vanity to bed to bureau and back again. She paused at the vanity and picked up the discarded gold chain. The diamond twisted in the air, flashing points of fire. Babs laid it carefully down.

She still could scarcely believe the disastrous end to the evening. She had dined in state but quite alone, while her husband chose to carouse with his hastily assembled friends rather than be in the same room with her.

It was her father's fault, of course. Her father was to blame for the entire ludicrous situation, from the fact of her marriage to the state of careful distance that was maintained between herself and the earl.

She had seen glimpses of interest in her husband's face from time to time when they conversed together or he accompanied her to various functions. She had begun to dare hope that she could win his affection.

But she had been shown quite brutally this evening that she would never stand as an individual in her husband's eyes. He would always see her as an extension of her father, and of her father's power over his life. Babs knew for a certainty that the situation would remain thus until her father's hold over the earl was broken. And she could not think of any other way to destroy that hold than to get her hands on the gaming vowels that were held by her father.

Unaware that his wife was contemplating a most reckless course of action, the Earl of Chatworth was doing some plotting of his own. He had requested the presence of certain acquaintances of his in order to discuss the means of bringing ruin upon his father-in-law. The meeting had been at times raucous, but for all that in deadly earnest.

Lord Chatworth was well-pleased with what had been decided. He knew that he owed a grave debt to these gentlemen that he would not easily be able to repay. "I must humbly proffer my thanks, gentlemen," he said quietly. "You shall make possible a matter of fine revenge."

One of the gentlemen waved aside the earl's gratitude. "By Jove, it would be the same for any one of us caught in such a contretemps. Imagine a tradesman attempting to force a House vote!"

"Give him the vote that he wishes, Marcus. You have our

word on it that it will be the disaster that you have outlined for the impudent bastard,'' said Simon Hadwicke.

''Aye, he'll mourn the day that he set up his doxy of a daughter as debt security,'' said another gentleman with a laugh.

The earl had been smiling, but at that his expression altered. He said quite coldly, ''The lady is my wife, sir.''

There was an astonished and pregnant silence.

Hadwicke made a soundless whistle, and his own astonishment was reflected in Viscount Taredell's startled and rolling eyes. So that was the way of it. His lordship was well and truly caught at last. Simon straightened in his chair, gesturing expansively with his empty wineglass. ''A toast, I say! A toast to his lordship and his lordship's lovely lady.''

The gentlemen, released from the uncomfortable moment, quickly joined in. The unfortunate comment was passed over and forgotten. But in the morning it would be in all the clubs that the Earl of Chatworth had made it bluntly clear that he would champion his wife's name.

The notorious rake and libertine had at last succumbed to a ruling love.

26

THE CARRIAGE'S IRON WHEELS clattered over the cobbles and the raucous sounds of London intruded clearly through the closed windows, but Babs was not attending. All of her being was concentrated on the purpose that had brought her into that part of London.

The hackney stopped. The moment was upon her and she felt her courage slip at the thought of what she intended to do. Barbara picked up her reticule and got out of the carriage. She handed up the fare to the driver.

Unable to delay any longer, the countess turned and walked up the front steps of her father's villa. She rang the bell and the door opened. The porter ushered her inside with a murmured greeting. The door was shut firmly—almost, to Babs' ears, with a sound of finality.

"Good morning. Is my father in?" asked Babs. She was amazed at how cool and matter-of-fact she sounded.

"No, mum. The master be at his place in the City," said the porter.

"I see." It was what Babs had hoped and counted upon. She had been prepared to seek an audience with her father, her excuse to have been that she had come to make a plea for the Earl of Chatworth. She stood as though reflecting, before she smiled again at the porter. "Perhaps I could leave a note, then? I know my way to the study."

The porter bowed. He did not follow her down the hall to the study, which Babs was glad of. She was nervous; every fiber of her being was taut with an awful suspense.

She went into the study and quietly shut the door. Still with her hand on the brass knob, she turned and contemplated

201

her father's private sanctum. The most notable feature of the
room was the massive desk that occupied the space between
the ceiling-high windows. There were few bookcases or any
other major pieces of furniture, except for a table pushed
against the papered wall that held several wine decanters and
glasses.

A large fireplace dominated the room opposite the desk.
There was a good fire laid in the hearth and Babs was glad
for its cheery yellow glow. But even with the reflected heat
of the flames, she could not seem to shake the cold trembling
of her limbs.

When Babs had decided upon her desperate course of
action, she had not had the slightest notion where her father
may have put what she wanted. But the desk drew her
attention. Its sheer weight and size proclaimed it an important
part of her father's conception of himself. Surely anything
as important as the Earl of Chatworth's gambling vowels
would be secreted inside one of its several drawers.

Babs tentatively tried one of the drawers. It slid open with
smooth efficiency. She let out her pent-up breath. Casting
a swift glance toward the closed door, she began to go
through the drawer. She sifted through the papers, nervously
and with swift-beating heart. She felt as though the clock
ticking on the mantel had become extraordinarily loud in a
silence that was broken only by her own shortened breaths
and the rustling of the drawer's contents.

The vowels went not in the drawer. She shoved the drawer
shut and jerked open the next, and the next.

Babs could have wept with vexation. Her hands were
shaking in earnest now. She could scarcely grasp the sheets
of business correspondence and other ordinary items that kept
appearing in drawer after drawer.

But at last her search was rewarded. Tucked away in a
battered box, as though to give the impression that the
contents were not very valuable, were those papers that she
had dared to come find.

Babs gave a sob of relief and closed the box. Hastily she
shut the drawer, very aware of how swiftly the time had

passed while she had been at her task. She started to put the small box into her reticule.

She looked quickly at the clock on the mantel. It showed that a scarce twenty minutes had passed since she had entered the study. The porter must have begun to wonder at the length of her supposed note, but Babs did not care. She knew that her father, a man of set habits when it came to the timing of his luncheon, was not due back to the villa for another half-hour. If she did not allow her courage to fail her, she might yet leave the villa and without the incriminating evidence on her person. Then, if she should by some ill chance run into her father, she could in all conscience say that she had come to plead with him on the Earl of Chatworth's behalf. Given her father's character, she knew how that admission would both please and amuse him. He would refuse her, naturally, and set her on her way with a mocking taunt. And she would be grateful to escape so lightly.

Babs opened the box. The sheer number of the slips astounded her. There must be scores of the vowels, all marked with the firm sweeping initials characteristic of her husband's hand. It was beyond her how a gentleman could so carelessly play at cards, but she had come to know in her short time in the London salons that such staggering debts were not uncommon among the *ton* of either sex. Deep play was the rule of the day, and none but the timid caviled at the stakes.

At least the Earl of Chatworth did not dip so badly these days, thought Babs. Her hand froze in the act of lifting a handful of the vowels. But she did not actually know that, she realized. She had only assumed it to be true because she rarely saw her husband at the card tables that were a common alternative entertainment to dancing at the functions they had attended. She had no way of knowing whether the earl frequented the lurid gaming hells that she had heard about, nor whether he indulged in the dice at his clubs.

Babs swallowed, suddenly sickened. She could very well be indulging in an exercise in futility if her husband was

continuing to paper the town with his gaming debts. Her
father would think nothing of collecting the new and adding
them to those he had originally used for blackmail. With
revulsion, she threw the handful of vowels into the fire. The
flames greedily lit upon the slips, which flared briefly before
turning to blackened ash. She started to throw the next
handful of vowels into the flames.

The study door burst open. Babs whirled, the vowels
scattering from her nerveless fingers. Her heart pounded in
sudden awful fear.

Cribbage stood in the doorway, his hand still tight on the
knob. His hard eyes slid from his daughter's whitened face
to the incriminating battered box which she had not attempted
to conceal. She faced him like a cornered cat, at once defiant
and frightened. Scattered about the hem of her skirt on the
carpet was further evidence of her treachery. He slowly
looked up and with the sheer force of his will captured her
green gaze. Without a word, he closed the door softly behind
him.

Lord Chatworth was disconcerted when upon his return
for luncheon he was waylaid in the entry hall by his wife's
maid.

The woman's eyes lit with relief at sight of his tall figure.
"My lord! Oh, how glad I am that you have come!"

The earl threw a questioning look at his butler. Smithers
gave the barest of shrugs and Lord Chatworth sighed. He
gave his beaver into the waiting hands of the butler and
proceeded to strip off his gloves. "Yes, Lucy? I presume
that you have a particular reason for expressing yourself with
such ecstasy at my appearance."

His lordship's sarcasm went awry of the mark. Far from
deflating the servantwoman's strange manners, it seemed to
encourage her to speak more freely. "My lord, I have been
beside myself. It is my lady—"

At last Lord Chatworth's attention was firmly attached.
"Lady Chatworth? Where is she?"

"That is just it, my lord," said Lucy, grateful that his
lordship seemed to follow her so quickly. "My lady made

an odd comment yesterday evening before I left her about making a visit to her father. Knowing what I do, I thought she was having a little joke. But this morning she went out without a word to anyone. And she has not been seen since.''

''That is true, my lord,'' Smithers said, ponderously. ''Though I did not witness her ladyship's departure myself, I am told that Lady Chatworth left sometime after breakfast. I only mention it as odd, because her ladyship requested that the footman procure a common hackney for her.''

''My God,'' said Lord Chatworth. He had no reason to believe that the maid's fears were justified, but instinctively he knew that what the woman feared was true. He was as certain as he breathed that Babs had gone to her father's villa, and he thought he could guess the reason behind her uncharacteristic start.

He rounded on the butler and gave swift orders to have his phaeton brought around immediately to the front. Without waiting for acknowledgment, he leapt the stairs three at a time.

Lord Chatworth returned downstairs in the space of ten minutes. He had changed swiftly from morning coat and town trousers to driving coat and buckskins. His expression was black and grim. He nodded at the intelligence conveyed by Smithers that his phaeton stood ready at the curb.

Lord Chatworth jumped up into the waiting carriage. He nodded curtly for the groom to let go of the leader's halter. With hardly a glance, he put the phaeton into the heavy traffic and set off at as smart a pace as the congested streets allowed.

Lord Chatworth curbed his impatience with difficulty but once succumbed to swearing furiously at a vehicle driven by a rather inept whipster. With a show of consummate ease, he whipped his horses and passed the offending carriage at a distance that left the other driver gaping in admiration.

Once free of the thoroughfares, Lord Chatworth sent his horses along at a greater pace. His face was carven in deep lines and his eyes were hard. The reins between his fingers slipped evenly and smoothly as he controlled his team. But his thoughts were not on his driving.

He was recalling the night that he had burst in upon his

wife, determined in his drunken fury to bed her, only to be stopped cold by the appalling sight of the welts that criss-crossed her slender back. Her father had beaten her merely because the wedding would take place at an earlier date than he had anticipated. What would Cribbage not do if he discovered his daughter in his house and plotting against his interests?

Lord Chatworth was physically sickened by the thought. He whipped up his horses again, thrusting them forward at a dangerous speed for even these outskirts of the metropolis.

When Cribbage's villa appeared, Lord Chatworth yanked his team down with a savagery unusual for one who was normally considerate of his animals. He pulled up to the curb, snubbed the reins, and leapt down from the seat. A young boy was loitering close by. Without breaking stride, Lord Chatworth tossed a large coin to him. "Walk them, and there will be a crown in it for you," he snapped.

"Aye, guv'nor!" The boy joyfully took hold of the leader's halter and began his appointed task.

Lord Chatworth ran up the steps to Cribbage's villa. He did not wait to ring the bell, but twisted the handle and thrust open the door. Ignoring the porter's bleated protest, he took hold of the servant by the front of his coat. "My wife, where is she?" he inquired savagely.

The porter gobbled with fright. He pointed a shaking finger in the direction of a closed door down the hall. "There, m'lord. But the master is not wanting to be disturbed. My lord!"

Lord Chatworth was unheeding as he raced down the hall. He kicked open the door. It slammed back against the wall, allowing him an unimpeded view of the occupants in the room. Babs clutched the mantel for support, her face averted, her bonnet dangling by its ribbons down her back. His father-in-law stood over her, his heavy legs apart, his fist half-raised.

"Cribbage!"

The man turned, surprisingly swift for one of his bulk. His enraged face further blackened. "You have no business here, sirrah. Get out!"

"On the contrary." The earl's voice was deadly in its cold steel. He had plunged his hand into his coat pocket and now raised a quite serviceable dueling pistol. "I have come for my wife."

"Your wife!" Cribbage barked a laugh. "Your whore, more like! For that is all she is to you, is it not, my lord? A bought woman and hardly a match for your pretty lady mistress. Oh, yes, I know of her ladyship and her trysts with you, my lord. Such hypocrites, you quality!"

Lord Chatworth's expression had grown very still, but his voice was gentle when he spoke to the woman who had straightened to stiff attention. "Babs, come here."

She cast one swift sideways glance at her father before she edged carefully past him. Then she ran to Lord Chatworth. He put his arm about her rigid shoulders and tightened his hold when he felt her violent trembling.

Lord Chatworth glanced down at her face, then swung his cold eyes to his father-in-law. "I should kill you where you stand, you blackguard," he said softly.

Cribbage threw out his arms. "Then do so, my lord." His voice was mockery itself. "Or do you lack the courage, as do so many of your ilk?"

Lord Chatworth felt his wife's fingers clutch at his lapel and he felt more than heard her breathless protest. The pistol did not waver in his hand.

The earl smiled, that peculiar arrogant smile. "It would give me great pleasure to blow a hole through you, Cribbage. But do you know, I suspect that the greater pleasure will be to bring you crashing to your ruin. That will exact the more satisfying revenge."

"Words, my lord, mere words. Now hear me, sirrah! Your whore failed in destroying the debts I hold over you. You shall pay for her betrayal and your own temerity in coming here. I demand payment upon the stroke of noon tomorrow, my lord."

Cribbage was breathing heavily. His fists flexed. "Do you hear, my lord? Payment in full!" The last was an enraged bellow as Lord Chatworth and his wife walked swiftly down the hall, past the gaping porter, and out the door.

Lord Chatworth handed Babs up into the phaeton and then bounded beside her. He tossed the street urchin a second crown. Without a backward glance, he struck up the team and clattered away.

27

BARBARA SAT STIFFLY beside the earl. Her head was in a whirl. She did not know what he was thinking. She cast a glance up at his stern profile, but his expression was so forbidding that she had not the courage to address him. She did not know how she could explain her actions or even to ask him how he had known where she had gone. However, that in a way mattered less than the fact that he had come after her.

Babs had never been more glad of anything in her life than when the door crashed open and the earl had stridden into her father's study. The look on his lordship's face had set her pulses fluttering with a strange fear, but his cold rage had not been directed at her.

Babs quickly glanced up at the earl's face and away again. Her father's contemptuous derision had smashed home the reality under which she lived. She had fallen desperately in love with her husband, but he did not want her. She was naught but an embarrassment and a trial to him, and that was all that she would ever be.

The Earl of Chatworth had lived up to every facet of their bargain. She supposed that she should be grateful, but Babs felt closer to despair than she had ever been before. It was she who had not kept the tone of their bargain. She had had the audacity to fall in love.

A choked sob escaped her.

Lord Chatworth glanced down at her bowed head. "Are you quite all right?" There was no gentleness in his tone.

Babs swallowed and her throat and whole chest burned with the repression of her grief. She tried to speak and for a nightmarish moment she thought she was going to totally disgrace herself. But at last she managed to get out an adequate reply. "Perfectly all right, my lord."

He frowned at her, but he did not speak to her again. That was the sum of their conversation during the return home.

When the phaeton stopped at the curb, Babs did not wait for the earl to come around and hand her down. She gathered her skirts and climbed down to the sidewalk.

"Babs!"

She heard him, but she did not pause. She ran up the front steps, pushed open the door, and dashed past the astounded footmen to the stairs. It was then that she heard the quick hard rap of his boots on the tiles in the entry hall. She swallowed a sob and climbed faster.

She had reached her bedroom door and her hand was on the brass knob when his heavy hand fell on her shoulder. She was spun ungently about.

The earl's gray eyes angrily bore down into hers. "Not by a long shot, my lady," he said softly. Still retaining his hold on her, he reached around her and opened the door. She had stiffened at his touch and perforce he had to pull her with him into the bedroom.

"My lady!" The maid had turned upon their entrance, a glad smile lighting her face. Her expression quickly altered at the earl's abrupt command to leave. Lucy cast an anxious glance at her mistress's pale face as she obeyed.

The earl kicked the bedroom door closed. He released his wife abruptly. Babs staggered, then righted herself. She crossed her arms, hugging herself in an unintentional show of fright. Her eyes were huge in her face.

"What was the meaning of that display, madam?" asked Lord Chatworth, his mouth white-rimmed with anger. His fingers flexed slightly with the force of the emotion within him.

Babs glanced swiftly at the movement of his hands. Her mouth went suddenly dry. "I—I don't know what you mean."

"You ran from me," he said with scarcely bridled anger. Babs thought she understood then. "I did not intend to embarrass you, my lord. I was not thinking of the servants or—''

''The devil with the servants!'' In one swift stride Lord Chatworth reached her and took hold of her shoulders. He shook her harshly. ''How dare you accuse me of such pretension! Yes, that is just the expression. I have seen it too many times before—that damnable trepidation in your eyes when you look at me. I can feel the shrinking of your body whenever I deign to touch you. My dear wife, who runs in such fear of me.''

''No! No!'' Babs started to cry. When he shook her again, her fingers clutched his coat. ''Pray do not! You do not understand!''

She was suddenly crushed against his chest. His arms were steel bands about her ribs and his cheek pressed against the top of her head. His breath ruffled her hair. ''Do I not?''

His voice was savage, but yet far less threatening than his previous tone. He pulled the bonnet completely free and tossed it aside. Putting a hand through her hair, he dragged back her head so that he could look into her face. His eyes smoldered with anger and something else. ''My lady, I understand far more than you suspect. My God, when I think what he would have done to you . . .''

Babs attempted to inject a note of lightness into her voice. ''I do apologize, my lord. I never intended to enact a Cheltenham tragedy for you.'' She started to pull out of the earl's slackened hold.

But Lord Chatworth's arm tightened about her once more, effectively imprisoning her.

''My lord!'' She looked up quickly, the protest dying in her throat at his expression. She had scarcely a second to register the meaning of the strange dark light in his eyes before his lips descended upon hers.

His mouth was demanding, possessing her and tasting of her as though she had no will to call her own. Babs had instinctively stiffened, but all too soon her thoughts were in confusion. His lips assaulted her inexperience, beating down what resistance was left in her. She had dreamed for so long of being held in his arms. For Babs, in those indescribable and chaotic moments, the difference between dream and reality blurred.

His lips, his hands, were everywhere. Her being was played to the erotic music that he evoked. Scalded by burning kisses and stroked to an ever-spiraling heat, Babs perceived only him. She did not know when a rough hand pulled the pins from her hair or when her dress was torn from her shoulders.

She felt softness give beneath her. Her fingertips slipped over bare, warm flesh and entangled in silky hair. The warmth that enveloped her shifted away. She opened her eyes confusedly. The earl stared down at her, braced with his muscular arms upon either side of her, his breath quickened. His half-hooded eyes were ablaze. "We shall do better than we have done," he promised softly. Then his head dipped and his lips caught hers again.

Babs moaned low in her throat. Her arms of their own volition wound about his neck. Slowly, the earl dropped into her embrace.

When Babs woke, she sighed a little. It had been such a peculiarly vivid dream. Never before had she dreamed of the earl with such clarity. The heat rose in her as she recalled certain details.

The significance struck her with horrible clarity. She started up, swiveling at the same time as she snatched the bedsheet close.

A lazy arm pinned her back against the bed. The earl smiled down into her horrified green eyes. He wore the peculiar smile that she particularly disliked.

"Surely my lady does not wish to rise so soon," he said, a note of laughter in his quiet voice.

"You . . . were . . . " Words failed her. She closed her eyes, feeling a burning shame. She had not dreamed it, after all. It had all been too ghastly, too wonderfully, real.

"Yes, my lady wife. It has been an altogether refreshing interlude, and easily one I could wish to prolong." His fingers twined in her glorious hair where it lay splashed across the white pillow.

Babs swallowed against the sudden jump of her heart into her throat. She opened her eyes to look up at her husband, but he was not looking directly at her. His gaze was still on her hair and there was an abstracted frown on his face.

As though he felt her wary scrutiny, the earl's glance turned to meet hers. His eyes filled with an unholy amusement. "My dear Babs, I may have seduced you, but I do not think that you can have many complaints. As I recall, you were not precisely unwilling."

A flush burned her face. It was true, what he said. She had been anything but unwilling. She had been altogether wanton. Babs wondered what her aunt might have said to that. Lady Azaela had warned her of what to expect of a gentleman, but she had not breathed a word of what to expect of herself.

Babs knew that she was in an untenable position, but she gathered what shreds of dignity she still possessed and said, "I have but one complaint, my lord. Our agreement was made for a marriage of convenience. I cannot recall anything said of seduction, willing or otherwise."

Lord Chatworth's face split in a dazzling grin. He shook his head admiringly. "True, my dear lady. But, then, our agreement was in some respects incredibly shortsighted."

Babs silently and wholeheartedly agreed. When she had made her pact with the Earl of Chatworth, she had then had no notion that she would fall in love with him, or that their agreement would become such a burden to her very happiness.

The earl sat up and in a single fluid motion pulled her up to sit beside him. With an elaborate care that made her bite her lip in vexation, he tucked the sheet chastely about her so that she was decently covered. He slanted his own peculiar smile down at her. "I hope that you are comfortable, lady wife."

"Quite comfortable," lied Babs. She was resting against his side, and his arm encircled her. The warmth of his long torso and of his arm was distracting to the coherence of her thoughts.

"I am glad of it, for we have business to discuss."

Lord Chatworth's voice had lost its intimate quality and the words were clipped. An icy stake was driven into the insulating warmth. Her mind cleared instantly. "Yes, my lord?"

Her chin was caught between hard fingers. Startled, she looked up into the cool expression of his eyes. "Understand me once and for all, Babs. I am Marcus to you, whether you will it or not. That is one thing that will come out of the sharing of this bed." His voice was harsh.

"I understand." He released her then and her lashes swept down to hide the swift angry tears. Her fingers folded and refolded the sheet covering her. She had thought the measure of her humiliation full before, but she was discovering that he had the capacity to exact more than she had ever thought possible.

"I am glad. As I told you, we shall deal better than we have done before. That is my promise."

Babs' eyes flew to his face, then away. She thought she understood all too well. The tenets of their agreement had come completely undone and what Lady Azaela had predicted and warned her of was coming to pass. The Earl of Chatworth had grown tired of possessing a wife in name only. Her pulse beat dully at the thought, whether in revulsion or in fascinated anticipation she was not certain. She had yearned for just such a thing to come to pass, after all. But of one thing she was quite certain: she loved him, and nothing at all could ever change that.

"However, our own considerations must be set aside yet awhile longer. Your father must be our primary concern just now. His ultimatum does change matters slightly," said Lord Chatworth. He reached to brush her hair back so that it no longer partially curtained her face. "Babs, what were you trying to accomplish this morning? You must have known that it was a futile gesture."

Babs held herself quite still. She did not want to meet his eyes. "I am grown weary of my father's interference, Marcus. I thought that if I could remove the vowels from his possession, then he could no longer blackmail you to do his bidding. And we would be free of him at last."

Lord Chatworth sighed. "My very foolish wife, did it never occur to you that as a man of honor, even if the vowels were destroyed, I could never have let go of proper payment? Can you not understand, Babs? A gentleman's debts of honor must be paid, no matter of the consequences to himself or to others."

Some part of her snapped loose of her careful control. "What I understand—and all too well, my lord—is that you have consistently refused any offer of help from me," she flashed. "I thought our agreement was to work together to be free of my father, but not once have you taken my help seriously. These last months I have been confused by your scorning of my aid, but at last I have come to the one unmistakable conclusion that makes any sense, and that is that I a my father's daughter, naught but an encumbrance and an embarrassment that must always remind you of your own humiliation. Your hatred of my father is quite strong, but a part of it has always been reserved for me as well, has it not, my lord?"

The anger in his eyes was unmistakable. She gasped when he rolled over to imprison her between his elbows. Shrinking back against the pillow, Babs held her breath. He bit off his answer to her accusation. "I should make you eat every last lying word, madam. But I have not the time, just now."

The earl eased himself away from her and left the bed. He walked across the room to his discarded clothing, completely unaware of the view that he afforded his wife or of the blushing aversion of her gaze. He dressed swiftly in his buckskins and shirt, then bent to pick up his boots, coat, and wrinkled neckcloth. When he had finished dressing, he regarded her unsmilingly. "I have a few matters to set in motion if I am to meet your father's deadline on the morrow. You must trust me, Babs. After it is all done, why, we shall continue this discussion. On that, lady wife, you have my word." Lord Chatworth strode to the door that connected her bedroom to the pretty sitting room and to his own bedroom beyond. The door crashed behind him.

Babs was left staring at the door. She could scarcely make any sense of what had just happened. She knew only that this morning she had made a complete and utter fool of herself, first by attempting to make right a matter that her husband would not allow her to involve herself in, and then by tumbling willy-nilly into his arms. She wasn't quite sure what he had meant in his parting words, but somehow there had been conveyed a threat, of that much she was certain. She pounded on the coverlet with frustration. What did it all mean, and more to the point, what, if anything, did the Earl of Chatworth feel for her?

28

THE EARL DID NOT RETURN until very late that evening. Babs had remained in the drawing room until long past her usual hour, waiting for his lordship.

When she heard his voice and his firm step in the entry hall, she flew to the drawing-room door. She stood just inside the opened door, her gaze rested on the earl's face. He looked drawn and deep lines bracketed his mouth. But when his eyes fell on her, he smiled. "Babs."

She felt the warmth rise in her at his easy recognition. She went to him and gently took his arm. "Come into the drawing room, Marcus. Smithers will bring you a cold collation," she said, throwing a look toward the butler. He nodded understanding and quietly relayed the order.

Babs and the earl entered the drawing room. She closed the door, gesturing him to sit down even though she had not yet done so. Lord Chatworth accepted her courtesy with a nod of acknowledgment and dropped into a chair with a sigh.

Babs seated herself on the settee opposite him. She had thought that she would be shy in his company after the passion they had shared, but she found that it was not so. She was far more concerned with the weariness in his face and his stillness than with her own belated modesty.

"Marcus? What has happened?"

The earl opened his eyes and lifted his head from its resting position against the back of the chair. His eyes were cool as he said, "The wheels are set in motion. After the vote tomorrow in the House, it is my hope that your father will be utterly ruined and I will have broken his hold on me at last."

Babs shivered at the cold satisfaction in his voice.

He noticed, and the mocking smile touched his lips. "Do I shock you, my dear wife?"

She shook her head quickly. "No, it is not that. I knew when we first met that you were a strong man, perhaps even as ruthless as my father. I knew also that it would take such ruthlessness to win free of him. I do not regret it in any way."

Lord Chatworth got up. He crossed the short distance between them to seat himself on the settee beside her. He took her hands. "Look at me, Babs." When she had raised her eyes to his face, he said, "I want you to thoroughly understand what I intend. I mean to bring your father to ruin. I have arranged for all of the cotton and wool on the market to be completely bought up. When the vote is taken, and if it goes the way that I think it will, then those same commodities will be offered to him at exorbitant rates. Cribbage will be forced to buy at the highest prices of the decade to keep his mills running. He cannot possibly do so without more capital. He will be forced to borrow whatever funds he can."

The earl's gray eyes gleamed. "He will come to me, Babs. My vowels will no longer be worthless scraps of paper to him, but instead represent a small fortune. And I shall redeem them, but only after extracting his signature on a written legal caveat that he will not again approach either of us or our heirs for the remainder of his life."

"I see nothing to object to in that," Babs said. She frowned a little and shook her head. "But I do not understand. You have said that you will bring ruin on my father."

"Babs, Cribbage will not be able to recover from such a financial blow. In a matter of months at most, he will be forced to begin the selling of his mills to repay his debts. Or he will end in a debtor's prison," Lord Chatworth said quietly.

There was a short silence as Babs absorbed his meaning. She felt a fleeting pity for her father, but it was not of him alone that she thought. The freedom that she had so wished for her husband had changed her own circumstances quite drastically. She disregarded his lordship's allusion to their heirs with regret, for surely he spoke only out of his sense of duty toward her. He could not really wish to remain married to the daughter of the man who had held him under threat of blackmail these several months.

Babs withdrew her hands from the earl's clasp and rose from the settee. She went to the mantel and stared into the fire. Without looking around, she said, "I have wished often for the destruction of my father's suffocating hold on me. You have made that possible."

She turned. Her wide green eyes were perfectly steady in expression. "I believe that you wished our agreement to be one of temporary duration, my lord. I shall not counter against a suit for divorce."

The earl slowly rose to his feet. There was an unreadable expression on his face. "Is that what you wish, Babs?"

"It is not a question of what I wish or do not wish, my lord," she said quietly. She felt the trembling begin deep inside of her. Her heart felt as though it was breaking, but she could not unsay the words, nor did she truly wish to do so. She loved the gentleman who stood watching her with all of her being. She would not hold him fettered by an agreement forged out of necessity. If she did so, she believed that he would eventually come to hate her.

Lord Chatworth crossed to stand beside her. He looked down into her somber eyes. "What is it that you wish, Babs?" he asked very softly.

"That is unfair question, my lord, as well you know. I came to you to form a bargain. You have upheld your end of it and now it is time for me to do the same," said Babs.

"And is that to be the end of it?" He reached up to smooth her hair and then his hand dropped gently to rest upon her shoulder. "Babs, our agreement fashioned the basis of an admirable partnership. But it was not all-encompassing. I think that point was made rather tellingly this afternoon. Or must I remind you of it?" He bent his head and would have taken her lips, but she ducked swiftly away.

Babs' voice wobbled with the determined control that she exerted upon herself. "Pray do not do this to me, Marcus. I do not think that I can bear it. What happened between us was a mistake. We should never have—"

"A mistake, my lady? I do not think of what we shared in such terms," said Lord Chatworth evenly, though his eyes smoldered with the beginning of temper.

"But, indeed, it was just that! Oh, perhaps it does not appear so to you. I should not expect a rakehell to understand. After all, what does one woman more or less mean to one grown so indifferent? For you are indifferent, are you not, Marcus? Your reputation—"

Lord Chatworth muttered an oath and caught her up in his arms. He kissed her thoroughly and with fierce possession. Babs pushed against him at first, but abruptly she gave in. No longer rigid in his arms, she gave back all that he wanted of her. The unexpected strength of her passion was electrifying.

When Lord Chatworth lifted his head, he was breathing quickly and his heart pounded. She lay her cheek against his waistcoat. His arms folded about her and he pressed his chin against her soft fragrant hair. "My dear lady wife, I do not wish to bring suit against you," he said hoarsely.

"Why? I have been a mettlesome nuisance and an encumbrance to you. You have often wished me to the devil, I know," said Babs.

"Damn you, Babs. What is it about you that has me so tied in knots?" he muttered. He took hold of her shoulders and moved her back from him so that he could stare grimly into her face. "I never thought to ever say this. But as it is already in all the clubs, I suspect that I have no choice but admit to it. I have fallen in love with my lady wife. I do not wish to let you go, Babs, unless that is your wish of me."

"You, Marcus?"

"Yes, I," he said, mocking the astonishment inherent in her voice. The twisted smile touched his face. "And what of you, Babs? Do you not also have a confession to make to me?"

Babs stared at his shirt front. Her heart was singing but she would not put an end to his suspense so soon. He had seduced her most heinously and then left her in dread uncertainty of his feelings toward her. Now she had the means to revenge herself a little. "I don't know what you mean, I'm sure," she said firmly.

"I am set down, indeed." His voice was quiet, so quiet that she cast a startled glance upward.

It was a mistake, as she quickly realized when he swooped down to capture her lips. Laughter bubbled up in her.

Lord Chatworth raised his head, his brows snapping together. He said mildly, "I did not realize that I was an object of amusement, madam."

Babs smiled at him, her wide green eyes filled with a wicked delight. "You can be such a fool, my love," she said affectionately. She laughed when he swept her back into his arms.

"I shall exact a fine payment for your impertinence, my lady," he growled.

Bab would have said something more, but he effectively silenced her. She was left dazed and breathless, a circumstance that the earl regarded with approval.